THE ADVENTURES OF RAGGEDY ANN AND ANDY

The Adventures of Raggedy Ann and Andy

Written and Illustrated by

JOHNNY GRUELLE

WORDSWORTH CLASSICS

For my husband

ANTHONY JOHN RANSON

with love from your wife, the publisher.
Eternally grateful for your unconditional love.

Readers who are interested in other titles from
Wordsworth Editions are invited to visit our website at
www.wordsworth-editions.com

For our latest list and a full mail-order service, contact
Bibliophile Books, 5 Datapoint, South Crescent, London E16 4TL
TEL: +44 (0)20 7474 2474 FAX: +44 (0)20 7474 8589
ORDERS: orders@bibliophilebooks.com
WEBSITE: www.bibliophilebooks.com

First published in 2014 by Wordsworth Editions Limited
8B East Street, Ware, Hertfordshire SG12 9HJ

ISBN 978 1 84022 725 3

Wordsworth Editions
is the company founded in 1987 by

MICHAEL TRAYLER

Typeset in Great Britain by Antony Gray
Printed and bound by Clays Ltd, St Ives plc

Contents

RAGGEDY ANN AND ANDY

Introduction

Marcella liked to play up in the attic at Grandma's quaint old house, way out in the country, for there were so many old forgotten things to find up there.

One day when Marcella was up in the attic and had played with the old spinning-wheel until she had grown tired of it, she curled up on an old horsehair sofa to rest.

'I wonder what is in that barrel, way back in the corner?' she thought, as she jumped from the sofa and climbed over two dusty trunks to the barrel standing back under the eaves.

It was quite dark back there, so when Marcella had pulled a large bundle of things from the barrel she took them over to the dormer window where she could see better. There was a funny little bonnet with long white ribbons. Marcella put it on.

In an old leather bag she found a number of tin-types of queer-looking men and women in old-fashioned clothes. And there was one picture of a very pretty little girl with long curls tied tightly back from her forehead and wearing a long dress and queer pantaloons which reached to her shoe-tops. And then out of the heap she pulled an old rag doll with only one shoe-button eye and a painted nose and a smiling mouth. Her dress was of soft material, blue with pretty little flowers and dots all over it.

Forgetting everything else in the happiness of her find, Marcella caught up the rag doll and ran downstairs to show it to Grandma.

'Well! Well! Where did you find her?' Grandma cried. 'It's old Raggedy Ann!' she explained as she hugged the doll to her breast. 'I had forgotten her. She has been in the attic for fifty years, I guess! Well! Well! Dear old Raggedy Ann! I will sew another button on her right away!' and Grandma went to the machine drawer and got her needle and thread.

Marcella watched the sewing while Grandma told how she had played with Raggedy Ann when she was a little girl.

'Now,' Grandma laughed, 'Raggedy Ann, you have two fine shoe-button eyes and with them you can see the changes that have taken place in the world while you have been shut up so long in the attic! For, Raggedy Ann, you have a new playmate and mistress now, and I hope you both will have as much happiness together as you and I used to have!'

Then Grandma gave Raggedy Ann to Marcella, saying very seriously, 'Marcella, let me introduce my very dear friend, Raggedy Ann. Raggedy, this is my granddaughter, Marcella!' And Grandma gave the doll a twitch with her fingers in such a way that the rag doll nodded her head to Marcella.

'Oh, Grandma! Thank you ever and ever so much!' Marcella cried as she gave Grandma a hug and kiss. 'Raggedy Ann and I will have just loads of fun.'

And this is how Raggedy Ann joined the doll family at Marcella's house. and there began the adventures of Raggedy Ann which are told in the following stories.

Raggedy Ann Learns a Lesson

One day the dolls were left all to themselves.

Their little mistress had placed them all around the room and told them to be nice children while she was away.

And there they sat and never even so much as wiggled a finger, until their mistress had left the room.

Then the soldier dolly turned his head and solemnly winked at Raggedy Ann.

And when the front gate clicked and the dollies knew they were alone in the house, they all scrambled to their feet.

'Now let's have a good time!' cried the tin soldier. 'Let's all go in search of something to eat!'

'Yes! Let's all go in search of something to eat!' cried all the other dollies.

'When Mistress had me out playing with her this morning,' said Raggedy Ann, 'she carried me by a door near the back of the house and I smelled something which seemed to me as if it would taste delicious!'

'Then you lead the way, Raggedy Ann!' cried the French dolly.

'I think it would be a good plan to elect Raggedy Ann as our leader on this expedition!' said the Indian doll.

At this all the other dolls clapped their hands together and shouted, 'Hurrah! Raggedy Ann will be our leader.'

So Raggedy Ann, very proud indeed to have the confidence and love of all the other dollies, said that she would be very glad to be their leader.

'Follow me!' she cried as her wobbly legs carried her across the floor at a lively pace.

The other dollies followed, racing about the house until they came to the pantry door. 'This is the place!' cried Raggedy Ann, and sure enough, all the dollies smelled something which they knew must be very good to eat.

But none of the dollies was tall enough to open the door and, although they pushed and pulled with all their might, the door remained tightly closed.

The dollies were talking and pulling and pushing and every once in a while one would fall over and the others would step on her in their efforts to open the door. Finally Raggedy Ann drew away from the others and sat down on the floor.

When the other dollies discovered Raggedy Ann sitting there, running her rag hands through her yarn hair, they knew she was thinking.

'Sh! Sh!' they said to each other and quietly went over near Raggedy Ann and sat down in front of her.

'There must be a way to get inside,' said Raggedy Ann.

'Raggedy says there must be a way to get inside!' cried all the dolls.

'I can't seem to think clearly today,' said Raggedy Ann. 'It feels as if my head were ripped.'

JOHNNY GRUELLE

At this the French doll ran to Raggedy Ann and took off her bonnet. 'Yes, there is a rip in your head, Raggedy!' she said, and pulling a pin from her skirt she pinned up Raggedy's head. 'It's not a very neat job, for I got some puckers in it!' she said.

'Oh, that is ever so much better!' cried Raggedy Ann. 'Now I can think quite clearly.'

'Now Raggedy can think quite clearly!' cried all the dolls.

'My thoughts must have leaked out of the rip before!' said Raggedy Ann.

'They must have leaked out before, dear Raggedy!' cried all the other dolls.

'Now that I can think so clearly,' said Raggedy Ann, 'I think the door must be locked and to get in we must unlock it!'

'That will be easy!' said the Dutch doll who says 'Mamma' when he is tipped backwards and forwards, 'for we will have the brave tin soldier shoot the key out of the lock!'

'I can easily do that!' cried the tin soldier, as he raised his gun.

'Oh, Raggedy Ann!' cried the French dolly. 'Please do not let him shoot!'

'No!' said Raggedy Ann. 'We must think of a quieter way!'

After thinking quite hard for a moment, Raggedy Ann sprang up and said: 'I have it!' And she caught up the Jumping Jack and held him up to the door; then Jack slid up his stick and unlocked the door.

Then the dollies all pushed and the door swung open.

My! Such a scramble! The dolls piled over one another in their desire to be the first at the goodies.

They swarmed upon the pantry shelves and in their eagerness spilled a pitcher of cream which ran all over the French dolly's dress.

The Indian doll found some cornbread and dipping it in the molasses he sat down for a good feast.

A jar of raspberry jam was overturned and the dollies ate of this until their faces were all purple.

The tin soldier fell from the shelf three times and bent one of his tin legs, but he scrambled right back up again.

Never had the dolls had so much fun and excitement, and they had all eaten their fill when they heard the click of the front gate.

They did not take time to climb from the shelves, but all rolled or jumped off on to the floor and scrambled back to their room as fast as they could run, leaving a trail of breadcrumbs and jam along the way.

Just as their mistress came into the room the dolls dropped in whatever positions they happened to be in.

'This is funny!' cried Mistress. 'They were all left sitting in their places around the room! I wonder if Fido has been shaking them up!'

Then she saw Raggedy Ann's face and picked her up. 'Why Raggedy Ann, you are all sticky! I do believe you are covered with jam!' and Mistress tasted Raggedy Ann's hand. 'Yes! It's JAM! Shame on you, Raggedy Ann! You've been in the pantry and all the others, too!' and with this the dolls' Mistress dropped Raggedy Ann on the floor and left the room.

When she came back she had on an apron and her sleeves were rolled up.

She picked up all the sticky dolls and putting them in a basket she carried them out under the apple tree in the garden.

There she had placed her little tub and wringer and she took the dolls one at a time, and scrubbed them with a

JOHNNY GRUELLE

scrubbing brush and soused them up and down and this way and that in the soap suds until they were clean.

Then she hung them all out on the clothes-line in the sunshine to dry.

There the dolls hung all day, swinging and twisting about as the breeze swayed the clothes-line.

'I do believe she scrubbed my face so hard she wore off my smile!' said Raggedy Ann, after an hour of silence.

'No, it is still there!' said the tin solder, as the wind twisted him around so he could see Raggedy. 'But I do believe my arms will never work without squeaking, they feel so rusted,' he added.

Just then the wind twisted the little Dutch doll and loosened his clothes-peg, so that he fell to the grass below with a sawdusty bump and as he rolled over he said, 'Mamma!' in a squeaky voice.

Late in the afternoon the back door opened and the little mistress came out with a table and chairs. After setting the table she took all the dolls from the line and placed them about the table.

They had lemonade with grape jelly in it, which made it a beautiful lavender colour, and little 'baby-teeny-weeny-cookies' with powdered sugar on them.

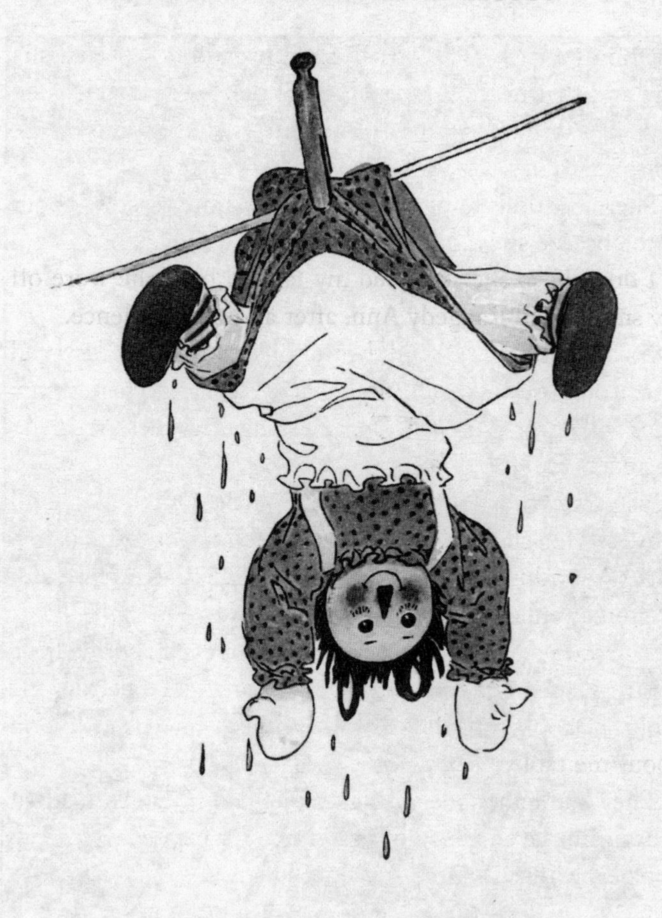

After this lovely dinner, the dollies were taken into the house, where they had their hair brushed and nice clean nighties put on.

Then they were placed in their beds and Mistress kissed each one good-night and tiptoed from the room.

JOHNNY GRUELLE

All the dolls lay as still as mice for a few minutes, then Raggedy Ann raised up on her cotton-stuffed elbows and said: 'I have been thinking!'

'Sh!' said all the other dollies, 'Raggedy has been thinking!'

'Yes,' said Raggedy Ann, 'I have been thinking; our mistress gave us the nice dinner out under the trees to teach us a lesson. She wished us to know that we could have had all the goodies we wished, whenever we wished, if we had behaved ourselves. And our lesson was that we must never take without asking what we could always have for the asking! So let us all remember and try never again to do anything which might cause those who love us any unhappiness!'

'Let us all remember,' chimed the other dollies.

And Raggedy Ann, with a merry twinkle in her shoe-button eyes, lay back in her little bed, her cotton head filled with thoughts of love and happiness.

Raggedy Ann and the Washing

'Why, Dinah! How could you!'

Mamma looked out of the window and saw Marcella run up to Dinah and take something out of her hand and then put her head in her arm and commence crying.

'What is the trouble, dear?' Mamma asked, as she came out of the door and knelt beside the little figure shaking with sobs.

Marcella held out Raggedy Ann. But such a comical looking Raggedy Ann!

Mamma had to smile in spite of her sympathy, for Raggedy Ann looked ridiculous!

Dinah's big eyes rolled out in a troubled manner, for Marcella had snatched Raggedy Ann from Dinah's hand as she cried, 'Why, Dinah! How could you?'

Dinah could not quite understand and, as she dearly loved Marcella, she was troubled.

Raggedy Ann was not in the least down-hearted and while

she felt she must look very funny she continued to smile, but with a more expansive smile than ever before.

Raggedy Ann knew just how it all happened and her remaining shoe-button eye twinkled.

She remembered that morning when Marcella came to the nursery to take the nighties off the dolls and dress them she had been cross.

Raggedy Ann thought at the time, 'Perhaps she has climbed out of bed backwards!' for Marcella complained to each doll as she dressed them.

And when it came Raggedy's time to be dressed, Marcella was very cross for she had scratched her finger on a pin when dressing the French doll.

So, when Marcella heard the little girl next door calling to her, she ran out of the nursery tossing Raggedy Ann away from her as she ran.

Now it happened Raggedy landed in the clothes hamper and there she lay all doubled up in a knot.

A few minutes afterwards Dinah came through the hall with an armful of clothes and piled them in the hamper on top of Raggedy Ann.

Then Dinah carried the hamper out to the back of the house where she did the washing.

Dinah dumped all the clothes into the boiler and poured water on them.

The boiler was then placed upon the stove.

When the water began to get warm, Raggedy Ann wiggled around and climbed up amongst the clothes to the top of the boiler to peep out. There was too much steam and she could see nothing. For that matter, Dinah could not see Raggedy Ann, either, on account of the steam.

So Dinah, using an old broom-handle, stirred the clothes

JOHNNY GRUELLE

in the boiler and the clothes and Raggedy Ann were stirred and whirled around until all were thoroughly boiled.

When Dinah took the clothes a piece at a time from the boiler and scrubbed them, she finally came upon Raggedy Ann.

Now Dinah did not know but that Marcella had placed Raggedy in the clothes hamper to be washed, so she soaped Raggedy well and scrubbed her up and down over the rough washboard.

Two buttons from the back of Raggedy's dress came off and one of Raggedy Ann's shoe-button eyes was loosened as Dinah gave her face a final scrub.

Then Dinah put Raggedy Ann's feet in the wringer and turned the crank. It was hard work getting Raggedy through the wringer, but Dinah was very strong. And of course it happened! Raggedy Ann came through as flat as a pancake.

It was just then, that Marcella returned and saw Raggedy.

'Why, Dinah! How could you!' Marcella had sobbed

as she snatched the flattened Raggedy Ann from the bewildered Dinah's hand.

Mamma patted Marcella's hand and soon got her to stop sobbing.

When Dinah explained that the first she knew of Raggedy being in the wash was when she took her from the boiler, Marcella began crying again.

'It was all my fault, Mamma!' she cried. 'I remember now that I threw dear old Raggedy Ann from me as I ran out of

the door and she must have fallen into the clothes hamper! Oh dear! Oh dear!' and she hugged Raggedy Ann tight.

Mamma did not tell Marcella that she had been cross and naughty for she knew Marcella felt very sorry. Instead Mamma put her arms around her and said, 'Just see how Raggedy Ann takes it! She doesn't seem to be unhappy!'

And when Marcella brushed her tears away and looked at Raggedy Ann, flat as a pancake and with a cheery smile upon her painted face, she had to laugh. And Mamma and Dinah had to laugh, too, for Raggedy Ann's smile was almost twice as broad as it had been before.

'Just let me hang Miss Raggedy on the line in the bright sunshine for half an hour,' said Dinah, 'and you won't know her when she comes off!'

So Raggedy Ann was pinned to the clothes-line, out in the bright sunshine, where she swayed and twisted in the breeze and listened to the chatter of the robins in a nearby tree.

Every once in a while Dinah went out and rolled and patted Raggedy until her cotton stuffing was soft and dry and fluffy and her head and arms and legs were nice and round again.

Then she took Raggedy Ann into the house and showed Marcella and Mamma how clean and sweet she was.

Marcella took Raggedy Ann right up to the nursery and told all the dolls just what had happened and how sorry she was that she had been so cross and peevish when she dressed them. And while the dolls said never a word they looked at their little mistress with love in their eyes as she sat in the little red rocking chair and held Raggedy Ann tightly in her arms.

And Raggedy Ann's remaining shoe-button eye looked

up at her little mistress in rather a saucy manner, but upon her face was the same old smile of happiness, good humour and love.

Raggedy Ann and the Kite

Raggedy Ann watched with interest the preparations.

A number of sticks were being fastened together with string and covered with light cloth.

Raggedy Ann heard some of the boys talk of 'the kite', so Raggedy Ann knew this must be a kite.

When a tail had been fastened to the kite and a large ball of heavy twine tied to the front, one of the boys held the kite up in the air and another boy walked off, unwinding the ball of twine.

There was a nice breeze blowing, so the boy with the twine called, 'Let 'er go' and started running.

Marcella held Raggedy up so that she could watch the kite sail through the air.

How nicely it climbed! But suddenly the kite acted strangely, and as all the children shouted advice to the boy with the ball of twine, the kite began darting this way and that, and finally, making four or five loop-the-loops, it crashed to the ground.

'It needs more tail on it!' one boy shouted.

Then the children asked each other where they might get more rags to fasten to the tail of the kite.

'Let's tie Raggedy Ann to the tail!' suggested Marcella. 'I know she would enjoy a trip way up in the sky!'

The boys all shouted with delight at this new suggestion. So Raggedy Ann was tied to the tail of the kite.

This time the kite rose straight in the air and remained steady. The boy with the ball of twine unwound it until the kite and Raggedy Ann were way, way up and far away. How Raggedy Ann enjoyed being up there! She could see for miles and miles! And how tiny the children looked!

Suddenly a great puff of wind came and carried Raggedy Ann streaming way out behind the kite! She could hear the wind singing on the twine as the strain increased.

Suddenly Raggedy Ann felt something rip. It was the rag to which she was tied. As each puff of wind caught her the rip widened.

When Marcella watched Raggedy Ann rise high above the field, she guessed how much Raggedy Ann enjoyed it, and wished that she, too, might have gone along. But after the kite had been up in the air for five or ten minutes, Marcella grew restless. Kites were rather tiresome. There was more fun in tea parties out under the apple tree.

'Will you please pull down the kite now?' she asked the boy with the twine. 'I want Raggedy Ann.'

'Let her ride up there!' the boy replied. 'We'll bring her home when we pull down the kite! We're going to get another ball of twine and let her go higher!'

Marcella did not like to leave Raggedy Ann with the boys, so she sat down upon the ground to wait until they pulled down the kite.

But while Marcella watched Raggedy Ann, a dot in the

JOHNNY GRUELLE

sky, she could not see the wind ripping the rag to which Raggedy was tied.

Suddenly the rag parted and Raggedy Ann went sailing away as the wind caught in her skirts.

Marcella jumped from the ground, too surprised to say anything. The kite, released from the weight of Raggedy Ann, began darting and swooping to the ground.

'We'll get her for you!' some of the boys said when they saw Marcella's troubled face, and they started running in the direction Raggedy Ann had fallen. Marcella and the other girls ran with them. They ran, and they ran, and they ran, and at last they found the kite upon the ground with one of the sticks broken, but they could not find Raggedy Ann anywhere.

'She must have fallen almost in your yard!' a boy said to Marcella, 'for the kite was directly over here when the doll fell!'

Marcella was heartbroken. She went into the house and lay on the bed. Mamma went out with the children and tried to find Raggedy Ann, but Raggedy Ann was nowhere to be seen.

When Daddy came home in the evening he tried to find Raggedy, but met with no success. Marcella had eaten hardly any dinner, nor could she be comforted by Mamma or Daddy. The other dolls in the nursery lay forgotten and were not put to bed that night, for Marcella lay and sobbed and tossed about her bed.

Finally she said a little prayer for Raggedy Ann, and went to sleep. And as she slept Marcella dreamed that the fairies came and took Raggedy Ann with them to Fairyland for a visit, and then sent Raggedy Ann home to her. She awakened with a cry. Of course Mamma came to her bed right away and said that Daddy would offer a reward in the morning for the return of Raggedy.

'It was all my fault, Mamma!' Marcella said. 'I should not have offered the boys dear old Raggedy Ann to tie on the tail of the kite! But I just know the fairies will send her back.'

Mamma took her in her arms and soothed her with cheering words, although she felt indeed that Raggedy Ann was truly lost and would never be found again.

Now, where do you suppose Raggedy Ann was all this time?

When Raggedy Ann dropped from the kite, the wind caught in her skirts and carried her along until she fell in the fork of the large elm tree directly over Marcella's house. When Raggedy Ann fell with a thud, face up in the fork of the tree, two robins who had a nest near by flew chattering away.

Presently the robins returned and scolded Raggedy Ann for lying so close to their nest, but Raggedy Ann only smiled at them and did not move.

When the robins quietened down and stopped their chiding, one of them hopped up closer to Raggedy Ann in order to investigate.

It was Mamma Robin. She called to Daddy Robin and told him to come. 'See the nice yarn! We could use it to line the nest with,' she said.

So the robins hopped closer to Raggedy Ann and asked if they might have some of her yarn hair to line their nest. Raggedy Ann smiled at them. So the two robins pulled and tugged at Raggedy Ann's yarn hair until they had enough to make their nest nice and soft.

Evening came and the robins sang their good-night songs, and Raggedy Ann watched the stars come out, twinkle all night and disappear in the morning light. In the morning

JOHNNY GRUELLE

the robins again pulled yarn from Raggedy Ann's head, and loosened her so she could peep from the branches, and when the sun came up Raggedy Ann saw she was in the trees in her own yard.

Now, before she could eat any breakfast, Marcella started out to find Raggedy Ann. And it was Marcella herself who found her. And this is how she did it.

Mamma Robin had seen Marcella with Raggedy Ann out in the yard many times, so she began calling, 'Cheery! Cheery!' and Daddy Robin started calling, 'Cheery! Cheery! Cheer up! Cheer up! Cheerily Cheerily! Cheery! Cheery!' And Marcella, looking up into the tree above the house to see the robins, discovered Raggedy Ann peeping down at her.

Oh, how her heart beat with happiness. 'Here is Raggedy Ann,' she shouted.

And Mamma and Daddy came out and saw Raggedy smiling at them, and Daddy got the clothes-prop and climbed out of the attic window and poked Raggedy Ann out of the tree and she fell right into Marcella's arms where she was hugged in a tight embrace.

'You'll never go up on a kite again, Raggedy Ann!' said Marcella, 'for I felt so lost without you. I will never let you leave me again.'

So Raggedy Ann went into the house and had breakfast with her little mistress, and Mamma and Daddy smiled at each other when they peeped through the door into the breakfast room, for Raggedy Ann's smile was wide and very yellow. Marcella, her heart full of happiness, was feeding Raggedy Ann part of her egg.

Raggedy Ann Rescues Fido

It was almost midnight and the dolls were asleep in their beds; all except Raggedy Ann.

Raggedy lay there, her shoe-button eyes staring straight up at the ceiling. Every once in a while Raggedy Ann ran her rag hand up through her yarn hair. She was thinking.

When she had thought for a long, long time, Raggedy Ann raised herself on her wobbly elbows and said, 'I've thought it all out.'

At this the other dolls shook each other and roused up saying, 'Listen! Raggedy has thought it all out!'

'Tell us what you have been thinking, dear Raggedy,' said the tin soldier. 'We hope they were pleasant thoughts.'

'Not very pleasant thoughts!' said Raggedy, as she brushed a tear from her shoe-button eyes. 'You haven't seen Fido all day, have you?'

'Not since early this morning,' the French dolly said.

'It has troubled me,' said Raggedy, 'and if my head was not stuffed with lovely new white cotton, I am sure it would have ached with the worry! When Mistress took me into the living-room this afternoon she was crying, and I heard her mamma say, "We will find him! He is sure to come home soon!" and I knew they were talking of Fido! He must be lost!'

The tin soldier jumped out of bed and ran over to Fido's basket, his tin feet clicking on the floor as he went. 'He is not here,' he said.

'When I was sitting in the window about noontime,' said the Indian doll, 'I saw Fido and a yellow scraggly dog playing out on the lawn and they ran out through a hole in the fence!'

'That was Priscilla's dog, Peterkins!' said the French doll.

'I know poor Mistress is very sad on account of Fido,' said the Dutch doll, 'because I was in the dining-room at supper-time and I heard her daddy tell her to eat her supper and he would go out and find Fido; but I had forgotten all about it until now.'

'That is the trouble with all of us except Raggedy Ann!' cried the little penny-doll, in a squeaky voice, 'She has to think for all of us!'

'I think it would be a good plan for us to show our love for Mistress by trying to find Fido!' exclaimed Raggedy.

'It is a good plan, Raggedy Ann!' cried all the dolls. 'Tell us how to set about it.'

'Well, first let us go out upon the lawn and see if we can track the dogs!' said Raggedy.

'I can track them easily!' the Indian doll said, 'for Indians are good at trailing things!'

'Then let us waste no more time in talking!' said Raggedy Ann, as she jumped from bed, followed by the rest.

The nursery window was open, so the dolls helped each other up on the sill and then jumped to the soft grass below.

They fell in all sorts of queer attitudes, but of course the fall did not hurt them.

At the hole in the fence the Indian doll picked up the trail of the two dogs, and the dolls, stringing out behind, followed him until they came to Peterkins' house. Peterkins was surprised to see the strange little figures in white nighties come trooping up the path to the dog house.

Peterkins was too large to sleep in the nursery, so he had a nice cosy dog house under the grape arbour.

'Come in,' Peterkins said when he saw and recognised the dolls, so all the dollies went into Peterkins' house and sat about while Raggedy told him why they had come.

'It has worried me, too!' said Peterkins, 'but I had no way of telling your mistress where Fido was, for she cannot understand dog language! For you see,' Peterkins continued, 'Fido and I were having the grandest romp over in the park when a great big man with a funny thing on the end of a stick came running towards us. We barked at him and Fido thought he was trying to play with us and went up too close and, do you know, that wicked man caught Fido in the thing at the end of the stick and carried him to a wagon and dumped him in with a lot of other dogs!'

'*The dog catcher!*' cried Raggedy Ann.

'Yes!' said Peterkins, as he wiped his eyes with his paws. 'It was the dog catcher! For I followed the wagon at a distance and I saw him put all the dogs into a big wire pen, so that none could get out!'

'Then you know the way there, Peterkins?' asked Raggedy Ann.

'Yes, I can find it easily,' Peterkins said.

'Then show us the way!' Raggedy Ann cried, 'for we must try to rescue Fido.'

JOHNNY GRUELLE

So Peterkins led the way up alleys and across streets, the dolls all pattering along behind him. It was a strange procession. Once a strange dog ran out at them, but Peterkins told him to mind his own business and the strange dog returned to his own yard.

At last they came to the dog catcher's place. Some of the dogs in the pen were barking at the moon and others were whining and crying.

There was Fido, all covered with mud, and his pretty red ribbon dragging on the ground. My, but he was glad to see the dolls and Peterkins! All the dogs came to the side of the pen and twisted their heads from side to side, gazing in wonder at the queer figures of the dolls.

'We will try and let you out,' said Raggedy Ann.

At this all the dogs barked joyfully.

Then Raggedy Ann, the other dolls and Peterkins went to the gate.

The catch was too high for Raggedy Ann to reach, but

Peterkins held Raggedy Ann in his mouth and stood up on his hind legs so that she could raise the catch.

When the catch was raised, the dogs were so anxious to get out they pushed and jumped against the gate so that it flew open, knocking Peterkins and Raggedy Ann into the mud. Such a yapping and barking was never heard in the neighbourhood as when the dogs swarmed out of the enclosure, jumping over one another and scrambling about in their mad rush to escape.

Fido picked himself up from where he had been rolled by the large dogs and helped Raggedy Ann to her feet. He, Peterkins, and all the dolls ran after the pack, turning the corner just as the dog catcher came running out of the house in his nightgown to see what was causing the trouble.

He stopped in astonishment when he saw the string of

dolls in white nighties pattering down the alley, for he could not imagine what they were.

Well, you may be sure the dolls thanked Peterkins for his kind assistance and they and Fido ran on home, for a faint light was beginning to show in the east where the sun was getting ready to come up.

When they got to their own house they found an old chair out in the yard and after a great deal of work they finally dragged it to the window and thus managed to get into the nursery again.

Fido was very grateful to Raggedy Ann and the other

dolls and before he went to his basket he gave them each a lick on the cheek.

The dolls lost no time in scrambling into bed and pulling up the covers, for they were very sleepy, but just as they were dozing off, Raggedy Ann raised herself and said, 'If my legs and arms were not stuffed with nice clean cotton I feel sure they would ache, but being stuffed with nice clean white cotton, they do not ache and I could not feel happier if my body were stuffed with sunshine, for I know how pleased and happy Mistress will be in the morning when she discovers Fido asleep in his own little basket, safe and sound at home.'

And as the dollies by this time were all asleep, Raggedy Ann pulled the sheet up to her chin and smiled so hard she ripped two stitches out of the back of her rag head.

Raggedy Ann and the Painter

When house-cleaning time came around, Mistress's mamma decided that she would have the nursery repainted and new paper put upon the walls. That was why all the dolls happened to be laid helter-skelter upon one of the high shelves.

Mistress had been in to look at them and wished to put them to bed, but as the painters were coming again in the early morning, Mamma thought it best that their beds be piled in the cupboard.

So the dolls' beds were piled into the cupboard, one on top of another, and the dolls were placed upon the high shelf.

When all was quiet that night, Raggedy Ann who was on the bottom of the pile of dolls spoke softly and asked the others if they would mind moving along the shelf.

'The cotton in my body is getting squashed as flat as a pancake!' said Raggedy Ann. But, although the tin soldier was piled so that his foot was pressed into Raggedy's face, she still wore her customary smile.

So the dolls began moving off to one side until Raggedy Ann was free to sit up.

'Ah, that's a great deal better!' she said, stretching her arms and legs to get the kinks out of them, and patting her dress into shape.

'Well, I'll be glad when morning comes!' she said finally, 'for I know Mistress will take us out in the yard and play with us under the trees.'

So the dolls sat and talked until daylight, when the painters came to work.

One of the painters, a young fellow, seeing the dolls, reached up and took Raggedy Ann down from the shelf.

'Look at this rag doll, Jim,' he said to one of the other painters, 'she's a daisy,' and he took Raggedy Ann by the hands and danced with her while he whistled a lively tune. Raggedy Ann's heels hit the floor thumpity-thump and she enjoyed it immensely.

The other dolls sat upon the shelf and looked straight before them, for it would never do to let grown-up men know that dolls were really alive.

'Better put her back upon the shelf,' said one of the other men. 'You'll have the little girl after you! The chances are that she likes that old rag doll better than any of the others!'

But the young painter twisted Raggedy Ann into funny attitudes and laughed and laughed as she looped about. Finally he got to tossing her up in the air and catching her. This was great fun for Raggedy and as she sailed up by the shelf the dolls all smiled at her, for it pleased them whenever Raggedy Ann was happy.

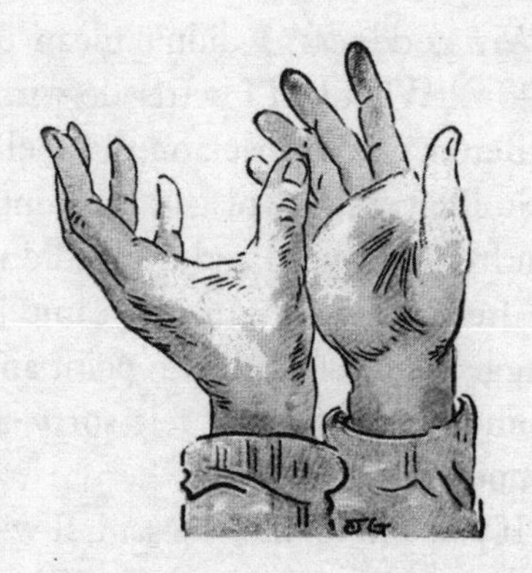

But the young fellow threw Raggedy Ann up into the air once too often and when she came down he failed to catch her and she came down *splash*, head first into a bucket of oily paint.

'I told you!' said the older painter, 'and now you are in for it!'

'My goodness! I didn't mean to do it!' said the young fellow. 'What had I better do with her?'

'Better put her back on the shelf!' replied the other.

So Raggedy was placed back upon the shelf and the paint ran from her head and trickled down upon her dress.

After breakfast, Mistress came into the nursery and saw Raggedy all covered with paint and she began crying.

The young painter felt sorry and told her how it had happened.

'If you will let me,' he said, 'I will take her home with me and clean her up tonight and then bring her back the day after tomorrow.'

So Raggedy was wrapped in a newspaper that evening and carried away.

All the dolls felt sad that night without Raggedy Ann near them.

'Poor Raggedy! I could have cried when I saw her all covered with paint!' said the French doll.

'She didn't look like our dear old Raggedy Ann at all!' said the tin soldier as he wiped the tears from his eyes so that they would not run down on his arms and rust them.

'The paint covered her lovely smile and nose and you could not see the laughter in her shoe-button eyes!' said the Indian doll.

And so the dolls talked that night and the next. But in the daytime when the painters were there, they kept very quiet.

The second day Raggedy was brought home and the dolls

were all anxious for night to come so that they could see and talk with Raggedy Ann.

At last the painters left and the house was quiet, for Mistress had been in and placed Raggedy on the shelf with the other dolls.

'Tell us all about it, Raggedy dear!' the dolls cried.

'Oh, I am so glad I fell in the paint!' cried Raggedy, after she had hugged all the dolls, 'for I have had the happiest time. The painter took me home and told his mamma how I happened to be covered with paint and she was very sorry. She took a rag and wiped off my shoe-button eyes and then I saw that she was a very pretty, sweet-faced lady, and she got some cleaner and wiped off most of the paint on my face.

'But you know,' Raggedy continued, 'the paint had soaked through my rag head and had made the cotton inside all sticky and soggy and I could not think clearly. And my yarn hair was all matted with paint.

'So the kind lady took off my yarn hair and cut the stitches out of my head, and took out all the painty cotton.

'It was a great relief, although it felt queer at first and my thoughts seemed scattered.

'She left me in her work-basket that night and hung me out upon the clothes-line the next morning when she had washed the last of the paint off.

'And while I hung out on the clothes-line, what do you think?'

'We could never guess!' all the dolls cried.

'Why a dear little Jenny Wren came and picked enough cotton out of me to make a cute little cuddly nest in the grape arbor!'

'Wasn't that sweet!' cried all the dolls.

JOHNNY GRUELLE

'Yes indeed it was!' replied Raggedy Ann. 'It made me very happy. Then when the lady took me into the house again she stuffed me with lovely nice new cotton, all the way from my knees up, and sewed me up and put new yarn on my head for hair and – and – and it's a secret!' said Raggedy Ann.

'Oh, tell us the secret!' cried all the dolls, as they pressed closer to Raggedy.

'Well, I know you will not tell anyone who would not be glad to know about it, so I will tell you the secret and why I am wearing my smile a trifle broader!' said Raggedy Ann.

The dolls all said that Raggedy Ann's smile was indeed a quarter of an inch wider on each side.

'When the dear lady put the new white cotton in my body,' said Raggedy Ann 'she went to the cupboard and came back with a paper bag. And she took from the bag ten or fifteen little candy hearts with mottos on them and she hunted through the candy hearts until she found a beautiful red one which she sewed up in me with the cotton! So that is the secret, and that is why I am so happy! Feel here,' said Raggedy Ann. All the dolls could feel Raggedy Ann's beautiful new candy heart and they were very happy for her.

After all had hugged each other good night and had cuddled up for the night, the tin soldier asked, 'Did you have a chance to see what the motto on your new candy heart was, Raggedy Ann?'

'Oh yes,' replied Raggedy Ann. 'I was so happy I forgot to tell you. It had printed upon it, in nice blue letters, I LOVE YOU.'

Raggedy Ann's Trip to the River

When Marcella had a tea party out in the orchard, of course all of the dolls were invited. Raggedy Ann, the tin soldier, the Indian doll and all the others – even the four little penny-dolls in the spool box. After a lovely tea party with ginger cookies and milk, of course the dolls were very sleepy, at least Marcella thought so, so she took all except Raggedy Ann into the house and put them to bed for the afternoon nap. Marcella told Raggedy Ann to stay there and watch the things.

As there was nothing else to do, Raggedy Ann waited for Marcella to return. And as she watched the little ants eating cookie crumbs Marcella had thrown to them, she heard all of a sudden the patter of puppy feet behind her. It was Fido.

The puppy dog ran up to Raggedy Ann and twisted his head about as he looked at her. Then he put his front feet out and barked in Raggedy Ann's face. Raggedy Ann tried to look very stern, but she could not hide the broad smile painted on her face.

'Oh, you want to play, do you?' the puppy dog barked, as he jumped at Raggedy Ann and then jumped back again.

The more Raggedy Ann smiled, the livelier Fido's antics became, until finally he caught the end of her dress and dragged her about.

This was great fun for the puppy dog, but Raggedy Ann did not enjoy it. She kicked and twisted as much as she could, but the puppy dog thought Raggedy was playing.

He ran out of the garden gate and down the path across the meadow, every once in a while stopping and pretending he was very angry. When he pretended this, Fido would give Raggedy Ann a great shaking, making her yarn head hit the ground 'ratty-tat-tat'. Then he would give his head a toss and send Raggedy Ann high in the air, where she would turn over two or three times before she reached the ground.

By this time, she had lost her apron and now some of her yarn hair was coming loose.

As Fido neared the brook, another puppy dog came running across the footbridge to meet him. 'What have you there, Fido?' said the new puppy dog as he bounced up to Raggedy Ann.

'This is Raggedy Ann,' answered Fido. 'She and I are having a lovely time playing.'

You see, Fido really thought Raggedy enjoyed being tossed around and whirled high up in the air. But of course she didn't. However, the game didn't last much longer. As Raggedy Ann hit the ground the new puppy dog caught her dress and ran with her across the bridge, Fido barking close behind him.

In the centre of the bridge, Fido caught up with the new puppy dog and they had a lively tug-of-war with Raggedy Ann stretched between then. As they pulled and tugged and flopped Raggedy Ann about, somehow she fell over the side of the bridge into the water.

The puppy dogs were surprised, and Fido was very sorry indeed, for he remembered how good Raggedy Ann had been to him and how she had rescued him from the dog-pound. But the current carried Raggedy Ann away and all Fido could do was to run along the bank and bark.

Now, you would have thought Raggedy Ann would sink, but no, she floated nicely, for she was stuffed with clean white cotton and the water didn't soak through very quickly.

After a while, the strange puppy and Fido grew tired of running along the bank and the strange puppy scampered home over the meadow, with his tail carried gaily over his back as if he had nothing to be ashamed of. But Fido walked home very sorry indeed. His little heart was broken to think that he had caused Raggedy Ann to be drowned.

But Raggedy Ann didn't drown – not a bit of it. In fact, she even went to sleep on the brook, for the motion of the current was very soothing as it carried her along – just like being rocked by Marcella.

So, sleeping peacefully, Raggedy Ann drifted along with the current until she came to a pool where she lodged against a large stone.

Raggedy Ann tried to climb upon the stone, but by this time the water had thoroughly soaked through Raggedy Ann's nice, clean, white cotton stuffing and she was so heavy she could not climb.

So there she had to stay until Marcella and Daddy came along and found her.

JOHNNY GRUELLE

You see, they had been looking for her. They had found pieces of her apron all along the path and across the meadow where Fido and the strange puppy dog had shaken them from Raggedy Ann. So from the bridge they followed the brook until they found her.

When Daddy fished Raggedy Ann from the water, Marcella hugged her so tightly to her breast the water ran from Raggedy Ann and dripped all over Marcella's apron. But Marcella was so glad to find Raggedy Ann again she didn't mind it a bit. She just hurried home and took off all of Raggedy Ann's wet clothes and placed her on a little red chair in front of the oven door, and then brought all of the other dolls in and read a fairy tale to them while Raggedy Ann steamed and dried.

When Raggedy Ann was thoroughly dry, Mamma said she thought the cake must be finished and she took from the oven a lovely chocolate cake and gave Marcella a large piece to have another tea party with.

That night when all the house was asleep, Raggedy Ann sat up in bed and said to the dolls who were still awake, 'I am so happy I do not feel a bit sleepy. Do you know, I believe the water soaked me so thoroughly my candy heart must have melted and filled my whole body, and I do not feel the least bit angry with Fido for playing with me so roughly!'

So all the other dolls were happy, too, for happiness is very easy to catch when we love one another and are sweet all through.

Raggedy Ann and the Strange Dolls

Raggedy Ann lay just as Marcella had dropped her – all sprawled out with her rag arms and legs twisted in ungraceful attitudes. Her yarn hair was twisted and lay partly over her face, hiding one of her shoe-button eyes.

Raggedy gave no sign that she had heard, but lay there smiling at the ceiling.

Perhaps Raggedy Ann knew that what the new dolls said was true. But sometimes the truth may hurt and this may have been the reason Raggedy Ann lay there so still.

'Did you ever see such an ungainly creature!'

'I do believe it has shoe buttons for eyes!'

'And yarn hair!'

'Mercy, did you ever see such feet!'

The Dutch doll rolled off the doll sofa and said 'Mamma' in his quavery voice, he was so surprised at hearing anyone speak so of beloved Raggedy Ann – dear Raggedy Ann, she of the candy heart, whom all the dolls loved.

Uncle Clem was also very much surprised and offended. He walked up in front of the two new dolls and looked them sternly in the eyes, but he could think of nothing to say so he pulled at his yarn moustache.

Marcella had only received the two new dolls that morning. They had come in the morning mail and were presents from an aunt.

Marcella had named the two new dolls Annabel-Lee and Thomas, after her aunt and uncle.

Annabel-Lee and Thomas were beautiful dolls and must have cost heaps and heaps of shiny pennies, for both were handsomely dressed and had *real* hair! Annabel's hair was of a lovely shade of auburn and Thomas's was golden yellow.

Annabel was dressed in soft, lace-covered silk and upon her head she wore a beautiful hat with long silk ribbons tied in a neat bow beneath her dimpled chin.

Thomas was dressed in an Oliver Twist suit of dark velvet with a lace collar. Both he and Annabel wore lovely black slippers and short stockings.

They were sitting upon two of the little red doll chairs where Marcella had placed them and where they could see the other dolls.

When Uncle Clem walked in front of them and pulled his moustache they laughed outright. 'Tee-hee-hee!' they snickered, 'he has holes in his knees!'

Quite true. Uncle Clem was made of worsted and the moths had eaten his knees and part of his kilt. He had a kilt, you see, for Uncle Clem was a Scotch doll.

Uncle Clem shook, but he felt so hurt he could think of nothing to say.

He walked over and sat down beside Raggedy Ann and brushed her yarn hair away from her shoe-button eye.

The tin soldier went over and sat beside them.

'Don't you mind what they say, Raggedy!' he said, 'They do not know you as we do!'

'We don't care to know her!' said Annabel-Lee as she primped her dress. 'She looks like a scarecrow!'

'And the soldier must have been made with a can opener!' laughed Thomas.

'You should be ashamed of yourselves!' said the French dolly, as she stood before Annabel and Thomas, 'You will make all of us sorry that you have joined our family if you continue to poke fun at us and look down upon us. We are all happy here together and share in each others' adventures and happiness.'

Now, that night Marcella did not undress the two new dolls, for she had no nighties for them, so she let them sit up in the two little red chairs so they would not crease their clothes. 'I will make nighties for you tomorrow!' she said as she kissed them good-night. Then she went over and gave

Raggedy Ann a good-night hug. 'Take good care of all my children, Raggedy!' she said as she went out.

Annabel and Thomas whispered together. 'Perhaps we have been too hasty in our judgement!' said Annabel-Lee. 'This Raggedy Ann seems to be a favourite with the mistress and with all the dolls!'

'There must be a reason!' replied Thomas. 'I am beginning to feel sorry that we spoke of her looks. One really cannot help one's looks after all.'

Now, Annabel-Lee and Thomas were very tired after their long journey and soon they fell asleep and forgot all about the other dolls.

When they were sound asleep, Raggedy Ann slipped quietly from her bed and awakened the tin soldier and

Uncle Clem and the three tiptoed to the two beautiful new dolls.

They lifted them gently so as not to wake them and carried them to Raggedy Ann's bed.

Raggedy Ann tucked them in snugly and lay down upon the hard floor.

The tin soldier and Uncle Clem both tried to coax Raggedy Ann into accepting their bed (they slept together), but Raggedy Ann would not hear of it.

'I am stuffed with nice soft cotton and the hard floor does not bother me at all!' said Raggedy.

At daybreak Annabel and Thomas awoke to find themselves in Raggedy Ann's bed and as they sat up and looked at each other each knew how ashamed the other felt, for they realised Raggedy Ann had generously given them her bed.

There Raggedy Ann lay; all sprawled out upon the hard floor, her rag arms and legs twisted in ungraceful attitudes.

'How good and honest she looks!' said Annabel. 'It must be her shoe-button eyes!'

'How nicely her yarn hair falls in loops over her face!' exclaimed Thomas. 'I did not notice how pleasant her face looked last night!'

'The others seem to love her ever and ever so much!' mused Annabel. 'It must be because she is so kind.'

Both new dolls were silent for a while, thinking deeply.

'How do you feel?' Thomas finally asked.

'Very much ashamed of myself!' answered Annabel, 'And you, Thomas?'

'As soon as Raggedy Ann awakens, I shall tell her just how much ashamed I am of myself, and if she can, I want her to forgive me!' Thomas said.

Love
one
another.
JOHNNY GRUELLE

'The more I look at her, the better I like her!' said Annabel.

'I am going to kiss her!' said Thomas.

'You'll awaken her if you do!' said Annabel.

But Thomas climbed out of bed and kissed Raggedy Ann on her painted cheek and smoothed her yarn hair from her rag forehead.

And Annabel-Lee climbed out of bed, too, and kissed Raggedy Ann.

Then Thomas and Annabel-Lee gently carried Raggedy Ann and put her in her own bed and tenderly tucked her in, and then took their seats in the two little red chairs.

After a while Annabel said softly to Thomas, 'I feel ever and ever so much better and happier!'

'So do I!' Thomas replied. 'It's like a whole lot of sunshine coming into a dark room, and I shall always try to keep it there!'

Fido had one fuzzy white ear sticking up over the edge of his basket and he gave his tail a few thumps against his pillow.

Raggedy Ann lay quietly in bed where Thomas and Annabel had tucked her. And as she smiled at the ceiling, her candy heart (with I LOVE YOU written on it) thrilled with contentment, for, as you have probably guessed, Raggedy Ann had not been asleep at all!

JOHNNY GRUELLE

Raggedy Ann and the Kittens

Raggedy Ann had been away all day.

Marcella had come early in the morning and dressed all the dolls and placed them about the nursery.

Some of the dolls had been put in the little red chairs around the little doll table. There was nothing to eat upon the table except a turkey, a fried egg and an apple, all made of plaster of Paris and painted in natural colours. The little teapot and other doll dishes were empty, but Marcella had told them to enjoy their dinner while she was away.

The French dolly had been given a seat upon the doll sofa and Uncle Clem had been placed at the piano.

Marcella picked up Raggedy Ann and carried her out of the nursery when she left, telling the dolls to 'be specially good children, while Mamma is away!'

When the door closed, the tin soldier winked at the Dutch-boy doll and handed the imitation turkey to the penny-dolls. 'Have some nice turkey?' he asked.

'No, thank you!' the penny-dolls said in little penny-doll, squeaky voices, 'we have had all we can eat!'

'Shall I play you a tune?' asked Uncle Clem of the French doll.

At this all the dolls laughed, for Uncle Clem could not begin to play any tune. Raggedy Ann was the only doll who had ever taken lessons, and she could play 'Peter, Peter, Pumpkin-Eater' with one hand.

In fact, Marcella had almost worn out Raggedy Ann's right hand teaching it to her.

'Play something lively!' said the French doll, as she giggled behind her hand, so Uncle Clem began hammering the eight keys on the toy piano with all his might until a noise was heard upon the stairs.

Quick as a wink, all the dolls took the same positions in which they had been placed by Marcella, for they did not wish really truly people to know that they could move about.

But it was only Fido. He put his nose in at the door and looked around.

All the dolls at the table looked steadily at the painted food, and Uncle Clem leaned upon the piano keys, looking just as unconcerned as when he had been placed there.

Then Fido pushed the door open and came into the nursery wagging his tail.

He walked over to the table and sniffed, in hopes Marcella had given the dolls real food and that some would still be left.

'Where's Raggedy Ann?' Fido asked, when he had satisfied himself that there was no food.

'Mistress took Raggedy Ann and went somewhere!' all the dolls answered in chorus.

JG

'I've found something I must tell Raggedy Ann about!' said Fido, as he scratched his ear.

'Is it a secret?' asked the penny-dolls.

'Secret nothing,' replied Fido. 'It's kittens!'

'How lovely!' cried all the dolls. 'Really live kittens?'

'Really live kittens!' replied Fido. 'Three little tiny ones, out in the barn!'

'Oh, I wish Raggedy Ann was here!' cried the French doll. 'She would know what to do about it!'

'That's why I wanted to see her,' said Fido, as he thumped his tail on the floor. 'I did not know there were any kittens and I went into the barn to hunt for mice and the first thing I knew Mamma Cat came bouncing right at me with her eyes looking green! I tell you I hurried out of there!'

'How did you know there were any kittens then?' asked Uncle Clem.

'I waited around the barn until Mamma Cat went up to the house and then I slipped into the barn again, for I knew there must be something inside or she would not have jumped at me in that way! We are usually very friendly, you know,' Fido confided. 'And what was my surprise to find three tiny little kittens in an old basket, way back in a dark corner!'

'Go and get them, Fido, and bring them up so we can see them!' said the tin soldier.

'Not me!' said Fido. 'If I had a suit of tin clothes on like you have I might do it, but you know cats can scratch very hard if they want to!'

'We will tell Raggedy when she comes in!' said the French doll, and then Fido went out to play with a neighbour dog.

So when Raggedy Ann returned to the nursery the dolls could hardly wait until Marcella had put on their nighties and left them for the night.

Then they told Raggedy Ann all about the kittens.

Raggedy Ann jumped from her bed and ran over to Fido's basket; he wasn't there.

Then Raggedy suggested that all the dolls go out to the barn and see the kittens. This they did easily, for the window was open and it was but a short jump to the ground.

They found Fido out near the barn watching a hole.

'I was afraid something might disturb them,' he said, 'for Mamma Cat went away about an hour ago.'

All the dolls, with Raggedy Ann in the lead, crawled through the hole and ran to the basket.

Just as Raggedy Ann started to pick up one of the kittens there was a lot of howling and yelping and Fido came bounding through the hole with Mamma Cat behind him. When Mamma Cat caught up with Fido he would yelp.

When Fido and Mamma Cat had circled the barn two or three times Fido managed to find the hole and escape to the

yard; then Mamma Cat came over to the basket and saw all the dolls.

'I'm s'prised at you, Mamma Cat!' said Raggedy Ann, 'Fido has been watching your kittens for an hour while you were away. He wouldn't hurt them for anything!'

'I'm sorry, then,' said Mamma Cat.

'You must trust Fido, Mamma Cat!' said Raggedy Ann, 'because he loves you and anyone who loves you can be trusted!'

'That's so!' replied Mamma Cat. 'Cats love mice, too, and I wish the mice trusted us more!'

The dolls all laughed at this joke.

'Have you told the folk up at the house about your dear little kittens?' Raggedy Ann asked.

'Oh, my, no!' exclaimed Mamma Cat. 'At the last place I lived the people found out about my kittens and, do you

know, all the kittens disappeared! I intend keeping then a secret!'

'But all the folk at this house are very kindly people and would dearly love your kittens!' cried all the dolls.

'Let's take them right up to the nursery,' said Raggedy Ann, 'and Mistress can find them there in the morning!'

'How lovely!' said all the dolls in chorus. 'Do, Mamma Cat! Raggedy Ann knows, for she is stuffed with nice clean white cotton and is very wise!'

So after a great deal of persuasion, Mamma Cat finally consented. Raggedy Ann took two of the kittens and carried them to the house while Mamma Cat carried the other.

Raggedy Ann wanted to give the kittens her bed, but Fido, who was anxious to prove his affection, insisted that Mamma Cat and the kittens should have his nice soft basket.

The dolls could hardly sleep that night; they were so anxious to see what Mistress would say when she found the dear little kittens in the morning.

Raggedy Ann did not sleep a wink, for she shared her bed with Fido and he kept her awake whispering to her.

In the morning when Marcella came to the nursery, the first thing she saw was the three little kittens.

She cried out in delight and carried them all down to show to Mamma and Daddy. Mamma Cat went trailing along, arching her back and purring with pride as she rubbed against all the chairs and doors.

Mamma and Daddy said the kittens could stay in the nursery and belong to Marcella, so Marcella took them back to Fido's basket while she hunted for names for them in a fairy-tale book.

Marcella finally decided upon three names: Prince Charming for the white kitty, Cinderella for the Maltese and Princess Golden for the kitty with the yellow stripes.

So that is how the three little kittens came to live in the nursery.

And it all turned out just as Raggedy Ann had said, for her head was stuffed with clean white cotton, and she could think exceedingly wise thoughts.

And Mamma Cat found out that Fido was a very good friend, too. She grew to trust him so much she would even let him help wash the kittens' faces.

Raggedy Ann and the Fairies' Gift

All the dolls were tucked snugly in their little beds for the night and the large house was very still.

Every once in a while Fido would raise one ear and partly open one eye, for his keen dog sense seemed to tell him that something was about to happen.

Finally he opened both eyes, sniffed the air and, getting out of his basket and shaking himself, he trotted across the nursery to Raggedy Ann's bed.

Fido put his cold nose in Raggedy Ann's neck. She raised her head from the little pillow.

'Oh! It's you, Fido!' said Raggedy Ann. 'I dreamed the tin soldier put an icicle down my neck!'

'I can't sleep,' Fido told Raggedy Ann. 'I feel that something is about to happen!'

'You have been eating too many bones lately, Fido, and they keep you awake,' Raggedy replied.

JOHNNY GRUELLE

'No, it isn't that. I haven't had any bones since the folk had beef last Sunday. It isn't that. Listen, Raggedy!'

Raggedy Ann listened.

There was a murmur as if someone were singing, far away.

'What is it?' asked Fido.

'Sh!' cautioned Raggedy Ann. 'It's music.'

It was indeed music, the most beautiful music Raggedy Ann had ever heard.

It grew louder, but still seemed to be *far* away.

Raggedy Ann and Fido could hear it distinctly and it sounded as if hundreds of voices were singing in unison.

'Please don't howl, Fido,' Raggedy Ann said as she put her two rag arms around the dog's nose. Fido usually 'sang' when he heard music.

But Fido did not sing this time; he was filled with wonder. It seemed as if something very nice was going to happen.

Raggedy Ann sat upright in bed. The room was flooded with a strange, beautiful light and the music came floating in through the nursery window.

Raggedy Ann hopped from her bed and ran across the floor, trailing the bedclothes after her. Fido followed close behind and together they looked out of the window across the flower garden.

There among the flowers were hundreds of tiny beings, some playing minute reed instruments and flower horns, while others sang. This was the strange, wonderful music Raggedy and Fido had heard.

'It's the fairies!' said Raggedy Ann. 'To your basket quick, Fido! They are coming this way!' And Raggedy Ann ran back to her bed, with the bedclothes still trailing behind her.

Fido gave three jumps and he was in his basket, pretending he was sound asleep, but one little black eye was peeping through a chink in the side.

Raggedy jumped into her bed and pulled the covers to her chin, but lay so that her shoe-button eyes could see towards the window.

Little fairy forms radiant as silver came flitting into the nursery, singing in far-away voices. They carried a little bundle. A beautiful light came from this bundle, and to Raggedy Ann and Fido it seemed like sunshine and moonshine mixed. It was a soft mellow light, just the sort of light you would expect to accompany fairy folk.

As Raggedy watched, her candy heart went pitty-pat against her cotton stuffing, for she saw a tiny pink foot sticking out of the bundle of light.

The fairy troop sailed across the nursery and through the door with their bundle and Raggedy Ann and Fido listened to their far-away music as they went down the hall.

Presently the fairies returned without the bundle and disappeared through the nursery window.

Raggedy Ann and Fido again ran to the window and saw the fairy troop dancing among the flowers.

The light from the bundle still hung about the nursery and a strange lovely perfume floated about.

When the fairies' music ceased and they had flown away, Raggedy Ann and Fido returned to Raggedy's bed to think it all out.

When old Mr Sun peeped over the garden wall and into the nursery, and the other dolls woke up, Raggedy Ann and Fido were still puzzled.

'What is it, Raggedy Ann?' asked the tin soldier and Uncle Clem, in one voice.

Before Raggedy Ann could answer, Marcella came running into the nursery, gathered up all the dolls in her arms and ran down the hall, Fido jumping beside her and barking shrilly.

'Be quiet!' Marcella said to Fido. 'It's asleep and you might wake it!'

Mamma helped Marcella arrange all the dolls in a circle around the bed so that they could all see what was in the bundle.

Mamma gently pulled back the soft covering and the dolls saw a tiny little fist as pink as coral, a soft little face with a cunning tiny pink nose, and a little head as bald as the French dolly's when her hair came off.

My, how the dollies all chattered when they were once again left alone in the nursery!

'A dear cuddly baby brother for Mistress!' said Uncle Clem.

'A beautiful bundle of love and fairy sunshine for everybody in the house!' said Raggedy Ann, as she went to the toy piano and joyously played 'Peter, Peter, Pumpkin-Eater' with one rag hand.

Raggedy Ann and the Chickens

When Marcella was called into the house she left Raggedy sitting on the chicken-yard fence. 'Now you sit quietly and do not stir,' Marcella told Raggedy Ann, 'If you move you may fall and hurt yourself!'

So Raggedy Ann sat quietly, just as Marcella told her, but she smiled at the chickens for she had fallen time and again and it had never hurt her in the least. She was stuffed with nice soft cotton, you see.

So, there she sat until a tiny little humming-bird, in search of flower honey hummed close to Raggedy Ann's head and hovered near the tall hollyhocks.

Raggedy Ann turned her rag head to see the humming-bird and lost her balance – *plump!* she went, down amongst the chickens.

The chickens scattered in all directions, all except Old Ironsides, the rooster.

He ruffled his neck feathers and put his head down close to the ground, making a queer whistling noise as he looked fiercely at Raggedy Ann.

But Raggedy Ann only smiled at Old Ironsides the rooster and ran her rag hand through her yarn hair for she did not fear him.

And then something strange happened, for when she made this motion the old rooster jumped up in the air and kicked his feet out in front, knocking Raggedy Ann over and over.

When Raggedy Ann stopped rolling she waved her apron at the rooster and cried, 'Shoo!' but instead of 'shooing', Old Ironsides upset her again.

Now, two old hens who had been watching the rooster jump at Raggedy ran up, and as one old hen placed herself before the rooster, the other old hen caught hold of Raggedy's apron and dragged her into the chicken-coop.

It was dark inside and Raggedy could not tell what was going on as she felt herself being pulled up over the nests.

But, finally Raggedy could sit up, for the old hen had stopped pulling her, and as her shoe-button eyes were very good, she soon made out the shape of the old hen in front of her.

'My! that's the hardest work I have done in a long time!' said the old hen, when she could catch her breath. 'I was afraid Mr Rooster would tear your dress and apron!'

'That was a queer game he was playing, Mrs Hen,' said Raggedy Ann.

The old hen chuckled way down in her throat, 'Gracious me! He wasn't playing a game, he was fighting you!'

'Fighting!' cried Raggedy Ann in surprise.

'Oh yes, indeed!' the old hen answered, 'Old Ironsides

the rooster thought you intended to harm some of the children chickens and he was fighting you!'

'I am sorry that I fell inside the pen, I wouldn't harm anything,' Raggedy Ann said.

'If we tell you a secret you must promise not to tell your mistress!' said the old hens.

'I promise! Cross my candy heart!' said Raggedy Ann.

Then the two old hens took Raggedy Ann way back into the farthest corner of the chicken coop. There, behind a box, they had built two nests and each old hen had ten eggs in her nest.

'If your folk hear of it they will take the eggs!' said the hens, 'and then we could not raise our families!'

Raggedy Ann felt the eggs and they were nice and warm.

'We just left the nests when you fell into the pen!' explained the old hens.

'But how can the eggs grow if you sit upon them?' said

Raggedy. 'If Fido sits on any of the garden, the plants will not grow, Mistress says!'

'Eggs are different!' one old hen explained. 'In order to make the eggs hatch properly, we must sit on them three weeks and not let them get cold at any time!'

'And at the end of the three weeks do the eggs sprout?' asked Raggedy Ann.

'You must be thinking of eggplant!' cried one old hen. 'These eggs hatch at the end of three weeks – they don't sprout – and then we have a lovely family of soft downy chickies; little puffballs that we can cuddle under our wings and love dearly!'

'Have you been sitting upon the eggs very long?' Raggedy asked.

'Neither one of us has kept track of the time,' said one

hen, 'so we do not know! You see, we never leave the nests except just once in a while to get a drink and to eat a little. So we can hardly tell when it is day and when it is night.'

'We were going out to get a drink when you fell in the pen!' said one old hen. 'Now we will have to sit upon the eggs and warm them up again!'

The two old hens spread their feathers and nestled down upon the nests.

'When you get them good and warm, I would be glad to sit upon the eggs to keep them warm while you get something to eat and drink!' said Raggedy. So the two old hens walked out of the coop to finish their meal which had been interrupted by Raggedy's fall and while they were gone, Raggedy Ann sat quietly upon the warm eggs. Suddenly down beneath her she heard something go, 'Pick, pick!' 'I hope it isn't a mouse!' Raggedy Ann said to herself, when she felt something move. 'I wish the old hens would come back.' But when they came back and saw the puzzled expression on her face, they cried, 'What is it?'

Raggedy Ann got to her feet and looked down and there were several little fluffy, cuddly baby chickies, round as little puffballs.

'Cheep! Cheep! Cheep!' they cried when Raggedy stepped out of the nest.

'Baby chicks!' Raggedy cried, as she stooped and picked up one of the little puffballs. 'They want to be cuddled!'

The two old hens, their eyes shining with happiness, got upon the nests and spread out their soft warm feathers, 'The other eggs will hatch soon!' said they.

So, for several days Raggedy helped the two hens hatch out the rest of the chickies, and just as they finished, Marcella came inside looking around.

'How in the world did you get in here, Raggedy Ann?' she cried. 'I have been looking all about for you! Did the chickens drag you in here?'

Both old hens down behind the box clucked softly to the chickies beneath them and Marcella overheard them.

She lifted the box away and gave a little squeal of surprise and happiness.

'Oh, you dear old Hennypennies!' she cried, lifting both old hens from their nests. 'You have hidden your nests away here and now you have one, two, three, four – twenty chickies!' and as she counted them, Marcella placed them in her apron; then catching up Raggedy Ann, she placed her over the new little chickies.

'Come on, old Hennypennies!' she said, and went out of the coop with the two old hens clucking at her heels.

Marcella called Daddy and Daddy rolled two barrels out under one of the trees and as they lay on their sides made a nice bed in each. Then he nailed slats across the front, leaving a place for a door. Each Hennypenny was then given ten little chickies and settled in her barrel. And all the dolls were happy when they heard of Raggedy's adventure and they did not have to wait long before they were all taken out to see the new chickies.

Raggedy Ann and the Mouse

Jeanette was a new wax doll, and like Henny, the Dutch doll, she could say 'Mamma' when anyone tipped her backwards or forwards. She had lovely golden brown curls of real hair. It could be combed and plaited, or curled or fluffed without tangling, and Raggedy Ann was very proud when Jeanette came to live with the dolls.

But now Raggedy Ann was very angry – in fact, Raggedy Ann had just ripped two stitches out of the top of her head when she took her rag hands and pulled her rag face down into a frown (but when she let go of the frown her face stretched right back into her usual cheery smile).

And *you* would have been angry, too, for something had happened to Jeanette.

Something or someone had stolen into the nursery that night when the dolls were asleep and nibbled all the wax from Jeanette's beautiful face – and now all her beauty was gone!

'It really is a shame!' said Raggedy Ann as she put her arms about Jeanette.

'Something must be done about it!' said the French doll as she stamped her little foot.

'If I catch the culprit, I will – well, I don't know what I will do with him!' said the tin soldier, who could be very fierce at times, although he was seldom cross.

'Here is the hole he came from!' cried Uncle Clem from the other end of the nursery. 'Come, see!'

All the dolls ran to where Uncle Clem was, down on his hands and knees.

'This must be the place!' said Raggedy Ann. 'We will plug up the hole with something so he will not come out again!'

The dolls hunted around and brought rags and pieces of paper and pushed them into the mouse's doorway.

'I thought I heard nibbling last night,' one of the penny-dolls said. 'You know I begged for an extra piece of pie last evening, when Mistress had me at the table, and it kept me awake!'

While the dolls were talking, Marcella ran downstairs with Jeanette and told Daddy and Mamma, who came upstairs with Marcella and hunted around until they discovered the mouse's doorway.

'Oh, why couldn't it have chewed on me?' Raggedy Ann asked herself when she saw Marcella's sorrowful face, for Raggedy Ann was never selfish.

'Daddy will take Jeanette downtown with him and have her fixed up as good as new,' said Mamma, so Jeanette was wrapped in soft tissue paper and taken away.

Later in the day Marcella came bouncing into the nursery with a surprise for the dolls. It was a dear fuzzy little kitten.

JOHNNY GRUELLE

Marcella introduced the kitten to all the dolls.

'Her name is Boots, because she has four little white feet!' said Marcella. So Boots, the happy little creature, played with the penny-dolls, scraping them over the floor and peeping out from behind chairs and pouncing upon them as if they were mice, and the penny-dolls enjoyed it hugely.

When Marcella was not in the nursery, Raggedy Ann wrestled with Boots and they would roll over and over upon the floor, Boots with her front feet around Raggedy Ann's neck and kicking with her hind feet.

Then Boots would arch her back and pretend she was very angry and walk sideways until she was close to Raggedy. Then she would jump at her and over and over they would roll, their heads hitting the floor bumpity-bump.

Boots slept in the nursery that night and was lonely for her mamma, for it was the first time she had been away from home.

Even though her bed was right on top of Raggedy Ann, she could not sleep. But Raggedy Ann was very glad to have Boots sleep with her, even if she was heavy, and when Boots began crying for her mamma, Raggedy Ann comforted her and soon Boots went to sleep.

One day Jeanette came home. She had a new coating of wax on her face and she was as beautiful as ever.

Now, by this time Boots was one of the family and did not cry at night. Besides Boots was told of the mouse in the corner and how he had eaten Jeanette's wax, so she promised to sleep with one eye open.

Late that night when Boots was the only one awake, out popped a tiny mouse from the hole. Boots jumped after the mouse and bumped against the toy piano, which made the keys tinkle so loudly it awakened the dolls.

They ran over to where Boots sat growling with the tiny mouse in her mouth.

My! how the mouse was squeaking!

Raggedy Ann did not like to hear it squeak, but she did not wish Jeanette to have her wax face chewed again, either.

So Raggedy Ann said to the tiny little mouse, 'You should have known better than to come here when Boots is with us. Why don't you go out in the barn and live where you will not destroy anything of value?'

'I did not know!' squeaked the little mouse. 'This is the first time I have ever been here!'

'Aren't you the little mouse who nibbled Jeanette's wax face?' Raggedy Ann asked.

'No!' the little mouse answered. 'I was visiting the mice inside the walls and wandered out here to pick up cake crumbs! I have three little baby mice at home down in the barn. I have never nibbled at anyone's wax face!'

'Are you a mamma mouse?' Uncle Clem asked.

'Yes!' the little mouse squeaked, 'and if the kitten will let me go I will run right home to my children and never return again!'

'Let her go, Boots!' the dolls all cried. 'She has three little baby mice at home! Please let her go!'

'No, indeed!' Boots growled. 'This is the first mouse I have ever caught and I will eat her!' At this the little mamma mouse began squeaking louder than ever.

'If you do not let the mamma mouse go, Boots, I shall not play with you again!' said Raggedy Ann.

'Raggedy will not play with Boots again!' said all of the dolls in an awed tone. Not to have Raggedy play with them would have been a sad punishment.

But Boots only growled.

The dolls drew to one side, while Raggedy Ann and Uncle Clem whispered together.

And while they whispered Boots would let the little mamma mouse run a short distance, then she would catch her again and box her about between her paws.

This she did until the poor little mamma mouse grew so tired she could scarcely run away from Boots.

Boots would let her get almost to the hole in the wall before catching her, for she knew she would not escape her.

As she watched the little mouse crawling towards the hole scarcely able to move, Raggedy Ann could not keep the tears from her shoe-button eyes.

Finally, as Boots started to spring after the little mouse again, Raggedy Ann threw her rag arms around the kitten's neck. 'Run, Mamma Mouse!' Raggedy Ann cried, as Boots whirled her over and over.

Uncle Clem ran and pushed the mamma mouse into the hole and then she was gone.

When Raggedy Ann took her arms from around Boots, the kitten was very angry. She laid her ears back and scratched Raggedy Ann with her claws.

But Raggedy Ann only smiled – it did not hurt her a bit for Raggedy was sewn together with a needle and thread and if that did not hurt, how could the scratch of a kitten? Finally Boots felt ashamed of herself and went over and lay down by the hole in the wall in hopes the mouse would return, but the mouse never returned. By then Mamma Mouse was out in the barn with her children, warning them to beware of kittens and cats.

Raggedy Ann and all the dolls then went to bed and Raggedy had just dozed off to sleep when she felt something jump upon her bed. It was Boots. She felt a warm little pink tongue caress her rag cheek. Raggedy Ann smiled happily to herself, for Boots had curled up on top of Raggedy Ann and was purring herself to sleep.

Then Raggedy Ann knew she had been forgiven for rescuing the mamma mouse and she smiled herself to sleep and dreamed happily of tomorrow.

Raggedy Ann's New Sisters

Marcella was having a tea party up in the nursery when Daddy called to her, so she left the dollies sitting around the tiny table and ran downstairs carrying Raggedy Ann with her.

Mamma, Daddy and a strange man were talking in the living-room and Daddy introduced Marcella to the stranger.

The stranger was a large man with kindly eyes and a cheery smile, as pleasant as Raggedy Ann's.

He took Marcella upon his knee and ran his fingers through her curls as he talked to Daddy and Mamma, so, of course, Raggedy Ann liked him from the beginning. 'I have two little girls,' he told Marcella. 'Their names are Virginia and Doris, and once when we were at the seaside they were playing in the sand and they covered up Freddy, Doris's boy-doll in the sand. They were playing that Freddy wanted to be covered with the clean white sand, just as the other bathers did. And when they had covered Freddy they took their little pails and shovels and went farther down the beach to play and forgot all about Freddy.

'Now when it was time for us to go home, Virginia and Doris remembered Freddy and ran down to get him, but the tide had come in and Freddy was far out under the water and they could not get him back. Virginia and Doris were very sad and they talked of Freddy all the way home.'

'It was too bad they forgot Freddy,' said Marcella.

'Yes, indeed it was!' the new friend replied as he took Raggedy Ann up and made her dance on Marcella's knee. 'But it turned out all right after all, for do you know what happened to Freddy?'

'No, what did happen to him?' Marcella asked.

'Well, first of all, when Freddy was covered with the sand, he enjoyed it immensely. And he did not mind it so much when the tide came up over him, for he felt Virginia and Doris would return and get him.

'But presently Freddy felt the sand above him move as if someone was digging him out. Soon his head was uncovered and he could look right up through the pretty green water, and what do you think was happening? The Tide Fairies were uncovering Freddy!

'When he was completely uncovered, the Tide Fairies swam with Freddy out to the Undertow Fairies. The Undertow Fairies took Freddy and swam with him out to the Roller Fairies. The Roller Fairies carried Freddy up to the surface and tossed him up to the Spray Fairies who carried him to the Wind Fairies.'

'And the Wind Fairies?' Marcella asked breathlessly.

'The Wind Fairies carried Freddy right to our garden and there Virginia and Doris found him, none the worse for his wonderful adventure!'

'Freddy must have enjoyed it and your little girls must

JOHNNY GRUELLE

have been very glad to get Freddy back again!' said Marcella. 'Raggedy Ann went up in the air on the tail of a kite one day and fell and was lost, so now I am very careful with her!'

'Would you let me take Raggedy Ann for a few days?' asked the new friend.

Marcella was silent. She liked the stranger friend, but she did not wish to lose Raggedy Ann.

'I will promise to take very good care of her and return her to you in a week. Will you let her go with me, Marcella?'

Marcella finally agreed and when the stranger friend left he placed Raggedy Ann in his briefcase.

'It is lonely without Raggedy Ann!' said the dollies each night. 'We miss her happy painted smile and her cheery ways!' they said.

And so the week dragged by . . . But, my! What a chatter there was in the nursery the first night after Raggedy Ann returned. All the dolls were so anxious to hug Raggedy Ann they could scarcely wait until Marcella had left them alone.

When they had squeezed Raggedy Ann almost out of shape and she had smoothed out her yarn hair, patted her apron out and felt her shoe-button eyes to see if they were still there, she said, 'Well, what have you been doing? Tell me all the news!'

'Oh we have just had the usual tea parties and games!' said the tin soldier. 'Tell us about yourself, Raggedy dear, we have missed you so much!'

'Yes! Tell us where you have been and what you have done, Raggedy!' all the dolls cried.

But Raggedy Ann just then noticed that one of the penny-dolls had a hand missing.

'How did this happen?' she asked as she picked up the doll.

'I fell off the table and landed on the tin soldier last night when we were playing. But don't mind a little thing like that, Raggedy Ann,' replied the penny-doll. 'Tell us of yourself! Have you had a nice time?'

'I shall not tell a thing until your hand is mended!' Raggedy Ann said.

So the Indian ran and brought a bottle of glue.

'Where's the hand?' Raggedy asked.

'In my pocket,' the penny-doll answered.

When Raggedy Ann had glued the penny-doll's hand in place and wrapped a rag around it to hold it until the glue dried, she said, 'When I tell you of this wonderful adventure, I know you will all feel very happy. It has made me almost burst my stitches with joy.'

The dolls all sat upon the floor around Raggedy Ann, the tin soldier with his arm over her shoulder.

'Well, first when I left,' said Raggedy Ann, 'I was placed in the stranger friend's briefcase. It was rather stuffy in there, but I did not mind it; in fact, I believe I must have fallen asleep, for when I awakened I saw the stranger friend's hand reaching in for me. He lifted me from the briefcase and danced me upon his knee. "What do you think of her?" he asked three other men sitting nearby.

'I was so interested in looking out of the window I did not pay any attention to what they said, for we were on a train and the scenery was just flying by! Then I was put back in the briefcase.

'When next I was taken out of the briefcase I was in a large, clean, light room and there were many, many girls all dressed in white aprons.

'The stranger friend showed me to another man and to the girls, who took off my clothes, cut my seams and took out my cotton. And what do you think! They found my lovely candy heart had not melted at all as I thought. Then they laid me on a table and marked all around my outside edges with a pencil on clean white cloth, and then the girls re-stuffed me and dressed me.

'I stayed in the clean, big, light room for two or three days and nights and watched my sisters grow from pieces of cloth into rag dolls just like myself!'

'Your *sisters*!' the dolls all exclaimed in astonishment. 'What do you mean, Raggedy?'

'I mean,' said Raggedy Ann, 'that the stranger friend had borrowed me from Marcella so that he could have patterns made from me. And before I left the big, clean, white room there where hundreds of rag dolls so like me you would not have been able to tell us apart.'

'We could have told *you* by your happy smile!' cried the French dolly.

'But all of my sister dolls have smiles just like mine!' replied Raggedy Ann.

'And shoe-button eyes?' the dolls all asked.

'Yes, shoe-button eyes!' Raggedy Ann replied.

'I would tell you from the others by your dress, Raggedy Ann,' said the French doll. 'Your dress is fifty years old! I could tell you by that!'

'But my new sister rag dolls have dresses just like mine, for the stranger friend had cloth made especially for them exactly like mine.'

'I know how we could tell you from the other rag dolls, even if you all look exactly alike!' said the Indian doll, who had been thinking for a long time.

'How?' asked Raggedy Ann with a laugh.

'By feeling for your candy heart! If the doll has a candy heart then it is you, Raggedy Ann!'

Raggedy Ann laughed. 'I am so glad you all love me as you do, but I am afraid you would still not be able to tell me from my new sisters (except that I am more worn) for each new rag doll has a candy heart, and on it is written, '*I love you*', the same words that are written on my own candy heart.'

'And there are hundreds and hundreds of the new rag dolls?' asked the little penny-dolls.

'Hundreds and hundreds of them, all named Raggedy Ann,' replied Raggedy.

'Then,' said the penny-dolls, 'we are indeed happy and proud for you! For wherever one of the new Raggedy Ann dolls goes there will go with her the love and happiness that *you* give to others.'

How Raggedy Andy Came

One day Daddy took Raggedy Ann down to his office and propped her up against some books upon his desk; he wanted to have her where he could see her cheery smile all day, for, as you must surely know, smiles and happiness are truly catching.

Daddy wished to catch a whole lot of Raggedy Ann's cheeriness and happiness and put all this down on paper, so that those who did not have Raggedy Ann dolls might see just how happy and smiling a rag doll can be.

So Raggedy Ann stayed at Daddy's studio for three or four days.

She was missed very, very much at home and Marcella really longed for her, but knew that Daddy was borrowing some of Raggedy Ann's sunshine, so she did not complain.

Raggedy Ann did not complain either, for in addition to the sunny, happy smile she always wore (it was painted on), Raggedy Ann had a candy heart, and of course no one (not even a rag doll) ever complains if they have such happiness about them.

One evening, just as Daddy was finishing his day's work, a messenger boy came with a package: a nice, soft lumpy package.

Daddy opened the nice, soft lumpy package and found a letter.

Grandma had told Daddy, long before this, that at the time Raggedy Ann was made, a neighbour lady had made a boy doll, Raggedy Andy, for her little girl, who always played with Grandma.

And when Grandma told Daddy this she wondered whatever had become of her little playmate and the boy doll, Raggedy Andy.

The letter was from the daughter of that little playmate who wrote to say that she was sending Raggedy Andy to be reunited with Raggedy Ann.

After reading the letter, Daddy opened the other package which had been inside the nice, soft, lumpy package and found – Raggedy Andy.

Raggedy Andy had been carefully folded up.

His soft, loppy arms were folded up in front of him and his soft, loppy legs were folded over his soft, loppy arms, and they were held this way by a rubber band.

Raggedy Andy must have wondered why he was being 'done up' this way, but it could not have caused him any worry, for in between where his feet came over his face Daddy saw his cheery smile.

After slipping off the rubber band, Daddy smoothed out the wrinkles in Raggedy Andy's arms and legs.

Then Daddy propped Raggedy Ann and Raggedy Andy up against books on his desk, so that they sat facing each other: Raggedy Ann's shoe-button eyes looking straight into the shoe-button eyes of Raggedy Andy.

They could not speak – not right out before a real person – so they just sat there and smiled at each other.

Daddy could not help reaching out his hands and feeling their throats.

Yes! There was a lump in Raggedy Ann's throat, and there was a lump in Raggedy Andy's throat. A cotton lump, to be sure, but a lump nevertheless.

'So, Raggedy Ann and Raggedy Andy, that is why you cannot talk, is it?' said Daddy. 'I will go away and let you have some time to yourselves, although it is good to sit and share your happiness by watching you.'

Daddy then took the rubber band and placed it around Raggedy Ann's right hand, and around Raggedy Andy's right hand, so that when he had it fixed properly they sat and held each other's hands.

Daddy knew they would wish to tell each other all the wonderful things that had happened to them since they had parted more than fifty years before.

So, locking his studio door, Daddy left the two old rag dolls looking into each other's eyes.

The next morning, when Daddy unlocked his door and looked at his desk, he saw that Raggedy Andy had fallen over so that he lay with his head in the bend of Raggedy Ann's arm.

The Nursery Dance

When Raggedy Andy was first brought to the nursery he was very quiet.

Raggedy Andy did not speak all day, but he smiled pleasantly to all the other dolls. There was Raggedy Ann, the French doll, Henny, the little Dutch doll, Uncle Clem, and a few others.

Some of the dolls were without arms and legs.

One had a cracked head. She was a nice doll, though, and the others all liked her very much. All of them had cried the night Susan (that was her name) fell off the toy box and cracked her china head.

Raggedy Andy did not speak all day.

But there was really nothing strange about this fact, after all. None of the other dolls spoke all day, either.

Marcella had played in the nursery all day and of course they did not speak in front of her.

Marcella thought they did, though, and often had them saying things which they really were not even thinking of.

For instance, when Marcella served water with sugar in

it and little oyster crackers for 'tea', Raggedy Andy was thinking of Raggedy Ann, and the French doll was thinking of one time when Fido was lost.

JOHNNY GRUELLE

Marcella took the French doll's hand, and passed a cup of 'tea' to Raggedy Andy, and said, 'Mr Raggedy Andy, will you have another cup of tea?' as if the French doll was talking.

And then Marcella answered for Raggedy Andy, 'Oh, yes, thank you! It is so delicious!'

Neither the French doll nor Raggedy Andy knew what was going on, for they were thinking deeply to themselves.

Nor did they drink the tea when it was poured for them. Marcella drank it instead.

Perhaps this was just as well, for most of the dolls were moist inside from the 'tea' of the day before.

Marcella did not always drink all of the tea, often she poured a little down their mouths.

Sugar and water, if taken in small quantities, would not give the dolls colic, Marcella would tell them, but she did not know that it made their cotton or sawdust insides quite sticky.

Quite often, too, Marcella forgot to wash their faces after a 'tea', and Fido would do it for them when he came into the nursery and found the dolls with sweets upon their faces.

Really, Fido was quite a help in this way, but he often missed the corners of their eyes and the backs of their necks where the 'tea' would run and get sticky. But he did his best and saved his little mistress a lot of work.

No, Raggedy Andy did not speak; he merely thought a great deal.

One can, you know, when one has been a rag doll as long as Raggedy Andy had. Years and years and years and years!

Even Raggedy Ann, with all her wisdom, did not really

know how long Raggedy Andy and she had been rag dolls.

If Raggedy Ann had a pencil in her rag hand and Marcella guided it for her, Raggedy Ann could count up to ten – sometimes. But why should one worry one's rag head about one's age when all one's life has been one happy experience after another, with each day filled with love and sunshine?

Raggedy Andy did not know his age, but he remembered many things that had happened years and years and years ago, when he and Raggedy Ann were quite young.

It was of these pleasant times Raggedy Andy was thinking all day, and this was the reason he did not notice that Marcella was speaking for him.

Raggedy Andy could patiently wait until Marcella put all the dollies to bed and left them for the night, alone in the nursery.

The day might have passed very slowly had it not been for the happy memories which filled Raggedy Andy's cotton-stuffed head.

But he did not even fidget.

Of course, he fell out of his chair once, and his shoe-button eyes went 'Click!' against the floor, but it wasn't his

fault. Raggedy Andy was so loppy he could hardly be placed in a chair so that he would stay, and Marcella jiggled the table.

Marcella cried for Raggedy Andy, '*Awaa! Awaa!*' and picked him up and snuggled him and scolded Uncle Clem for jiggling the table.

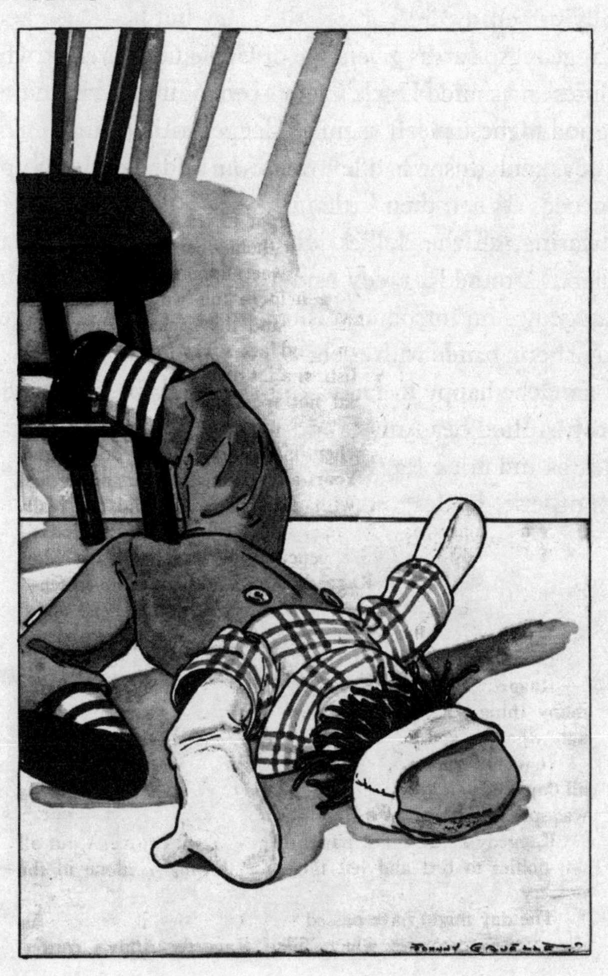

Through all this Raggedy Andy kept right on thinking his pleasant thoughts, and really did not know he had fallen from the chair.

You see how easy it is to pass over the little bumps of life if we are happy inside.

And so Raggedy Andy was quiet all day, and so the day finally passed.

Raggedy Andy was given one of Uncle Clem's clean white nighties and shared Uncle Clem's bed. Marcella kissed them all good night and left them to sleep until morning.

But as soon as she had left the room all the dolls sat up in their beds. When their little mistress's footsteps passed out of hearing, all the dollies jumped out of their beds and gathered around Raggedy Andy.

Raggedy Ann introduced them one by one and Raggedy Andy shook hands with each.

'I am very happy to know you all!' he said, in a voice as kindly as Raggedy Ann's, 'and I hope we will all like each other as much as Raggedy Ann and I have always liked each other!'

'Oh, indeed we shall!' the dollies all answered. 'We love Raggedy Ann because she is so kindly and happy, and we know we shall like you too, for you talk like Raggedy Ann and have the same cheery smile!'

'Now that we know each other so well, what do you say to a game, Uncle Clem?' Raggedy Andy cried, as he caught Uncle Clem and danced about the floor.

Henny, the Dutch doll, dragged the little square music box out into the centre of the room and wound it up. Then all, catching hands, danced in a circle around it, laughing and shouting in their tiny doll voices.

'That was lots of fun!' Raggedy Andy said, when the music had stopped and all the dolls had taken seats upon the floor facing him. 'You know I have been shut away in a trunk up in an attic for years and years and years.'

'Wasn't it very lonely in the trunk all that time?' Susan asked in her queer little cracked voice. You see, her head had been cracked.

'Oh, not at all,' Raggedy Andy replied, 'for there was always a nest of mice down in the corner of the trunk. Cute little mamma and daddy mice, and lots of little teeny-weeny baby mice. And when the mamma and daddy mice were away, I used to cuddle the tiny little baby mice!'

'No wonder you were never lonely!' said Uncle Clem, who was very kind and loved everybody and everything.

'No, I was never lonely in the old trunk in the attic, but it is far more pleasant to be out again and living here with all you nice friends!' said Raggedy Andy.

And all the dolls thought so too, for already they loved Raggedy Andy's happy smile and knew he would prove to be as kindly and lovable as Raggedy Ann.

The Spinning-Wheel

One night, after all the household had settled down to sleep, Raggedy Andy sat up in bed and tickled Uncle Clem.

Uncle Clem twisted and wiggled in his sleep until finally he could stand it no longer and woke up.

'I dreamed that someone told me the funniest story!' said Uncle Clem; 'but I cannot remember what it was!'

'I was tickling you!' laughed Raggedy Andy.

When the other dolls in the nursery heard Raggedy Andy and Uncle Clem talking, they too sat up in their beds.

'We've been so quiet all day,' said Raggedy Andy. 'Let's have a good romp!'

This suggestion suited all the dolls, so they jumped out of their beds and ran over towards Raggedy Andy's and Uncle Clem's little bed.

Raggedy Andy, always ready for fun, threw his pillow at Henny, the Dutch doll.

Henny did not see the pillow coming towards him so he was knocked head over heels.

Henny always said 'Mamma' when he was tilted backwards or forwards, and when the pillow rolled him over and over, he cried, 'Mamma. Mamma. Mamma!'

It was not because it hurt him, for you know Santa Claus always sees to it that each doll he makes in his great workshop is covered with a very magical wish, and this wish always keeps them from getting hurt.

Henny could talk just as well as any of the other dolls when he was standing up, sitting, or lying down, but if he was being tipped forward and backward, all he could say was, 'Mamma.'

This amused Henny as much as it did the other dolls, so when he jumped to his feet he laughed and threw the pillow back at Raggedy Andy.

Raggedy Andy tried to jump to one side, but forgot that he was on the bed, and he and Uncle Clem went tumbling to the floor.

Then all the dolls ran to their beds and brought their pillows and had the jolliest pillow fight imaginable.

The excitement ran so high and the pillows flew so fast, the floor of the nursery was soon covered with feathers. It was only when all the dolls had stopped to rest and put the feathers back into the pillow cases that Raggedy Andy discovered he had lost one of his arms in the scuffle.

The dolls were worried over this and asked, 'What will Marcella say when she sees that Raggedy Andy has lost an arm?'

'We can push it up his sleeve!' said Uncle Clem. 'Then when Raggedy Andy is taken out of bed in the morning, Marcella will find his arm is loose!'

'It has been hanging by one or two threads for a day or more!' said Raggedy Andy. 'I noticed the other day that sometimes my thumb was turned clear around to the back, and I knew then that the arm was hanging by one or two threads and the threads were twisted.'

Uncle Clem pushed Raggedy Andy's arm up through his sleeve, but every time Raggedy Andy jumped about, he lost his arm again.

'This will never do!' said Raggedy Ann. 'Raggedy Andy is lopsided with only one arm and he cannot join in our games as well as if he had two arms!'

'Oh, I don't mind that!' laughed Raggedy Andy. 'Marcella will sew it on in the morning and I will be all right, I'm sure!'

'Perhaps Raggedy Ann can sew it on now!' suggested Uncle Clem.

'Yes, Raggedy Ann can sew it on!' all the dolls cried. 'She can play "Peter, Peter, Pumpkin-Eater" on the toy piano and she can sew!'

'I will gladly try,' said Raggedy Ann, 'but there are no needles or thread in the nursery, and I have to have a thimble so the needle can be pressed through Raggedy Andy's cloth!'

'Marcella always gets a needle from Mamma!' said the French doll.

'I know,' said Raggedy Ann, 'but we cannot waken Mamma to ask her!'

The dolls all laughed at this, for they knew very well that even had Mamma been awake, they would not have asked her for needle and thread, because they did not wish her to know they could act and talk just like real people.

'Perhaps we can get the things out of the machine drawer!' Henny suggested.

'Yes,' cried Susan, 'let's all go and get the things out of the machine drawer! Come on, everybody!'

And Susan, although she had only a cracked head, ran out of the nursery door followed by all the rest of the dolls.

Even the tiny little penny-dolls clicked their china heels upon the floor as they followed the rest, and Raggedy Andy, carrying his loose arm, thumped along in the rear.

Raggedy Andy had not lived in the house as long as the others; so he did not know the way to the room in which the machine stood.

After much climbing and pulling, the needle and thread and thimble were taken from the drawer, and all raced back again to the nursery. Uncle Clem took off Raggedy Andy's shirt, and the other dolls all sat around watching while Raggedy Ann sewed the arm on again.

Raggedy Ann had only taken two stitches when she began laughing so hard she had to pause. Of course when Raggedy Ann laughed, all the other dolls laughed too, for laughter, like yawning, is very catching.

'I was just thinking!' said Raggedy Ann. 'Remember, way, way back, a long, long time ago, I sewed this arm on once before?' she asked Raggedy Andy.

'I do remember, now that you mention it,' said Raggedy Andy, 'but I cannot remember how the arm came off!'

'Tell us about it!' all the dolls cried.

'Let's see!' Raggedy Ann began. 'Your mistress left you over at our house one night, and after everyone had gone to bed, we went up into the attic!'

'Oh, yes! I do remember now!' Raggedy Andy laughed. 'We played with the large whirligig!'

'Yes,' Raggedy Ann said. 'The large spinning-wheel. We held on to the wheel and went round and round! And when we were having the most fun, your feet got fastened between the wheel and the rod which held the wheel in position and there you hung, head down!'

'I remember, you were working the pedal and I was sailing around very fast,' said Raggedy Andy, 'and all of a sudden the wheel stopped!'

'We would have laughed at the time,' Raggedy Ann explained to the other dolls, 'but you see it was quite serious. My mistress had put us both to bed for the night, and if she had discovered us right up in the attic, she would have wondered how in the world we got there! So there was nothing to do but get Raggedy Andy out of the tangle!'

'But you pulled me out all right!' Raggedy Andy laughed.

'Yes, I pulled and I pulled until I pulled one of Raggedy Andy's arms off,' Raggedy Ann said. 'And then I pulled and pulled until finally his feet came out of the wheel and we both tumbled to the floor!'

'Then we ran downstairs as fast as we could and climbed into bed, didn't we!' Raggedy Andy laughed.

'Yes, we did!' Raggedy Ann replied. 'And when we jumped into bed, we remembered that we had left Raggedy Andy's arm lying up on the attic floor, so we had to run back up there and get it! Remember, Raggedy Andy?'

'Yes! Wasn't it lots of fun?'

'Indeed it was!' Raggedy Ann agreed.

'Raggedy Andy wanted to let the arm remain off until the next morning, but I decided it would be better to have it sewn on, just as it had been when Mistress put us to bed.

So, just like tonight, we went to the pincushion and found a needle and thread and I sewed it on for him!'

'There!' Raggedy Ann said, as she wound the thread around her hand and pulled, so that the thread broke near Raggedy Andy's shoulder. 'It's sewn on again, good as new!'

'Thank you, Raggedy Ann!' said Raggedy Andy, as he threw the arm about Raggedy Ann's neck and gave her a hug.

'Now we can have another game!' Uncle Clem cried as he helped Raggedy Andy into his shirt and buttoned it up for him.

Just then the little cuckoo clock on the nursery wall went, 'Whirrr!' the little door opened, and the little bird put out his head and cried, 'Cuckoo! cuckoo! cuckoo! cuckoo!'

'No more games!' Raggedy Ann said. 'We must be very quiet from now on. The folk will be getting up soon!'

'Last one in bed is a monkey!' cried Raggedy Andy.

There was a wild scramble as the dolls rushed for their beds, and Susan, having to be careful of her cracked head, was the monkey. So Raggedy Andy, seeing that Susan was slow about getting into her bed, jumped out and helped her.

Then, climbing into the little bed which Uncle Clem shared with him, he pulled the covers up to his eyes and, after pretending to snore a couple of times, he lay very quiet, thinking of the kindness of the doll friends about him, until Marcella came and took him down to breakfast.

And all the other dolls smiled at him as he left the room, for they were very happy to know that their little mistress loved him as much as they did.

The Taffy Pull

'I know how we can have a whole lot of fun!' Raggedy Andy said to the other dolls. 'We'll have a taffy pull!'

'What do you mean, Raggedy Andy?' asked the French doll.

'He means a tug of war, don't you, Raggedy Andy?' asked Henny.

'No,' Raggedy Andy replied, 'I mean a taffy pull!'

'If it's lots of fun, then show us how to play the game!' Uncle Clem said. 'We like to have fun, don't we?' And Uncle Clem turned to all the other dolls as he asked the question.

'It really is not a game,' Raggedy Andy explained. 'You see, it is only a taffy pull.

'We take sugar and water and butter and a little vinegar and put it all on the stove to cook. When it has cooked until it strings when you lift some up in a spoon, or gets hard when you drop some of it in a cup of water, then it is ready.

'Then it must be placed upon buttered plates until it has

cooled a little, and then each one takes some of the candy and pulls and pulls until it gets real white. Then it is called "Taffy".'

'That will be loads of fun!'

'Show us how to begin!'

'Let's have a taffy pull!'

'Come on, everybody!' the dolls cried.

'Just one moment!' Raggedy Ann said. She had remained quiet before, for she had been thinking very hard, so hard, in fact, that two stitches had burst in the back of her rag head. The dolls, in their eagerness to have the taffy pull, were dancing about Raggedy Andy, but when Raggedy Ann spoke, in her soft cottony voice, they all quieted down and waited for her to speak again.

'I was just thinking,' Raggedy Ann said, 'that it would be very nice to have the taffy pull, but suppose some of the folk smell the candy while it is cooking.'

'There is no one at home!' Raggedy Andy said. 'I thought of that, Raggedy Ann. They have all gone over to Cousin Jenny's house and will not be back until the day after tomorrow. I heard Mamma tell Marcella.'

'If that is the case, we can have the taffy pull and all the fun that goes with it!' Raggedy Ann cried, as she started for the nursery door.

After her ran all the dollies, their little feet pitter-patting across the floor and down the hall.

When they came to the stairway Raggedy Ann, Raggedy Andy, Uncle Clem and Henny threw themselves down the stairs, turning over and over as they fell.

The other dolls, having china heads, had to be much more careful; so they slid down the banisters or jumped from one step to another.

JOHNNY GRUELLE.

Raggedy Ann, Raggedy Andy, Uncle Clem and Henny piled in a heap at the bottom of the steps, and by the time they had untangled themselves and helped each other up, the other dolls were down the stairs.

To the kitchen they all raced. There they found the fire in the stove still burning.

Raggedy Andy brought a small stew kettle, while the others brought the sugar and water and a large spoon. They could not find the vinegar and decided not to use it, anyway.

Raggedy Andy stood upon the stove and watched the candy, dipping into it every once in a while to see if it had cooked long enough, and stirring it with the large spoon.

At last the candy began to string out from the spoon when it was held above the stew kettle, and after trying a few drops in a cup of cold water, Raggedy Andy pronounced it 'done'.

Uncle Clem pulled out a large platter from the pantry, and Raggedy Ann dipped her rag hand into the butter jar and buttered the platter.

The candy, when it was poured into the platter, was a lovely golden colour and smelled delicious to the dolls. Henny could not wait until it cooled, so he put one of his chamois-leather hands into the hot candy.

Of course it did not burn Henny, but when he pulled his hand out again, it was covered with a great ball of candy, which strung out all over the kitchen floor and got on to his clothes.

Then, too, the candy cooled quickly, and in a very short time Henny's hand was encased in a hard ball of candy. Henny couldn't wiggle any of his fingers on that hand and he was sorry he had been so hasty.

While waiting for the candy to cool, Raggedy Andy said,

'We must rub butter upon our hands before we pull the candy, or else it will stick to our hands as it has done to Henny's hands and will have to wear off!'

'Will this hard ball of candy have to wear off of my hand?' Henny asked. 'It is so hard, I cannot wiggle any of my fingers!'

'It will either have to wear off, or you will have to soak your hand in water for a long time, until the candy on it melts!' said Raggedy Andy.

'Dear me!' said Henny.

Uncle Clem brought the poker then and, asking Henny to put his hand upon the stove leg, he gave the hard candy a few sharp taps with the poker and chipped the candy from Henny's hand.

'Thank you, Uncle Clem!' Henny said, as he wiggled his fingers. 'That feels much better!'

Raggedy Andy told all the dolls to rub butter upon their hands.

'The candy is getting cool enough to pull!' he said.

Then, when all the dolls had their hands nice and buttery, Raggedy Andy cut them each a nice piece of candy and showed them how to pull it.

'Take it in one hand this way,' he said, 'and pull it with the other hand, like this!'

When all the dolls were supplied with candy they sat about and pulled it, watching it grow whiter and more silvery the longer they pulled.

Then, when the taffy was real white, it began to grow harder and harder, so the smaller dolls could scarcely pull it any more.

When this happened, Raggedy Andy, Raggedy Ann, Uncle Clem and Henny, who were larger, took the little dolls' candy and mixed it with what they had been pulling until all the taffy was snow white.

Then Raggedy Andy pulled it out into a long rope and held it while Uncle Clem hit the ends a sharp tap with the edge of the spoon.

This snipped the taffy into small pieces, just as easily as you might break icicles with a few sharp taps of a stick.

The small pieces of white taffy were placed upon the buttered platter again and the dolls all danced about it, singing and laughing, for this had been the most fun they had had for a long, long time.

'But what shall we do with it?' Raggedy Ann asked.

'Yes, what shall we do with it!' Uncle Clem said. 'We can't let it remain in the platter here upon the kitchen floor! We must hide it, or do something with it!'

'While we are trying to think of a way to dispose of it, let us be washing the stew kettle and the spoon!' said practical Raggedy Ann.

'That is a very happy thought, Raggedy Ann!' said Raggedy Andy. 'For it will clean the butter and candy from our hands while we are doing it!'

So the stew kettle was dragged to the sink and filled with water, the dolls all taking turns scraping the candy from the sides of the kettle, and scrubbing the inside with a cloth.

When the kettle was nice and clean and had been wiped dry, Raggedy Andy found a roll of waxed paper in the pantry upon one of the shelves.

'We'll wrap each piece of taffy in a nice little piece of paper,' he said, 'then we'll find a nice paper bag, and put all the pieces inside the bag, and throw it from the upstairs window when someone passes the house so that someone may have the candy!'

All the dolls gathered about the platter on the floor, and once Raggedy Andy had cut the paper into neat squares, the dolls wrapped the taffy in the papers.

Then the taffy was put into a large bag, and with much pulling and tugging it was finally dragged up into the nursery, where a window overlooked the street.

Then, just as a little boy and a little girl, who looked as though they did not ever have much candy, passed the house, the dolls all gave a push and sent the bag tumbling to the pavenment.

The two children laughed and shouted, 'Thank you,' when they saw that the bag contained candy, and the dolls, peeping from behind the lace curtains, watched the two happy-faced children eating the taffy as they skipped down the street.

When the children had passed out of sight, the dolls climbed down from the window.

'That was lots of fun!' said the French doll, as she

smoothed her skirts and sat down beside Raggedy Andy.

'I believe Raggedy Andy must have a candy heart too, like Raggedy Ann!' said Uncle Clem.

'No!' Raggedy Andy answered, 'I'm just stuffed with white cotton and I have no candy heart, but someday perhaps I shall have!'

'A candy heart is very nice!' Raggedy Ann said. (You know, she had one.) 'But one can be just as nice and happy and full of sunshine without a candy heart.'

'I almost forgot to tell you,' said Raggedy Andy, 'that when pieces of taffy are wrapped in little pieces of paper, just as we wrapped them, they are called "Kisses".'

The Rabbit Chase

'Well, what shall we play tonight?' asked Henny, the Dutch doll, when the house was quiet and the dolls all knew that no one else was awake. Raggedy Andy was just about to suggest a good game, when Fido, who sometimes slept in a basket in the nursery, growled.

All the dollies looked in his direction.

Fido was standing up with his ears sticking as straight in the air as loppy silken puppy-dog ears can stick up.

'He must have been dreaming!' said Raggedy Andy.

'No, I wasn't dreaming!' Fido answered. 'I heard something go, "Scratch! Scratch!" as plain as I hear you!'

'Where did the sound come from, Fido?' Raggedy Andy asked when he saw that Fido really was wide awake.

'From outside somewhere!' Fido answered. 'And if I could get out without disturbing all the folk, I'd run out and see what it might be! Perhaps I had better bark!'

'Please do not bark!' Raggedy Andy cried as he put his rag arm around Fido's nose. 'You will awaken everybody in the house. We can open a door or a window for you and let you out, if you must go!'

'I wish you would. Listen! There it is again: "Scratch! Scratch!" What can it be?'

'You may soon see!' said Raggedy Andy. 'We'll let you out, but please don't sit at the door and bark and bark to get back in again, as you usually do, for we are going to play a good game and we may not hear you!'

'You can sleep out in the shed after you have found out what it is,' said Raggedy Andy.

As soon as the dolls opened the door for Fido, he went running across the lawn, barking in a loud shrill voice. He ran down behind the shed and through the garden, and then back towards the house again.

Raggedy Andy and Uncle Clem stood looking out of the door, the rest of the dolls peeping over their shoulders, so when something came jumping through the door, it hit Uncle Clem and Raggedy Andy and sent them flying against the other dolls behind them.

All the dolls went down in a wiggling heap on the floor.

It was surprising that the noise and confusion did not waken Daddy and the rest of the folk, for just as the dolls were untangling themselves from each other and getting upon their feet, Fido came jumping through the door and sent the dolls tumbling again.

Fido ceased barking when he came through the door.

'Which way did he go?' he asked, when he could get his breath.

'What was it?' Raggedy Andy asked in return.

'It was a rabbit!' Fido cried. 'He ran right in here, for I could smell his tracks!'

'We could feel him!' Raggedy Andy laughed.

'I could not tell you which way he went,' Uncle Clem said, 'except I feel sure he came through the door and into the house!'

None of the dolls knew into which room the rabbit had run.

Finally, after much sniffing, Fido traced the rabbit to the nursery, where, when the dolls followed, they saw the rabbit crouching behind the rocking horse.

Fido whined and cried because he could not get to the rabbit and bite him.

'You should be ashamed of yourself, Fido!' cried Raggedy Ann. 'Just see how the poor bunny is trembling!'

'He should not come scratching around our house if he doesn't care to be chased!' said Fido.

'Why don't you stay out in the woods and fields where you really belong?' Raggedy Andy asked the rabbit.

'I came to leave some Easter eggs!' the bunny answered in a queer little quavery voice.

'An Easter bunny!' all the dolls cried, jumping about and clapping their hands. 'An Easter bunny!'

'Well!' was all Fido could say, as he sat down and began wagging his tail.

'You may come out from behind the rocking horse now, Easter bunny!' said Raggedy Andy. 'Fido will not hurt you, now that he knows, will you, Fido?'

'Indeed I won't!' Fido replied. 'I'm sorry that I chased

you! And I remember now, I had to jump over a basket out by the shed! Was that yours?'

'Yes, it was full of Easter eggs and coloured grasses for the little girl who lives here!' the bunny said.

When the Easter bunny found out that Fido and the dolls were his friends, he came out from behind the rocking horse and hopped across the floor to the door.

'I must go and see if any of the eggs are broken, for if they are, I will have to run home and colour some more! I was just about to make a nice nest and put the eggs in it when Fido came bouncing out at me!'

And with a squeeky little laugh the Easter bunny, followed by Fido and all the dolls, hopped across the lawn towards the shed.

There they found the basket. Four of the lovely coloured Easter eggs were broken.

'I will run home and colour four more. It will only take a

few minutes, so when I return and scratch again to make a nest, please do not bark at me!' said the Easter bunny.

'I won't! I promise!' Fido laughed.

'May we go with you and watch you colour the Easter eggs?' Raggedy Andy begged.

'Indeed you may!' the Easter bunny answered. 'Can you run fast?'

Then down through the garden and out through a crack in the fence the Easter bunny hopped, with a long string of dolls trailing behind.

When they came to the Easter bunny's home, they found Mamma Easter Bunny and a lot of little teeny-weeny bunnies who would someday grow up to be big Easter bunnies like their mamma and daddy bunny. The Easter bunny told them of his adventure with Fido, and all joined in his laughter when they found it had turned out well at the end.

The Easter bunny put four eggs on to boil and while these were boiling he mixed up a lot of pretty colours.

When the eggs were boiled, he dipped the four eggs into the pretty coloured dye and then painted lovely flowers on them.

When the Easter bunny had finished painting the eggs he put them in his basket and, with all the dolls running along beside him, he returned to the house.

'Why not make the nest right in the nursery?' Raggedy Andy asked.

'That would be just the thing! Then the little girl would wonder and wonder how I could ever get into the nursery without awakening the rest of the folk, for she will never suspect that you dolls and Fido let me in!'

So with Raggedy Andy leading the way, they ran up to

the nursery and there, in one corner, they watched the Easter bunny make a lovely nest and put the Easter eggs in it.

And in the morning when Marcella came in to see the dolls you can imagine her surprise when she found the pretty gift of the Easter bunny.

'How in the world did the bunny get inside the house and into this room without waking Fido?' she laughed.

And Fido, pretending to be asleep, slowly opened one eye and winked over the edge of his basket at Raggedy Andy.

And Raggedy Andy smiled back at Fido, but never said a word.

The New Tin Gutter

All day Saturday the men had worked out upon the eaves of the house and the dolls facing the window could see them.

The men made quite a lot of noise with their hammers, for they were putting new gutters around the eaves, and pounding upon tin makes a great deal of noise.

Marcella had not played with the dolls all that day, for she had gone visiting; so when the men hammered and made a lot of noise, the dolls could talk to each other without fear of anyone hearing or knowing they were really talking to each other.

'What are they doing now?' Raggedy Andy asked.

He was lying with his head beneath a little bed quilt, just as Marcella had dropped him when she left the nursery; so he could not see what was going on.

'We can only see the men's legs as they pass the window,' answered Uncle Clem. 'But they are putting new shingles or something on the roof!'

After the men had left their work and gone home to supper and the house was quiet, Raggedy Andy cautiously moved his head out from under the little bed quilt and, seeing that the coast was clear, sat up.

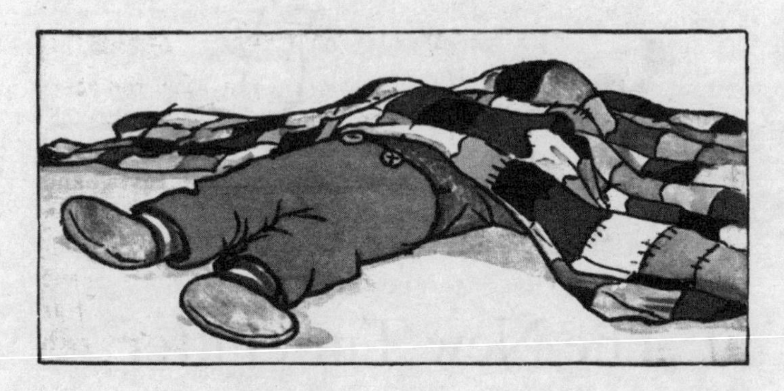

This was a signal for all the dolls to sit up and smooth out the wrinkles in their clothes.

The nursery window was open; so Raggedy Andy lifted the penny-dolls to the sill and climbed up beside them.

Leaning out, he could look along the new shiny tin gutter the men had put in place.

'Here's a grand place to have a lovely slide!' he said as he gave one of the penny-dolls a scoot down the shiny tin gutter.

'Whee! See her go!' Raggedy Andy cried.

All the other dolls climbed upon the window sill beside him.

'Scoot me too!' cried the other little penny-doll in her squeeky little voice, and Raggedy Andy took her in his rag hand and gave her a great swing which sent her scooting down the shiny tin gutter, 'Kerswish!'

Then Raggedy Andy climbed into the gutter himself and, taking a few steps, spread out his feet and went scooting down the shiny tin.

The other dolls followed his example and scooted along behind him.

When Raggedy Andy came to the place where he expected to find the penny-dolls lying, they were nowhere about.

'Perhaps you scooted them farther than you thought!' Uncle Clem said.

'Perhaps I did!' Raggedy Andy said. 'We will look around the bend in the eaves!'

'Oh dear!' he exclaimed when he had peeped around the corner of the roof, 'the gutter ends here and there is nothing but a hole!'

'They must have scooted right into the hole,' Henny, the Dutch doll said.

Raggedy Andy lay flat upon the shiny tin and looked down into the hole.

'Are you down there, penny-dolls?' he called.

There was no answer.

'I hope their heads were not broken!' Raggedy Ann said.

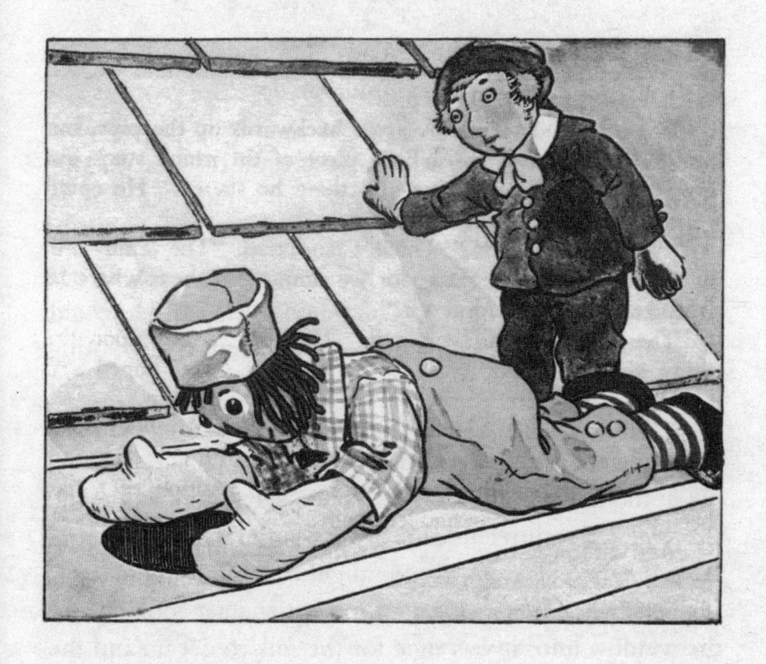

'I'm so sorry I scooted them!' Raggedy Andy cried, as he brushed his hand over his shoe-button eyes.

'Maybe if you hold to my feet, I can reach down the hole and find them and pull them up again!' he added.

Uncle Clem and Henny each caught hold of a foot of Raggedy Andy and let him slide down into the hole.

It was a rather tight fit, but Raggedy Andy wiggled and twisted until all the dolls could see of him were his two feet.

'I can't find them!' he said in muffled tones. 'Let me down farther and I think I'll be able to reach them!'

Now Henny and Uncle Clem thought that Raggedy Andy meant for them to let go of his feet and this they did.

Raggedy Andy kept wiggling and twisting until he came to a bend in the pipe and could go no farther.

'I can't find them!' he cried. 'They have gone farther down the pipe! Now you can pull me up!'

'We can't reach you, Raggedy Andy!' Uncle Clem called down the pipe. 'Try to wiggle back up a bit and we will catch your feet and pull you up!'

Raggedy Andy tried to wiggle backwards up the pipe, but his clothes caught upon a little piece of tin which stuck out from the inside of the pipe and there he stayed. He could neither go down nor come back up.

'What shall we do?' Uncle Clem cried, 'The folk will never find him down there, for we cannot tell them where he is, and they will never guess!'

The dolls were all very sad. They stayed out upon the shiny new tin gutter until it began raining and hoped and hoped that Raggedy Andy could get back up to them.

Then they went inside the nursery and sat looking out the window until it was time for the folk to get up and the house to be astir. Then they went back to the position each had been in when Marcella had left them.

And although they were very quiet, each one was so sorry to lose Raggedy Andy, and each felt that he would never be found again.

'The rain must have soaked his cotton through and through!' sighed Raggedy Ann. 'For all the water from the house runs down the shiny tin gutters and down the pipe into a rain barrel at the bottom!'

Then Raggedy Ann remembered that there was an opening at the bottom of the pipe.

'Tomorrow night, if we have a chance, we dolls must take a stick and see if we can reach Raggedy Andy from the bottom of the pipe and pull him down to us!' she thought.

Marcella came up to the nursery and played all day,

JOHNNY GRUELLE

watching the rain patter upon the new tin gutter. She wondered where Raggedy Andy was, although she did not get worried about him until she had asked Mamma where he might be.

'He must be just where you left him!' Mamma said.

'I cannot remember where I left him!' Marcella said. 'I thought he was with all the other dolls in the nursery, though!'

All day Sunday it rained and all of Sunday night, and on Monday morning when Daddy set off to work it was still raining.

As Daddy walked out of the front gate, he turned to wave goodbye to Mamma and Marcella and then he saw something.

Daddy came right back into the house and telephoned the men who had put in the new shiny tin gutters.

'The drainpipe is plugged up. One of you must have left something in the eaves, and it has washed down into the pipe so that the water pours over the gutter in sheets!'

'We will send a man right up to fix it!' the men said.

So along about ten o'clock that morning one of the men came to fix the pipe.

But although he punched a long pole down the pipe, and punched and punched, he could not dislodge whatever it was that plugged the pipe and kept the water from running through it.

Then the man measured with his stick, so that he knew just where the place was, and with a pair of tin shears he cut a section from the pipe and found Raggedy Andy.

Raggedy Andy was punched quite out of shape and all jammed together, but when the man straightened out the funny little figure, Raggedy Andy looked up at him with his customary happy smile.

The man laughed and carried little water-soaked Raggedy Andy into the house.

'I guess your little girl must have dropped this rag doll down into the drainpipe!' the man said to Mamma.

'I'm so glad you found him!' Mamma told the man. 'We have hunted all over the house for him! Marcella could not remember where she put him; so when I get him nice and dry, I'll hide him in a nice easy place for her to find, and she will not know he has been out in the rain all night!'

So Mamma put Raggedy Andy behind the radiator and there he sat all afternoon, steaming and drying out.

And as he sat there he smiled and smiled, even though there was no one to see him.

He felt very happy within and he liked to smile, anyway, because his smile was painted on.

And another reason Raggedy Andy smiled was because he was not lonely. Inside his shirt were the two little penny-dolls.

The man had punched Raggedy Andy farther down into the pipe, and he had been able to reach the two little dolls and tuck them into a safe place.

'Won't they all be surprised to see us back again!' Raggedy Andy whispered as he patted the two little penny-dolls with his soft rag hands.

And the two little penny-dolls nestled against Raggedy Andy's soft cotton stuffed body, and thought how nice it was to have such a happy, sunny friend.

Dr Raggedy Andy

Raggedy Andy, Raggedy Ann, Uncle Clem and Henny were not given medicine. Because, you see, they had no mouths.

That is, mouths through which medicine could be poured.

Their mouths were either painted on, or were sewn on with yarn. Sometimes the medicine spoon would be touched to their faces but none of the liquid would be tipped out. Except accidentally.

But the French doll had a lovely mouth for taking medicine; it was open and showed her teeth in a dimpling smile. She also had soft brown eyes which opened and closed when she was tilted backwards or forwards.

The medicine which was given the dolls had great curing properties.

It would cure the most stubborn case of croup, measles, whooping cough or any other ailment the dolls had wished upon them by their little mistress.

Some days all the dolls would be put to bed with measles but in the course of half an hour they would have every other ailment in the *Home Doctor* book.

The dolls enjoyed it very much, for, you see, Marcella always tried the medicine first to see if it was strong enough before she gave any to the dolls.

So the dolls really did not get as much of the medicine as their little mistress.

The wonderful remedy was made from a very old recipe handed down from ancient times. This recipe is guaranteed to cure every ill a doll may have.

The medicine was made from brown sugar and water. Perhaps you may have used it for your dollies.

The medicine was also used as 'tea' and 'soda-water', except when the dolls were supposed to be ill.

Having nothing but painted or yarn mouths, the ailments of Raggedy Andy, Raggedy Ann, Uncle Clem and Henny, the Dutch doll, mostly consisted of sprained wrists, arms and legs, or perhaps a headache and a toothache.

None of them knew they had the trouble until Marcella had wrapped up the 'injured' rag arm, leg or head, and had explained in detail just what was the matter.

Raggedy Andy, Raggedy Ann, Uncle Clem or Henny were just as happy with their heads tied up for the toothache as they were without their heads tied up.

Not having teeth, naturally they could not have the toothache, but if they could furnish amusement for Marcella by having her pretend they had the toothache, then that made them very happy.

So this day, the French doll was quite ill. She started out with the croup, and went through the measles, whooping cough and yellow fever in an hour.

The attack came on quite suddenly.

The French doll was sitting quietly in one of the little red chairs, smiling the prettiest of dimpling smiles at Raggedy Andy, and thinking of the romp the dolls would have that night after the house grew quiet, when Marcella discovered that the French doll had the croup and put her to bed.

The French doll closed her eyes when put to bed, but the rest of her face did not change expression. She still wore her happy smile.

Marcella mixed the medicine very 'strong' and poured it into the French doll's open mouth.

She was given a dose every minute or so.

It was during the yellow-fever stage that Marcella was called to supper and left the dolls in the nursery alone.

Marcella did not play with them again that evening; so

the dolls all remained in the same position until Marcella and the rest of the folk went to bed.

Then Raggedy Andy jumped from his chair and wound up the little music box. 'Let's start with a lively dance!' he cried.

When the music started tinkling he caught the French doll's hand and danced away across the nursery floor before he discovered that her soft brown eyes remained closed, as they were when she lay upon the 'sick' bed.

All the dolls gathered around Raggedy Andy and the French doll.

'I can't open my eyes!' she said.

Raggedy Andy tried to open the French doll's eyes with his soft rag hands, but it was no use.

They shook her. This sometimes has the desired effect when dolls do not open their eyes. They shook her again and again. It was no use, her eyes remained closed.

'It must be the sticky, sugary medicine!' said Uncle Clem.

'I really believe it must be!' the French doll replied. 'The medicine seemed to settle in the back of my head when I was lying down, and I can still feel it there!'

'That must be it, and now it has hardened and keeps your pretty eyes from working!' said Raggedy Ann. 'What shall we do?'

Raggedy Andy and Raggedy Ann walked over to a corner of the nursery and thought and thought. They pulled their foreheads down into wrinkles with their hands, so that they might think harder.

Finally Raggedy Ann cried, 'I've thought of a plan!' and went skipping from the corner out to where the other dolls sat about the French doll.

'We must stand her upon her head, then the medicine will run into her hair, for there is a hole in the top of her head. I remember seeing it once when her hair came off!'

'No sooner said than done!' cried Uncle Clem, as he took the French doll by the waist and stood her upon her head.

'That should be long enough!' Raggedy Ann said, when Uncle Clem had held the French doll in this position for five minutes.

But when the French doll was again placed upon her feet her eyes still remained tightly closed.

All this time, Raggedy Andy had been in the corner, thinking as hard as his rag head would think.

He thought and thought, until the yarn hair upon his head stood up in the air and wiggled.

'If the medicine did not run up into her hair when she stood upon her head,' thought Raggedy Andy, 'then it is because the medicine could not run; so, if the medicine cannot run, it is because it is too sticky and thick to run out of the hole in the top of her head.' He also thought a lot more.

At last he turned to the others and said out loud, 'I can't seem to think of a single way to help her open her eyes

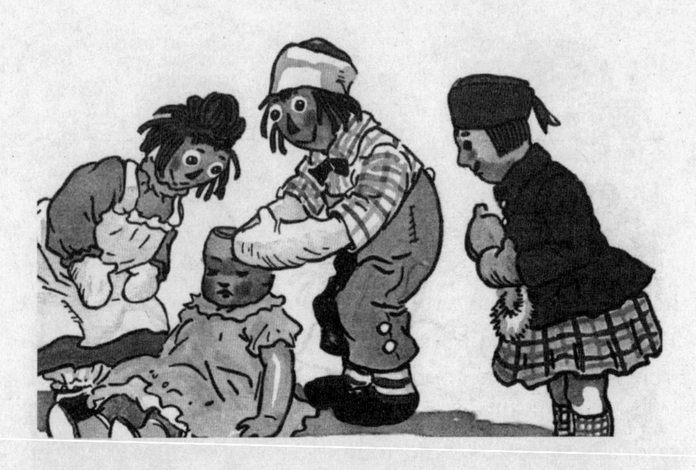

unless we take off her hair and wash the medicine from inside her china head.'

'Why didn't I think of that?' Raggedy Ann asked. 'That is just what we shall have to do!'

So Raggedy Ann caught hold of the French doll's feet, and Raggedy Andy caught hold of the French doll's lively curls, and they pulled and they pulled.

Then the other dolls caught hold of Raggedy Ann and Raggedy Andy and pulled and pulled, until finally, with a sharp 'R-R-Rip!' the French doll's hair came off, and the dolls who were pulling went tumbling over backwards.

Laughingly they scrambled to their feet and sat the French doll up, so they might look into the hole in the top of her head.

Yes, the sticky medicine had grown hard and would not let the French doll's eyes open.

Raggedy Andy put his hand inside and pushed on the eyes so that they opened.

This was all right, only now the eyes would not close when the French doll lay down. She tried it.

So Raggedy Andy ran down into the kitchen and brought up a small tin cup full of warm water and a tiny rag.

With these he loosened the sticky medicine and washed the inside of the French doll's head nice and clean.

There were lots of cooky and cracker crumbs inside her head, too.

Raggedy Andy washed it all nice and clean, and then wet the glue which made the pretty curls stay on.

So when her hair was placed upon her head again, the French doll was as good as new.

'Thank you all very much!' she said, as she tilted backwards and forwards, and found that her eyes worked very easily.

Raggedy Andy again wound up the little music box and, catching the French doll about the waist, started a rollicking dance which lasted until the roosters in the neighbourhood began their morning crowing.

Then, knowing the folk might soon be astir, the dolls ended their playing, and all took the same positions they had been in when Marcella left them the night before.

And so Marcella found them.

The French doll was in bed with her eyes closed, and her happy dimpling smile lighting up her pretty face.

And to this day, the dollies' little mistress does not know that Raggedy Andy was the doctor who cured the French doll of her only ill.

Raggedy Andy's Smile

Raggedy Andy's smile was gone.

Not entirely, but enough to make his face seem one-sided.

If one viewed Raggedy Andy from the left side, one could see his smile.

But if one looked at Raggedy Andy from the right side, one could not see his smile. So Raggedy Andy's smile was gone.

It really was not Raggedy Andy's fault.

He felt just as happy and sunny as ever, and perhaps would not have known the difference had not the other dolls told him he had only one half of his cheery smile left.

Nor was it Marcella's fault. How was she to know that Dickie would feed Raggedy Andy orange juice and take off most of his smile?

And besides taking off one half of Raggedy Andy's smile, the orange juice left a great brown stain upon his face.

Marcella was very sorry when she saw what Dickie had done.

Dickie would have been sorry, too, if he had been more than two years old, but when one is only two years old, one has very few sorrows.

Dickie's only sorrow was that Raggedy Andy was taken from him, and he could not feed Raggedy Andy more orange juice.

Marcella kissed Raggedy Andy more than she did the rest of the dolls that night, when she put them to bed, and this made all the dolls very happy. It always gave them great pleasure when any of their number was hugged and kissed, for there was not a selfish doll among them.

Marcella hung up a tiny stocking for each of the dollies, and placed a tiny little china dish for each of the penny-dolls beside their little spool box bed.

For, as you probably have guessed, it was Christmas Eve, and Marcella was in hopes Santa Claus would see the tiny stockings and place something in them for each dollie.

Then, when the house was very quiet, the French doll told Raggedy Andy that most of his smile was gone.

'Indeed!' said Raggedy Andy. 'I can still feel it! It must be there!'

'Oh, but it really is gone!' Uncle Clem said. 'It was the orange juice!'

'Well, I still feel just as happy,' said Raggedy Andy, 'so let's have a jolly game of some sort! What shall it be?'

'Perhaps we had best try to wash your face!' said practical Raggedy Ann. She always acted as a mother to the other dolls when they were alone.

'It will not do a bit of good!' the French doll told Raggedy Ann, 'for I remember I had orange juice spilled upon a nice white frock I had one time, and the stain would never come out!'

'That is too bad!' Henny, the Dutch doll, said. 'We shall miss Raggedy Andy's cheery smile when he is looking straight at us!'

'You will have to stand on my right side, when you wish to see my smile!' said Raggedy Andy, with a cheery little chuckle way down in his soft cotton inside.

'But I wish everyone to understand,' he went on, 'that I am smiling just the same, whether you can see it or not!'

And with this, Raggedy Andy caught hold of Uncle Clem and Henny, and made a dash for the nursery door, followed by all the other dolls.

Raggedy Andy intended jumping down the stairs, head over heels, for he knew that neither he, Uncle Clem nor Henny would break anything by jumping down stairs.

But just as they got almost to the door, they dropped to the floor in a heap, for there, standing watching the whole performance, was a man.

All the dolls fell in different attitudes, for it would never do for them to let a real person see that they could act and talk just like real people.

Raggedy Andy, Uncle Clem and Henny stopped so suddenly they fell over each other and Raggedy Andy, being in the lead and pulling the other two, slid right through the door and stopped at the feet of the man.

A cheery laugh greeted this and a chubby hand reached down and picked up Raggedy Andy and turned him over.

Raggedy Andy looked up into a cheery round face, with a jolly red nose and red cheeks, and all framed in white whiskers which looked just like snow.

Then the jovial round man walked into the nursery and picked up all the dolls and looked at them. He made no noise when he walked, and this was why he had taken the dolls by surprise at the head of the stairs.

The jolly man with the snow-white whiskers placed all the dolls in a row and from a small case in his pocket he took a tiny bottle and a little brush. He dipped the little brush in the tiny bottle and touched all the dolls' faces with it.

He had purposely saved Raggedy Andy's face until the last. Then, as all the dolls watched, the cheery white-whiskered man touched Raggedy Andy's face with the magic liquid, and the orange-juice stain disappeared, and in its place came Raggedy Andy's rosy cheeks and cheery smile.

And, turning Raggedy Andy so that he could face all the other dolls, the cheery fellow showed him that all the other dolls had new rosy cheeks and newly-painted faces. They all looked just like new dollies. Even Susan's cracked head had been made whole.

Henny, the Dutch doll, was so surprised he fell over backwards and said, 'Squeek!'

When the cheery man with the white whiskers heard this, he picked Henny up and touched him with the paint-brush in the centre of the back, just above the place where Henny had the little mechanism which made him say 'Mamma' when he was new. And when the visitor touched Henny and tipped him forwards and backwards, Henny was just as good as new and said, 'Mamma', very prettily.

Then the jolly stranger put something in each of the tiny doll stockings, and something in each of the little china plates for the two penny-dolls.

Then, as quietly as he had entered, he left, merely turning at the door and shaking his finger at the dolls in a cheery, mischievous manner.

Raggedy Andy heard him chuckling to himself as he went down the stairs.

Raggedy Andy tiptoed to the door and over to the head of the stairs.

Then he motioned for the other dolls to come.

There, from the head of the stairs, they watched the cheery white-whiskered figure take pretty things from a large sack and place them about the chimneyplace.

'He does not know that we are watching him,' the dolls all thought, but when the jolly man had finished his task, he turned quickly and laughed right up at the dolls, for he had known that they were watching him all the time.

Then, again shaking his finger at them in his cheery manner, the rosy-cheeked white-whiskered man swung the sack to his shoulder, and with a whistle such as the wind makes when it plays through the chinks of a window, he was gone – up the chimney.

The dolls were very quiet as they walked back into the nursery and sat down to think it all over, and as they sat there thinking, they heard out in the night the tinkle, tinkle, tinkle of tiny sleigh bells, growing fainter and fainter as the sleigh disappeared in the distance.

Without a word, but filled with a happy wonder, the dolls climbed into their beds, just as Marcella had left them, and pulled the covers up to their chins.

And Raggedy Andy lay there, his little shoe-button eyes looking straight towards the ceiling and smiling a joyful smile – not a half-smile this time, but a full-size smile.

The Wooden Horse

Santa Claus left a whole lot of toys.

A wooden horse, covered with Canton flannel and touched lightly with a paintbrush dipped in black paint to give him a dappled grey appearance, was one of the presents.

With the wooden horse came a beautiful red wagon with four yellow wheels. My! The paint was pretty and shiny.

The wooden horse was hitched to the wagon with a patent leather harness; and he, himself, stood proudly upon a red platform running on four little nickel wheels.

It was true that the wooden horse's eyes were as far apart as a camel's and made him look quite like one when viewed from in front, but he had soft leather ears and a silken mane and tail.

He was nice to look upon, was the wooden horse. All the dolls patted him and smoothed his silken mane and felt his shiny patent leather harness the first night they were alone with him in the nursery.

The wooden horse had a queer voice; the dolls could hardly understand him at first, but when his bashfulness wore off, he talked quite plainly.

'It is the first time I have ever tried to talk,' he explained when he became acquainted, 'and I guess I was talking down in my stomach instead of my head!'

'You will like it here in the nursery very much!' said Raggedy Andy. 'We have such jolly times and love each other so much I know you will enjoy your new home!'

'I am sure I shall!' the wooden horse answered. 'Where I came from, we – the other horses and myself – just stood silently upon the shelves and looked and looked straight ahead, and never so much as moved our tails.'

'See if you can move your tail now!' Henny, the Dutch doll, suggested.

The wooden horse started to roll across the nursery floor and if Raggedy Ann had not been in the way, he might have bumped into the wall. As it was, the wooden horse rolled against Raggedy Ann and upset her but could go no farther when his wheels ran against her rag foot.

When the wooden horse upset Raggedy Ann, he stood

JOHNNY GRUELLE

still until Uncle Clem and Henny and Raggedy Andy lifted him off Raggedy Ann's feet. 'Did I flick my tail?' he asked when Raggedy Ann stood up and smoothed her apron.

'Try it again!' said Raggedy Ann. 'I couldn't see!' She laughed her cheery rag-doll laugh, for Raggedy Ann, no matter what happened, never lost her temper.

The wooden horse started rolling backwards at this and knocked Henny over upon his back, causing him to cry, 'Mamma!' in his squeeky voice.

Uncle Clem, Raggedy Ann and the tin soldier all held on to the wooden horse and managed to stop him just as he was backing out of the nursery door towards the head of the stairs.

Then the dolls pulled the wooden horse back to the centre of the room. 'It's funny,' he said, 'that I start moving backwards or forwards when I try to flick my tail!'

'I believe it is because you have stood so long upon the shelf without moving,' Raggedy Andy suggested. 'Suppose you try moving forward!'

Uncle Clem, who was standing in front of the wooden horse, jumped to one side so hastily his feet slipped out from under him, just as if he had been sliding upon slippery ice.

The wooden horse did not start moving forward as Uncle Clem had expected; instead, his silken tail flicked gaily up over his back.

'Whee! There, you flicked your tail!' cried all the dolls as joyfully as if the wooden horse had done something truly wonderful.

'It's easy now!' said the wooden horse. 'When I wish to move forwards or backwards I'll try to flick my tail and then I'll roll along on my shiny wheels; then when I wish to flick my tail I'll try to roll forwards or backwards, like this!' And instead of rolling forward, the wooden horse flicked his tail. 'I wanted to flick my tail then!' he said in surprise. 'Now I'll roll forward!' And sure enough, the wooden horse rolled across the nursery floor.

When he started rolling upon his shiny wheels, Raggedy Andy cried, 'All aboard!' and, taking a short run, he leaped upon the wooden horse's back. Uncle Clem, Raggedy Ann, Henny, the Dutch doll, and Susan, the doll whose head was no longer cracked, all scrambled up into the pretty red wagon.

The wooden horse thought this was great fun and round and round the nursery he circled. His shiny wheels and the pretty yellow wheels of the red wagon creaked so loudly none of the dolls heard the cries of the tiny penny-dolls who were too small to climb aboard. Finally, as the wagon-load of dolls passed the penny-dolls, Raggedy Andy noticed the two little midgets standing together and missing the fun; so, leaning way over to one side as the horse swept by them, Raggedy Andy caught both the penny-dolls in his strong rag arms and lifted them to a seat upon the broad back of the wooden horse.

'Hooray!' cried all the dolls when they saw Raggedy Andy's feat. 'It was just like a Wild West Show!'

'We must all have all the fun we can together!' said Raggedy Andy.

'Good for you!' cried Uncle Clem. 'The more fun we can give each other, the more fun each one of us will have!'

The wooden horse made the circle of the nursery a great many times, for it pleased him very much to hear the gay laughter of the dolls and he thought to himself, 'How happy I will be, living with such a jolly crowd.'

But just as he was about to pass the door again, there was a noise upon the stairs and the wooden horse, hearing it, stopped so suddenly Raggedy Andy and the penny-dolls went clear over his head and the dolls in the front of the wagon took Raggedy Andy's seat upon the horse's back.

They lay just as they fell, for they did not wish anyone to suspect that they could move or talk.

'Ha! Ha! Ha! I knew you were having a lot of fun!' cried a cheery voice.

At this, all the dolls immediately scrambled back into their former places, for they recognised the voice of the French dollie.

But what was their surprise to see her dressed in a lovely fairy costume, her pretty curls flying out behind, as she ran towards them.

Raggedy Andy was just about to climb upon the horse's back again when the French doll leaped there herself and, balancing lightly upon one foot, stood in this position while the wooden horse rolled around the nursery as fast as he could go.

Raggedy Andy and the two penny-dolls ran after the wagon and, with the assistance of Uncle Clem and Raggedy Ann, climbed aboard.

When the wooden horse finally stopped the dolls all said, 'This is the most fun we have had for a *long* time!'

The wooden horse, a thrill of happiness running through his wooden body, cried, 'It is the most fun I have *ever* had!'

And the dolls, while they did not tell him so, knew that he had had the most fun because he had given *them* the most pleasure.

For, as you must surely know, they who are the most unselfish are the ones who gain the greatest joy; because they give happiness to others.

Making 'Angels' in the Snow

'Whee! It's good to be back home again!' said Raggedy Andy to the other dolls, as he stretched his feet out in front of the little toy stove and rubbed his rag hands briskly together, as if to warm them.

All the dolls laughed at Raggedy Andy for doing this, for they knew there had never been a fire in the little toy stove in all the time it had been in the nursery. And that was a long time.

'We are so glad and happy to have you back home again with us,' the dolls told Raggedy Andy, 'for we have missed you very, very much!'

'Well,' Raggedy Andy replied, as he held his rag hands over the tiny lid of the stove and rubbed them again, 'I have missed all of you, too, and wished many times that you had been with me to share in the pleasures and frolics I've had.'

And as Raggedy Andy continued to hold his hands over the little stove, Uncle Clem asked him why he did it.

JOHNNY GRUELLE

Raggedy Andy smiled and leaned back in his chair. 'Really,' he said, 'I wasn't paying any attention to what I was doing! I've spent so much of my time while I have been away drying out my soft cotton stuffing it seems as though it has almost become a habit.'

'Were you wet most of the time, Raggedy Andy?' the French doll asked.

'Nearly all the time!' Raggedy Andy replied. 'First I would get sopping wet and then I'd freeze!'

'Freeze!' exclaimed all the dolls in one breath.

'Dear me, yes!' Raggedy Andy laughed. 'Just see here!' And Raggedy Andy pulled his sleeve up and showed where his rag arm had been mended. 'That was quite a rip!' he smiled.

'Dear! Dear! How in the world did it happen? On a nail?' Henny, the Dutch doll, asked as he put his arm about Raggedy Andy.

'Froze!' said Raggedy Andy.

The dolls gathered around Raggedy Andy and examined the rip in his rag arm.

'It's all right now!' he laughed. 'But you should have seen me when it happened! I was frozen into one solid cake of ice all the way through, and when Marcella tried to limber up my arm before it had thawed out, it went, 'Pop!' and just bursted.

'Then I was placed in a pan of nice warm water until the icy cotton inside me had melted, and then I was hung up on a line above the kitchen stove, out at Grandma's.'

'But how did you happen to get so wet and then freeze?' asked Raggedy Ann.

'Out across the road from Grandma's home, way out in the country, there is a lovely pond,' Raggedy Andy explained.

'In the summertime pretty flowers grow about the edge, the little green frogs sit upon the pond lilies and beat upon their tiny drums all through the night, and the twinkling stars wink at their reflections in the smooth water. But when Marcella and I went out to Grandma's, last week, Grandma met us with a sleigh, for the ground was covered with starry snow. The pretty pond was covered with ice, too, and upon the ice was a soft blanket of the white, white snow. It was beautiful!' said Raggedy Andy.

'Grandma had a lovely new sledge for Marcella, a red one with shiny runners.

'And after we spent some time with Grandma, we went out to the pond for a slide.

'It was heaps of fun, for there was a little hill at one end of the pond so that when we coasted down we went scooting across the pond like an arrow.

'Marcella would turn the sledge sideways, just for fun, and she and I would fall off and go sliding across the ice upon our backs, leaving a clean path of ice, where we pushed aside the snow as we slid. Then Marcella showed me how to make "angels" in the soft snow!'

'Oh, tell us how, Raggedy Andy!' shouted all the dollies.

'It's very easy!' said Raggedy Andy. 'Marcella would lie down upon her back in the snow and put her hands back up over her head, then she would bring her hands in a circle down to her sides, like this.' And Raggedy Andy lay upon the floor of the nursery and showed the dollies just how it was done. 'Then,' he added, 'when she stood up it would leave the print of her body and legs in the white, white snow, and where she had swooped her arms there were the angel's wings!'

'It must have looked just like an angel!' said Uncle Clem.

'Indeed it was very pretty!' Raggedy Andy answered. 'Then Marcella made a lot of angels by placing me in the snow and working my arms; so you see, what with falling off the sledge so much and making so many angels, we both were wet, but I was completely soaked through. My cotton just became soppy and I was ever so much heavier! Then Grandma, just as we were having a most delightful time, came to the door and 'Ooh-hooed' to Marcella to come and get a nice new doughnut. So Marcella, thinking to return in a minute, left me lying upon the sledge and ran through the snow to the house. And there I stayed and stayed until I began to feel stiff and could hear the cotton inside me go, 'Tic! Tic!' as it began to freeze.

'I lay upon the sledge until after the sun went down. Two little chicadees came and sat upon the sledge and talked to me in their cute little bird language, and I watched the sky in the west get golden red, then turn into a deep crimson purple and finally a deep blue, as the sun went farther down around the bend of the earth. After it had been dark for some time, I heard someone coming through the snow and could see the yellow light of a lantern. It was Grandma.

'She pulled the sledge back to the house and did not see that I was upon it until she turned to go into the kitchen; then she picked me up and took me inside.

'He's frozen as stiff as a board!' she told Marcella as she handed me to her. Marcella did not say why she had forgotten to come for me, but I found out afterwards that it was because she was so wet. Grandma made her change her clothes and shoes and stockings and would not permit her to go out and play again.

'Well, anyway,' concluded Raggedy Andy, 'Marcella tried to limber my arm and, being almost solid ice, it just burst. And that is the way it went all the time we were out at Grandma's; I was wet nearly all the time. But I wish you could all have been with me to share in the fun.'

And Raggedy Andy again leaned over the little toy stove and rubbed his rag hands briskly together.

Uncle Clem went to the waste-paper basket and came back with some scraps of yellow and red paper. Then, taking off one of the tiny lids, he stuffed the paper in part of the way, as if the flames were 'shooting up'!

Then, as all the dolls' merry laughter rang out, Raggedy Andy stopped rubbing his hands, and catching Raggedy Ann about the waist, he went skipping across the nursery floor with her, whirling so fast neither saw they had gone out through the door until it was too late. For coming to the head of the stairs, they both went head over heels, 'blumpity, blump!' over and over, until they wound up, laughing, at the bottom.

'Last one up is a cry baby!' cried Raggedy Ann, as she scrambled to her feet. And with her skirts in her rag hands she went racing up the stairs to where the rest of the dollies stood laughing.

'Hurrah, for Raggedy Ann!' cried Raggedy Andy generously. 'She won!'

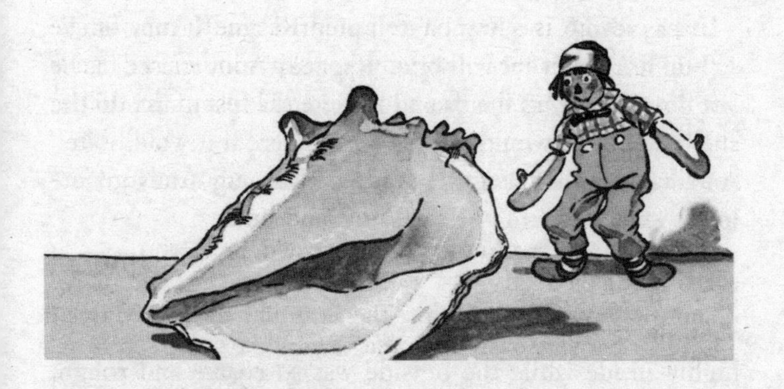

The Singing Shell

For years and years the beautiful shell had been upon the floor in Grandma's front room. It was a large shell with many points upon it. These were coarse and rough, but the shell was most beautiful inside.

Marcella had seen the shell time and time again and often admired its lovely colouring, which could be seen when one looked inside the shell.

So one day, Grandma gave the beautiful shell to Marcella to have for her very own, up in the nursery.

'It will be nice to place before the nursery door so the wind will not blow the door to and pinch anyone's fingers!' Grandma laughed.

So Marcella brought the shell home and placed it in front of the nursery door. Here the dolls saw it that night, when all the house was still, and stood about it wondering what kind of toy it might be.

'It seems to be nearly all mouth!' said Henny, the Dutch doll. 'Perhaps it can talk.'

'It has teeth!' the French doll pointed out. 'It may bite!'

'I do not believe it will bite,' Raggedy Andy mused, as he got down upon his hands and knees and looked up into the shell. 'Marcella would not have it up here if it would bite!' And, saying this, Raggedy Andy put his rag arm into the lovely shell's mouth.

'It doesn't bite! I knew it wouldn't!' he cried. 'Just feel how smooth it is inside!'

All the dolls felt and were surprised to find it polished so highly inside while the outside was so coarse and rough. With the help of Uncle Clem and Henny, Raggedy Andy turned the shell upon its back, so that all the dolls might look in.

The colouring consisted of dainty pinks, creamy whites and pale blues, all running together just as the colouring in an opal runs from one shade into another. Raggedy Andy, stooping over to look farther up inside the pretty shell, heard something.

'It's whispering!' he said, as he raised up in surprise.

All the dolls took turns putting their ears to the mouth of the beautiful shell. Yes, truly it whispered, but they could not catch just what it said.

Finally Raggedy Andy suggested that all the dolls lie down upon the floor directly before the shell and keep very quiet.

'If we don't make a sound we may be able to hear what it says!' he explained.

So the dolls lay down, placing themselves flat upon the floor directly in front of the shell from where they could see and admire its beautiful colouring.

Now the dolls could be very, very quiet when they really wished to be, and it was easy for them to hear the faint whispering of the shell.

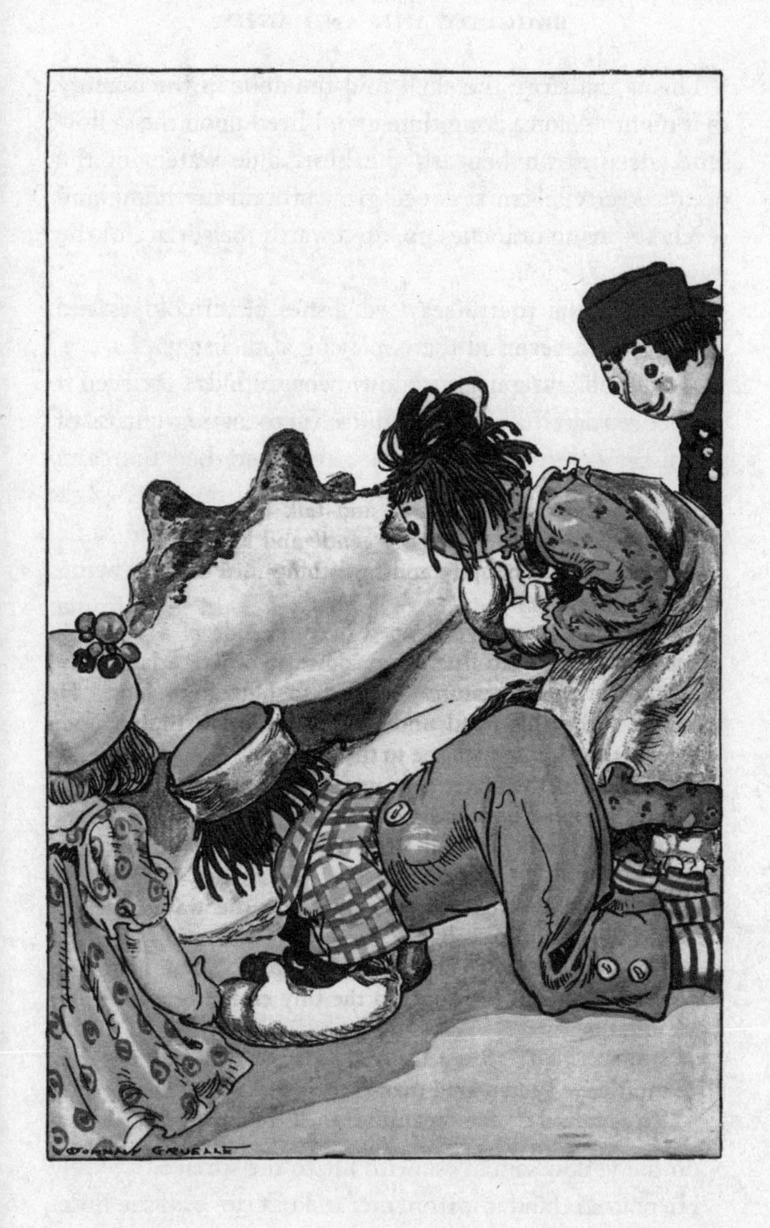
JOHNNY GRUELLE

This is the story the shell told the dolls in the nursery that night: 'A long, long time ago, I lived upon the yellow sand, deep down beneath the blue, blue waters of the ocean. Pretty silken seaweed grew around my home and reached waving branches up, up towards the surface of the water.

'Through the pretty seaweed, fishes of all colours and shapes darted here and there, playing at their games.

'It was still and quiet way down where I lived, for even if the ocean roared and pounded itself into an angry mass of tumbling waves up above, this never disturbed the calm waters down below.

'Many times, little fishes or other tiny sea people came and hid within my pretty house when they were being pursued by larger sea creatures. And it always made me very happy to give them this protection. They would stay inside until I whispered that the larger creature had gone, then they would leave me and return to their play.

'Elegant little sea horses with slender, curving bodies often went sailing above me, or would come to rest upon my back. It was nice to lie and watch the tiny things curl their little tails about the seaweed and talk together, for the sea horses like one another and are gentle and kind to each other, sharing their food happily and smoothing their little ones with their cunning noses.

'But one day a diver leaped over the side of a boat and came swimming headfirst down, down to where I lay. My! How the tiny sea creatures scurried to hide from him. He scooped me up with his hand, and giving his feet a thump upon the yellow sand, rose with me to the surface.

'He poured the water from me, and out came all the little creatures who had been hiding there!'

Raggedy Andy wiggled upon the floor, he was so interested.

'Did the tiny creatures get back into the water safely?' he asked the beautiful shell.

'Oh, yes!' the shell whispered in reply. 'The man held me over the side of the boat, so the tiny creatures went safely back into the water!'

'I am so glad!' Raggedy Andy said, with a sigh of relief. 'He must have been a kindly man!'

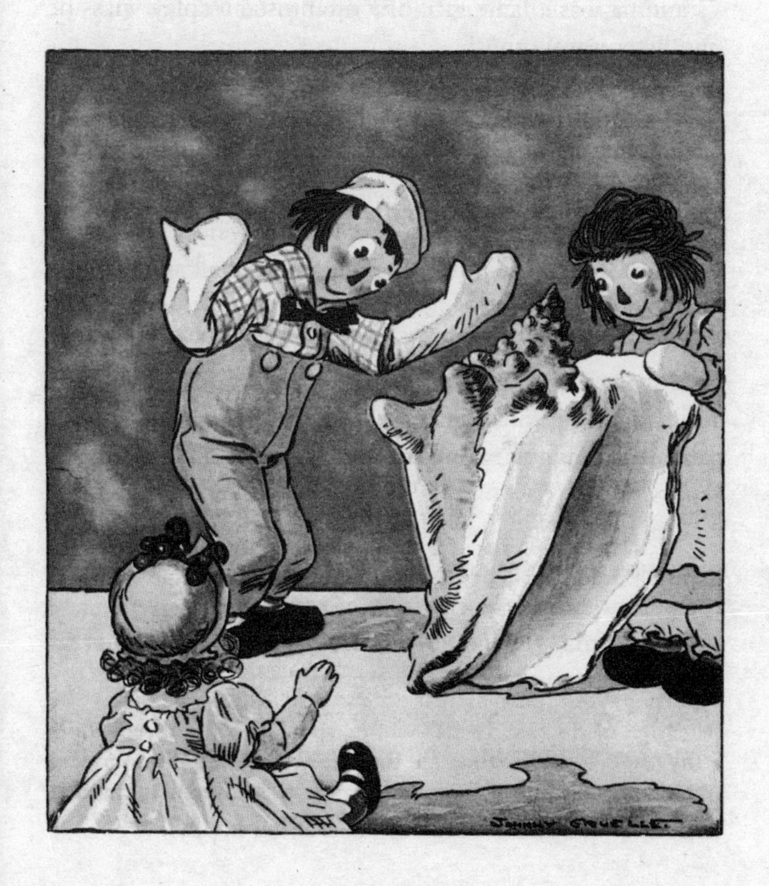

'Yes, indeed!' the beautiful shell replied. 'So I was placed along with a lot of other shells in the bottom of the boat and every once in a while another shell was placed among us. We whispered together and wondered where we were going. We were finally sold to different people and I have been at Grandma's house for a long, long time.'

'You lived there when Grandma was a little girl, didn't you?' Raggedy Ann asked.

'Yes,' replied the shell, 'I have lived there ever since Grandma was a little girl. She often used to play with me and listen to me sing.'

'Raggedy Ann can play "Peter, Peter, Pumpkin-Eater" on the piano, with one hand,' said Uncle Clem, 'but none of us can sing. Will you sing for us?' he asked the shell.

'I sing all the time,' the shell replied, 'for I cannot help singing, but my singing is a secret and so is very soft and low. Put your head close to the opening in my shell and listen!'

The dolls took turns doing this, and heard the shell sing softly and very sweetly.

'How strange and far away it sounds!' exclaimed the French doll. 'Like fairies singing in the distance! The shell must be singing the songs of the mermaids and the water-fairies!'

'It is queer that anything so rough on the outside could be so pretty within!' said Raggedy Andy. 'It must be a great pleasure to be able to sing so sweetly!'

'Indeed it is,' replied the beautiful shell, 'and I get a great happiness from singing all the time.'

'And you will bring lots of pleasure to us, by being so happy!' said Raggedy Andy. 'For although you may not enter into our games, we will always know that you are happily singing, and that will make us all happy!'

'I will tell you the secret of my singing,' said the shell. 'When anyone puts his ear to me and listens, he hears the reflection of his own heart's music, singing; so, you see, while I say that I am singing all the time, in reality I sing only when someone full of happiness hears his own singing as if it were mine.'

'How unselfish you are to say this!' said Raggedy Andy. 'Now we are ever so much more glad to have you with us. Aren't we?' he asked, turning to the rest of the dolls.

'Yes, indeed!' came the answer from all the dolls, even the tiny penny-dolls.

'That is why the shell is so beautiful inside!' said Raggedy Ann. 'Those who are unselfish may wear rough clothes, but inside they are always beautiful, just like the shell, and reflect to others the happiness and sunny music within their hearts!'

I LOVE YOU

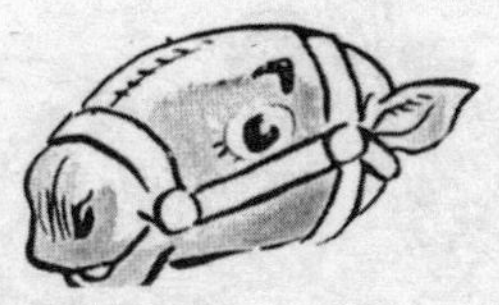

Raggedy Ann and Andy and the Camel with the Wrinkled Knees

CHAPTER 1

Raggedy Ann and Raggedy Andy lay in their little doll-beds, smiling up through the dark at the top of the play-house. It was very still and quiet in the playhouse, but the Raggedys were not even a teeny-weeny speck lonely, for they were thinking so many nice kindly thoughts. And, you know, when one thinks only lovely, kindly thoughts there is no time to become lonely.

The playhouse was an old piano-box which had been made nice and cosy. There was an old rug upon the floor, two doll-beds, three little chairs and a table with pretty little play teacups and saucers and plates on it.

Raggedy Ann and Raggedy Andy lay upon the doll-beds just where Marcella had left them that afternoon. One of Raggedy Ann's legs was twisted up over the other, but it wasn't the least bit uncomfortable, for Raggedy Ann's legs were stuffed with nice white, soft cotton and they could be

twisted in any position and it did not trouble Raggedy Ann. No indeed! Neither Raggedy Ann nor Raggedy Andy had moved since they had been placed in the little doll-beds, and now it was late at night. Marcella had forgotten to take the Raggedys into the house, but the Raggedys did not mind that either. They just smiled up at the top of the playhouse and listened to the tiny sounds which came from the little creatures out in the grass and flowers.

At first Raggedy Ann was so busy thinking nice kindly thoughts she did not notice. Then when Johnny Cricket stopped squeeking upon his tiny fiddle Raggedy Ann knew something was about to happen. Her little candy heart with the words 'I love you' printed upon it went pitty-pat against her nice cotton-stuffed body. And Raggedy Ann heard great big footsteps coming up the path, 'Thump! thump! thump.'

'Hmm!' Raggedy Ann whispered to Raggedy Andy, 'I wonder who that can be?'

The great big footsteps came up to the playhouse and went on, 'Thump! thump! thump!'

Raggedy Andy jumped out of the little doll-bed and tiptoed to the door. The night was dark, but Raggedy Andy had two very good shoe-button eyes and as they were black shoe-button eyes Raggedy Andy could see very well in the dark. And what do you think? Raggedy Andy saw a great big man reach right into one of the windows of the house and take something and run! The man ran right by the piano-box playhouse and Raggedy Andy could have jumped out and touched him if he had wished. But Raggedy Andy was so surprised to see anyone reach into another person's house and take something, he could think of nothing to do or say; and so the man jumped over the back fence and ran across the field!

'Did you see, Raggedy Ann?' Raggedy Andy asked.

'Yes!' said Raggedy Ann, very decidedly, 'we must run up to the house and find out what that man was doing!'

So, smoothing the wrinkles out of her apron and jiggling her legs to get the twists out of them, Raggedy Ann joined Raggedy Andy and they ran up to the house and climbed upon a chair so that they could peep over the sill into the window.

When Raggedy Ann and Raggedy Andy peeped up over the window-sill, all the dolls remained very quiet, for they thought it was the man returning; but when they realised it was Raggedy Ann's and Raggedy Andy's faces peeping in at them, they all jumped up and ran to them.

'What do you think, Raggedy Ann?' Uncle Clem cried. 'Someone reached into the window and took the French doll! Wasn't that a rude thing to do?'

'My! My! My!' was all Raggedy Ann could say for awhile. Then, after she sat and pulled her rag forehead down into a lot of wrinkles, Raggedy Ann was able to think of something to do.

'Raggedy Andy!' said Raggedy Ann. 'We must run after the man and make him bring the French doll back here!'

'That is just what I was thinking!' Raggedy Andy replied, as he climbed up on the window-sill. 'Come on, Raggedy Ann!'

Little Henny, the Dutch doll, wanted to go with Raggedy Ann and Raggedy Andy, but Raggedy Ann said, 'No, Henny, you must stay here and take care of the rest of the dolls! You see, you are the only young man left!' This pleased Henny so much he tried to stick out his chest so far that he fell over backwards and cried, 'M-a-m-m-a!' in his quavery voice.

Raggedy Andy knew just which way the strange man had run, for he had watched him, so after jumping from the window and catching hold of her hand, Raggedy Andy raced with Raggedy Ann over the yard, climbed through a hole in the fence and scooted across the field.

Raggedy Ann and Raggedy Andy ran until they came to the centre of the field, and all the way they had followed the man's trail where he had bent down the grass and field flowers. But when they came to the centre of the field, the grass and flowers were not bent down, and Raggedy Ann and Raggedy Andy stopped.

'Now isn't that strange, Raggedy Ann?' Raggedy Andy asked. 'He hasn't gone beyond here and still he isn't here!'

'Then if he isn't here,' Raggedy Ann answered, 'he must have gone on, Raggedy Andy.'

'But how could he, Raggedy Ann, when we can see that his footsteps end right here?' Raggedy Andy asked.

'Why! He must have gone up in the air, that's what, Raggedy Andy!' Raggedy Ann replied.

'Then we can follow him no farther!' Raggedy Andy cried, as he dropped his rag arms to his sides and looked very sad. 'What shall we do, Raggedy Ann?'

'Let's sit down and think as hard as we can, Raggedy Andy,' said Raggedy Ann. 'Even if we rip sixteen stitches out of our heads thinking so hard, let's try to think of what we had better do.'

So Raggedy Andy sat down beside her and threw one arm about Raggedy Ann's shoulders. And there they sat and thought and thought, just as hard as they could, until Raggedy Andy felt five stitches rip in his rag head and Raggedy Ann felt five stitches rip in her rag head, but neither one could think of anything to do.

'For,' Raggedy Ann said out loud, 'if we can't fly, how can we follow him?' This also puzzled Raggedy Andy and he said so.

Then Raggedy Ann and Raggedy Andy held their breath; for, coming towards them through the flowers and tall grasses they saw a dim, greenish-blue light. And as the pretty light (it was just like a Will-o'-the-wisp) came up to them they saw that a pretty fairy carried it at the end of a waving stick! No wonder Raggedy Ann and Raggedy Andy held their breath, she was such a pretty little fairy creature and it seemed so strange that at last they were getting to see a real live fairy. Very often all the dolls had wished that they might see a fairy. Now a very lovely fairy stood before Raggedy Ann and Raggedy Andy! Maybe, very often, beautiful fairies stand in front of us

© JOHNNY GRUELLE

and whisper to us but we are unable to see or hear them; who knows? But Raggedy Ann and Raggedy Andy could not only see this pretty little fairy creature, but they could hear her too.

'Why do you hold your breath, Raggedy Ann and Raggedy Andy?' the pretty little fairy asked, and there was a sly little tinkle to her voice which made Raggedy Ann and Raggedy Andy know that the pretty little fairy knew why they held their breath.

But Raggedy Ann laughed and said, 'We are holding our breath, because we have never seen a real live beautiful fairy before, and we did not wish to frighten you away.' And this made the pretty little fairy laugh out loud.

'Of course, I knew why, Raggedy Ann and Raggedy Andy,' she said. 'But now that we are good friends, please do not hold your breath any longer. For, I know why you are sitting out in the centre of the field and I know just how you can follow the man who took the French doll.'

'I thought the man might be Santa Claus,' Raggedy Ann said. 'But then after I had ripped five stitches in my rag head thinking, I knew it could not be Santa who took the French doll, for he only takes dolls when they need mending and the French doll was always kept just as good as new. Except when Marcella fed her chocolate drops and got chocolate around her dolly mouth.'

'No, it wasn't Santa Claus,' Raggedy Andy said.

'No, it wasn't Santa Claus,' the pretty little fairy agreed. 'But now the thing to do is for you two to follow the strange man. And in order to do that, you must be able to fly, for he flew away from here, you know.'

'That is just what I thought,' Raggedy Ann said.

'Raggedy Ann can think ever so much better than I can,'

Raggedy Andy told the fairy. 'For Raggedy Ann has a lovely candy heart and I guess that's why.'

The pretty little fairy laughed at this and said, 'Granny Balloon-Spider lives near here and I will ask her to build you a nice fluffy balloon so that you can follow the man who took the French doll.' And the pretty little fairy led the way until they came to a cunning little cottage and there stood Granny out on the porch waiting for them.

'Will you spin Raggedy Ann and Raggedy Andy a nice fluffy balloon in which they can fly after the man who took the French doll?' the pretty little fairy asked Granny.

'Indeed, I will be very glad to spin them a balloon!' Granny replied. 'But in order to carry them through the air I will have to spin such a large balloon that it will take me several days.'

© JOHNNY GRUELLE

'Oh, I shall fix that all right, Granny,' the pretty little fairy laughed. 'If you will bring your little spinning-wheel out here onto the porch, I will say a magic charm over it, and you will be able to spin the balloon in a very short time!'

So, when Granny Balloon-Spider brought the cunning little spinning-wheel out upon the porch, the pretty little fairy waved her fairy light over it and sang, 'Little cunning spinning-wheel, spin and whir and sing; spin a silken balloon to carry Raggedy Ann and Raggedy Andy up in the air in search of the French doll!' And Granny put her little red-slippered foot upon the treadle of the spinning-wheel and the cunning little spinning-wheel looked like solid silver it whirled so fast. And before you could recite 'The House that Jack Built' the little silken balloon was finished.

The pretty little fairy fastened a silken thread to Raggedy Ann's hand and one to Raggedy Andy's hand and touched the silken balloon with her fairy light; then the silken balloon rose into the air and carried Raggedy Ann and Raggedy Andy with it.

'Goodbye and thank you!' Raggedy Ann and Raggedy Andy called down to the little fairy and Granny Balloon-

Spider, and the little fairy waved her fairy light until the silken balloon had carried our two friends way up above a feathery cloud.

And as the gentle breeze blew them along, ever so gently, Raggedy Ann and Raggedy Andy twisted and swung about at the ends of the silken threads tied to their rag hands.

'Isn't it lovely, Raggedy Andy?' Raggedy Ann asked. 'I can scarcely believe we are not dreaming!'

'It is ever so much nicer than floating on water!' Raggedy Andy replied.

CHAPTER 2

Raggedy Ann and Raggedy Andy floated through the air, carried along by the silken balloon, until they could see the great, round, golden sun peeping up over the rim of the earth.

'Good-morning, Mr Sun!' Raggedy Ann laughed; but of course the sun did not answer, for he was thousands of miles away and did not hear. Then Raggedy Ann noticed that they were drifting closer and closer to the ground, and after a while the silken balloon caught in a low branch of a tree and there Raggedy Ann and Raggedy Andy hung, dangling by the silken cords the fairy had tied to their hands.

'Well, here we are,' laughed Raggedy Andy, 'but how will we get down to the ground?'

'That is what has been bothering me, too,' Raggedy Ann said. 'Of course it would not hurt either of us to drop from here to the ground, if we could only untie the silken cords the fairy tied about our hands.'

And so Raggedy Ann and Raggedy Andy hung there dangling and twisting about until finally Raggedy Andy laughed and asked, 'Do you know what, Raggedy Ann?'

'No, what, Raggedy Andy?' Raggedy Ann asked in reply.

'Why,' Raggedy Andy said. 'If we can't get down, then let's get up!' And with this, Raggedy Andy twisted his legs up over the branch and was soon sitting upon it. Then he pulled Raggedy Ann up beside him. When they had their hands in front of them, it was an easy matter to untie the silken cord.

'There we are!' laughed Raggedy Andy. 'Now all we have to do, is to jump from the tree and continue our search for the French doll!' So Raggedy Ann and Raggedy Andy stood up on the branch and joined hands.

'One for the money, two for the show, three to make ready and here she goes!' they both sang and jumped. 'Blump! Blump!' they struck against the ground and rolled over.

'Didn't hurt me a speck!' laughed Raggedy Ann.

'Me neither!' laughed Raggedy Andy as he sat up and dusted his clothes.

'Ha!' came a voice from behind the tree, and as they looked Raggedy Ann and Raggedy Andy saw the queerest creature come walking towards them. It was a camel, made out of Canton flannel and stuffed with sawdust, but he had evidently been played with so much that his legs were no longer straight and stiff. Instead, the Canton-flannel camel's legs were wrinkled and so wobbly, it seemed that he would pitch forward upon his head at each step. When the camel came up to Raggedy Ann and Raggedy Andy, he sat down beside them, and in doing this his knees gave way with him and he rolled over upon his side.

'Wup!' Raggedy Andy said, as he helped the camel to sit up. 'You almost fell over that time.'

'Indeed I did,' the camel laughed. 'My legs are not what they used to be. See how wrinkled my knees are?'

Raggedy Andy tried to smooth out the wrinkles in the

©
JOHNNY GRUELLE

camel's knees, but the camel smiled and said, 'It doesn't do a bit of good trying to get the wrinkles out. They come back again just as soon as I stand up,' he sighed. 'You see when I was brand-new, I was made with sticks in each leg, but these sticks were the sticks which are made to put in meat when it is tied up and roasted, and each stick had a point on the end. Well, sir, after I had been played with for a few weeks, those pointed sticks punched right up through my back and I wasn't safe for a little boy to play with. So the little boy's mother pulled the meat sticks out of my legs, and that made me sag down until my knees grew terribly wrinkled!'

'That is too bad!' Raggedy Ann said, as she patted the camel's head.

'Four bad, my dear!' the camel corrected.

'Oh, I didn't mean the number of legs you had, I meant that I felt sorry,' Raggedy Ann laughed.

'Ha, ha! Now I understand,' the camel smiled. 'But really, it isn't quite as bad as one would imagine, for when I had sticks in my legs I had to walk stiff-legged and that wasn't a bit graceful; but now I can walk along very softly without going "thump! thump! thump!" And it is ever so much more comfortable when I lie down now than it was when I had to stick my legs out stiffly at the side.'

'When you said, "Thump! thump! thump!" it reminded me of something!' said Raggedy Ann.

'What was it?' the camel with the wrinked knees asked.

Then Raggedy Ann told him how she had heard the man's footsteps go 'thump! thump! thump!' the night before.

The camel with the wrinkled knees scratched his head with the loppiest leg and asked, 'Was he a large man, with two legs and two arms, dressed in clothing?'

©
JOHNNY GRUELLE

'The very man!' cried Raggedy Andy. 'I was looking out of the playhouse door when the man reached into the window and took her!'

'Then, I am sure I can tell you how to find him!' the camel with the wrinkled knees cried, excitedly. 'For I know it is the same man who took me out of the little boy's playhouse one night. I ran away from him. Someday I'm going back home, for I had lots of good times with my little boy owner!'

'Hurry and tell us how to find the mean man, please!' Raggedy Ann begged. 'For we must rescue the French doll and return home as soon as we can.'

'Well,' the camel with the wrinkled knees said, 'Do you see that great big tree way over there?'

'Yes!' Raggedy Ann and Raggedy Andy both cried.

'Well,' the camel said, 'you mustn't go that way! You must go this way. Then when you get to this way you must turn and go that way until you come to this way again. Then take the first turn this way, until you come to that way and after walking that way ten minutes you turn and go this way. Then you are there.'

'Hmm!' mused Raggedy Ann and Raggedy Andy. 'We should be able to find it in the dark after such a *good* description of the way to reach there!'

'That's the funny part of the whole thing,' the camel with the wrinkled knees laughed. 'I ran away from the man at night when it was very, very dark, and I could easily find my way back in the dark, but I would get lost in the daytime!'

'Then I suppose we will have to go alone,' Raggedy Ann said.

'I'd like to return with you and help rescue the French

doll,' the camel with the wrinkled knees said. 'But I know I should never be able to find the way in the light.'

'Maybe if you would shut your eyes you could lead us to the place where the man lives,' Raggedy Andy suggested.

'Ha!' the camel laughed. 'How can I shut my eyes, when they are shoe buttons just like Raggedy Ann's?'

'I never thought of that!' Raggedy Andy said. 'But be quiet – Raggedy Ann is trying to think of some way!'

'I never said a word!' the camel replied.

'Yes, you did!' Raggedy Andy said. 'You are talking now, and it disturbs Raggedy Ann while she is thinking! So please remain very quiet and don't even cough, because sometimes Raggedy Ann rips a great many stitches out of her head and the cotton stuffing shows after she has thought really, really hard. Just sit quietly and wait, as I am doing, and pretty soon you will be surprised to find out how well Raggedy Ann can think. Why, I remember one time when we were having a – '

'I shan't say a word!' the camel promised.

'Yes, you say that you will not say anything, but just the minute you say that, can't you see that you are saying something?'

'Well! How can you tell that I shan't say a word unless I tell you that I shan't say a word? Just you tell me that, Mr Raggedy Andy!' the camel replied.

'This is no time to guess riddles,' Raggedy Andy said. 'If we were guessing riddles, I know one I bet you could never, never guess. But what I have asked you to do is to remain very quiet, for the more quiet you remain the sooner Raggedy Ann will be able to think of something to do.'

'Then I shall remain positively quiet, Raggedy Andy, so let's not quarrel about it.'

'I shan't quarrel with you,' Raggedy Andy replied, 'but you continually start – '

'I've thought of a good scheme!' Raggedy Ann cried, as she jumped to her feet. 'If the camel with the wrinkled knees cannot shut his eyes and if he cannot show us the way to the man's place in the daytime, then we must cover his eyes with a hanky. Then it will be just the same as if it were dark!'

'I only see one thing wrong with your idea, Raggedy Ann,' the camel said.

'What is it?' Raggedy Ann asked.

'Why,' the camel replied, 'If we tie something over the man's eyes, don't you see we will be where he is without having to go there!'

'Silly!' Raggedy Andy cried, 'Raggedy Ann means to tie something over your eyes instead of the man's eyes!'

'Oh!' the camel with the wrinkled knees laughed, as Raggedy Ann tied her pocket hanky over the camel's shoe-button eyes, 'now I see!'

When Raggedy Ann had finished tying her pocket hanky over the camel's eyes she said, 'Now we had better start.'

'Turn me around three times,' the camel said, 'so that I

won't get all mixed up in my directions. Then you had better get up on my back, for I shall go just as fast as I possibly can and you may not be able to keep up with me.'

Raggedy Ann turned the camel with the wrinkled knees around three times, then she and Raggedy Andy climbed upon his back.

'Hold tight!' the camel cried. 'Here we go!' and with this he started walking, slowly at first, then faster and faster, until soon his wobbly, wrinkled legs were hitting the ground, 'Clumpity clumpity, clumpity,' and he was running surprisingly fast.

Raggedy Ann and Raggedy Andy held on tight, becasue the camel bounced them up and down a great deal as he jumped along.

'Where are we now?' the camel asked, after he had run steadily for five minutes. Raggedy Ann and Raggedy Andy looked about them.

'Why!' they cried in surprise, 'we are right back where we started from! You must have run in a large circle!'

'Maybe I did,' the camel replied, 'Of course I cannot see where I am running, but I know perfectly well that I am going in the right direction.'

'But, Mr Camel,' Raggedy Ann exclaimed, as she slid from the camel's back, 'how can you be going in the right direction when you return to the place where we started from? Can't you see, that we might just as well have stood still and saved you all that running?'

'Maybe we had better try it again!' the camel panted. 'I am certain that I am not mistaken!'

So Raggedy Ann and Raggedy Andy again climbed upon the camel's back and again the camel carried them at a run for five minutes.

'Now where are we?' the camel asked.

'We are right where we started from!' Raggedy Andy cried. 'I don't believe you know where you are trying to go!'

'Of course I don't!' the camel agreed. 'But do not let that fool you! I have run exactly the same as I did when I came from the man's place!'

'Ahhhhh!' Raggedy Ann exclaimed. 'I know what's the trouble, Mr Camel! You have been running just the same as you did when you came from the man's place, so in order to return to the man's place, don't you see – you must run backwards!'

'Of course!' the camel chuckled. 'It's funny I didn't think of running backwards before!' The camel couldn't run quite as fast backwards as he did frontwards, but he covered a lot of ground. After running backwards for five minutes, the camel again asked, 'Where are we now?'

'I do not know!' Raggedy Ann and Raggedy Andy both answered.

'Then,' said the camel, 'we must be getting somewhere!'

CHAPTER 3

When the camel with the wrinkled knees had rested for a few minutes, he again started running backwards and was jumping along very fast when Raggedy Ann cried suddenly, 'Whoa!'

The camel immediately stopped and Raggedy Ann and Raggedy Andy, not expecting him to stop so suddenly, rolled off his back and turned over and over in the grass.

'Why did you cry, "Whoa"?' the camel wished to know when Raggedy Ann and Raggedy Andy had picked themselves up and came back to him.

'There's a little girl standing over there crying,' Raggedy Ann said. 'We must go over and see what is the trouble.'

Raggedy Ann took the hanky from the camel's eyes and the three walked over towards the little girl. When the little girl saw them she stopped crying and said, 'Don't come any closer, or the snapdragons will catch you!'

'Hmm,' mused Raggedy Andy. 'Snapdragons – who's afraid of snapdragons? Not me!' And with that, he walked right up to the little girl.

Raggedy Ann, when she saw that nothing happened to Raggedy Andy, also walked up to the little girl.

'The snapdragons are nothing but flowers,' Raggedy Andy said, and indeed this was true, for all about the little girl's feet pretty flowers were twined.

'How long have you been standing here, little girl?' Raggedy Ann asked.

'For a long, long time,' the little girl replied. 'Every time

I try to walk away the snapdragons catch my feet and hold me.'

'Nonsense!' Raggedy Andy exclaimed. 'Take my hand and we will walk over to where there are no snapdragons!'

But when the little girl did this and Raggedy Andy tried to walk, he found that the snapdragons also fastened themselves around his legs.

And when Raggedy Ann caught hold of Raggedy Andy's

hand and pulled, the snapdragons wrapped themselves around her feet and held her.

'You see!' the little girl cried. 'Now you are prisoners too, and we will never get away from them!'

When the camel saw that Raggedy Ann had become a prisoner too, he turned and walked still farther away from the snapdragons and sat down to think it over. Although the camel with the wrinkled knees sat and tried to think for a long, long time, he could not think of a way to rescue his friends from the snapdragons. Even though he scratched his head with his left hind leg he could not think of a way.

'I wonder how long we will have to stay here before we are rescued?' Raggedy Ann mused out loud.

'We may have to stay here years and years!' the little girl wailed. Then she told Raggedy Ann and Raggedy Andy all about herself. 'My name is Jenny,' the little girl began, 'and my brother's name is Jan. We used to live in a little cottage right in the centre of the deep, deep woods. The little cottage was no larger than a big dry-goods box, but that was large enough for Jan and me. You see, we lived there all by ourselves.'

'Didn't you have a mamma or a daddy?' Raggedy Ann asked in surprise.

'No,' Jenny replied, as she brushed a tear from her eye. 'Mamma and Daddy went over to see Grandma one day, and they never came back. So Jan and I went into the deep, deep woods to hunt for Mamma and Daddy, but we could not find them. And we could not find our way back home – so when we discovered the dear little cottage, which was no larger than a dry-goods box, Jan and I lived there!'

'But where is Jan now?' Raggedy Andy wanted to know.

'I was just about to tell you!' Jenny replied. 'In the deep,

deep woods, as you surely must know, there are gnomes and elves and fairies! And besides the fairies and gnomes and elves there are other little creatures. Sometimes Jan and I could not see the little fairies and gnomes and elves or other little creatures, but we could hear them singing or laughing or talking. Then, at other times, we could see them, but we could not hear them. Then sometimes we could see and hear them, too. And so, one day, Jan went out to the back of the little cottage to get a pail of water from the spring and when he came back into the house there was the queerest little man-creature with him we had ever seen!'

'What was it?' Raggedy Ann asked.

'It was a loonie!' Jenny answered. 'And if you have never seen a loonie, do not ever long to see one, for they are not as as elves and gnomes or fairies! Instead, loonies have large eyes which roll around every which way, and long red noses and crooked legs. They are funny-looking little creatures and really make you laugh when you see them. And that is just what Jan and I did, when the loonie walked into our little house with Jan. And do you know?' Jenny said, 'when we laughed at the little loonie, it made him so angry, he just bounced all around our little house and yelled at us.'

'I'll just bet, when you laughed at him that made him hopping mad,' said Raggedy Andy.

'Yes,' Jenny said, 'that is just what happened, and we did not know that such a small creature could be so strong. And before either Jan or I could do a thing, the little loonie caught Jan's feet and dragged him right out of the cottage and away through the woods!'

'Couldn't Jan catch hold of bushes, so the loonie couldn't pull him?' Raggedy Andy asked.

'Oh, yes,' Jenny replied. 'But the little loonie was so

strong, he just pulled Jan's hands away from the bushes and ran with him so fast I could not follow.' And Jenny began crying again.

'Please do not cry,' Raggedy Ann begged, as she wiped the little girl's eyes with her apron. 'We will help you find Jan. And when we catch the loonie we will spank him hard. Won't we, Raggedy Andy?'

'Indeed we will,' Raggedy Andy promised.

'And after I had searched and searched for Jan, all through the deep, deep woods, and could not find him, I came out across this field, and just the minute I stopped among the snapdragons, they twined around my feet and I could not move.'

'And you have never found out where the loonie took Jan?' Raggedy Andy asked.

'I suppose he took Jan to the town of the loonies,' Jenny answered. 'But even though I asked everyone I met in the deep woods, they could not tell me how to get to Loonie Town.'

'Perhaps someone could have told you,' Raggedy Ann suggested. 'But maybe they knew that if you went there alone, you would be captured and made a prisoner just as Jan was.'

Jenny was just about to reply to Raggedy Ann when she saw a funny old horse, not much larger than the camel with the wrinkled knees.

'What are you all standing around for?' the old horse asked as he came up to the edge of the patch of snapdragons. 'Is there going to be a parade?'

'You'd better come over here and sit down with me,' the camel with the wrinkled knees called. 'I am trying to think.'

The old horse walked over to where the camel sat and lay down beside him. 'My, I'm tired,' the horse sighed.

'Have you walked far?' the camel with the wrinkled knees asked.

'No, not very far,' the old horse replied, 'but you see, I am so old, the least bit of exercise wears me out and I have to lie down and rest.'

'I am trying to think of a way to rescue my friends there,' the camel said, as he pointed to Raggedy Ann, Raggedy Andy and Jenny.

'Have they been captured?' the tired old horse wanted to know.

'Certainly,' the camel replied. 'They are standing right in a whole lot of snapdragons and can't get away.'

'Hmm,' the tired old horse said, as he slowly got to his feet and stretched, 'I will look into this.' And from his trouser pocket he took a case and from the case a pair of old-fashioned spectacles.

When he had put the spectacles on his nose he walked up and looked at the snapdragons. 'Well, I'll declare!' he cried as he jumped back suddenly and upset the camel. 'Just put on my spectacles,' he said, as he handed them to the camel.

When the camel with the wrinkled knees had looked at the snapdragons through the spectacles he turned and ran as hard as his wobbly legs would let him. And the tired old horse ran after him. After an exciting chase clear across the field, the tired old horse finally managed to catch the camel's string tail between his teeth and stop him.

'Silly!' the tired old horse cried, as he took his spectacles away from the camel, 'I didn't mean to give you the spectacles to keep. I just loaned them to you.' And the tired old horse placed the spectacles on his own nose and slowly walked back towards Raggedy Ann and the others.

'I did not mean to keep your spectacles,' the camel with the wrinkled knees tried to explain, as he followed the tired old horse.

'Then why did you run?' the tired old horse asked. 'That's what I want to know.'

'Because,' the camel replied, 'I feared that the snapdragons were not flowers at all but were real live dragons! Chinese dragons!'

The tired old horse turned and looked the camel with the wrinkled knees up and down, from his feet to his head. Then shaking his head sadly the tired old horse walked among the snapdragons and lay down.

'Now you are in a pickle too!' Raggedy Andy cried. 'How can you rescue us when you are captured just the same as we are?'

The tired old horse rolled over upon his back and kicked his four feet in the air. 'If I can roll all the way over, I'm worth a fortune,' he said.

'I wouldn't give fivepence for you now!' the camel cried, as he sat down at the edge of the clump of snapdragons.

After kicking about for a few minutes, the tired old horse

succeeded in rolling over. 'Whee!' the tired old horse cried, 'I'm worth a fortune!' and with that he began prancing and kicking up his heels and frisking all about Raggedy Ann and Raggedy Andy and Jenny.

'You be careful there, Mr Horse,' Raggedy Ann cautioned. 'First thing you know, you'll kick Jenny!'

CHAPTER 4

The tired old horse stopped kicking up his heels and walked up to Jenny and looked at her intently through his spectacles. Then he took them off and wiped them with a red bandanna handkerchief. 'Ha!' he cried, when he looked at Jenny without his spectacles, 'I thought I recognised you. You used to live in the little cottage in the centre of the deep, deep woods, didn't you?'

'Why, yes,' Jenny replied. 'How did you know?'

'Because,' the tired old horse said, 'I used to be driven through the deep, deep woods every day, to haul wood for my master until I got so old and tired I couldn't haul wood any more; then my master turned me loose to live by myself and he got a young horse to take my place. I used to see you almost every day. You and Jan,' the horse continued. 'Why don't you return to the cosy little cottage?'

'Because,' Raggedy Andy replied, 'can't you see? Jenny has been captured by the snapdragons, and so have we, and so have you.'

'Nonsense!' the tired old horse laughed. 'All you have to do is just walk away from the snapdragons like this.'

'Huh!' the camel with the wrinkled knees cried, when he saw that the tired old horse couldn't budge. 'Now you are in for it, just like the rest of them.'

The tired old horse looked at his feet and all about him in a surprised sort of way. Then a broad smile spread over his kindly face and he put on his spectacles. When the spectacles were firmly placed upon his nose, the horse ran in circles around Raggedy Ann, Raggedy Andy and Jenny.

'There! You see?' the tired old horse said, as he stopped in front of Jenny. 'I couldn't budge before, because I did not have on my magic spectacles, and the snapdragons looked just like snapdragons! But now that I have on my magic spectacles, the snapdragons are only violets, so of course they cannot get around my feet and hold me!'

'Then will we have to wear magic spectacles before we can get away from the snapdragons?' Jenny wished to know.

'Oh, no,' the tired old horse replied, 'I shall eat all the violets which look to you like snapdragons. In that way, I shall have a fine meal and they won't tangle around your feet.' And without another word, the tired old horse started eating, and in a short time Jenny was able to walk over and sit down beside the camel with the wrinkled knees.

'My, goodness,' she said, 'it feels good to be able to sit down again.'

It did not take the tired old horse very long to eat the violets around Raggedy Ann and Raggedy Andy's feet and so, very soon, they were all standing together beside the camel with the wrinkled knees.

The tired old horse took off his spectacles and put them in his pocket.

'Now,' he said, as he rubbed his forefeet together, just as a man does when he is about to say something interesting, 'we will talk about Jenny and Jan.'

'We must help Jenny find Jan, don't you think so?' Raggedy Ann asked.

'Indeed, that is just what I was going to say!' cried the tired old horse. 'When I used to haul wood through the deep, deep woods past Jenny's little cottage I used to see her and Jan playing there together almost every day.'

'But I do not remember seeing you,' Jenny laughed.

'There was a good reason, my dear,' the tired old horse laughed. 'At that time I was just an ordinary horse and you were bewitched by some tribe of fairies, or gnomes, or elves, or something. Anyway, I could see you, but you could not see me, nor could you see my master or the cart of wood I used to haul. Could you?'

'No. I do not remember seeing the cart, or your master,' Jenny replied.

'There, you see!' the tired old horse said to Raggedy Ann. 'Well, one day I was hauling wood for my master and I saw the loonie come out of your little cottage dragging Jan. And although I wanted to run after the loonie and rescue Jan, I could not do so, because I was hitched to the cart. But I watched until I saw exactly where the loonie took Jan, and I'll bet you anything I can find the spot where he took Jan inside a great tree.'

'Then let us lose no time in going there!' Raggedy Andy cried, as he jumped to his feet. 'There is no question Jan has been in prison all this time.'

'I will take Jenny upon my back, because she is the heaviest, and the camel can take Raggedy Ann and Raggedy Andy upon his back, and we will run like the wind until we come to the deep, deep woods.'

'But,' said the camel with the wrinkled knees, 'I was taking Raggedy Ann and Raggedy Andy to show them where the man had taken the French doll. And the only way I can find the place is to be blindfolded and run backwards, and if I do that, how can I follow you, Mr Horse?'

'I tell you what we'll do,' Raggedy Ann suggested. 'Let us do as the tired old horse says, then when we have rescued Jan from the loonies, we will all search for the man who carried away the French doll, Babette.'

This was agreeable to the camel with the wrinkled knees and soon he and the tired old horse were racing across the fields towards the deep, deep woods. In a few moments they came to the deep, deep woods and followed a winding path until they came to the little cottage where Jenny and Jan had lived. And a few yards beyond this, the tired old horse sat down under a great tree.

'Whew,' he cried, as he took off his hat and fanned himself, 'that surely made me tired! Well, anyway, here is the tree into which the loonie took Jan.'

'And if I am not mistaken,' the camel with the wrinkled knees said, 'this is also the place where I was running backwards to. Just put your handkerchief over my eyes and let me see.'

When Raggedy Ann had bound her handkerchief over the camel's eyes, he said, 'Yes, sir, this is the very spot!' And he handed Raggedy Ann her hanky.

'What I can't understand is how the loonie could drag Jan into the tree when there isn't a single hole in the tree,' Raggedy Andy said. Everyone walked around the large tree, but there appeared no hole of any sort in the tree.

'Are you sure you haven't made a mistake, Mr Horse?' Raggedy Andy asked.

'I am sure,' the tired old horse replied. 'And besides, doesn't the camel say this is the place he was trying to run to?'

The tired old horse took off his hat again and scratched his head. 'Ah,' he said, 'I have it. We must blindfold the camel with the wrinkled knees and follow him into the tree; for I am sure it is a magic tree, or at least the entrance into the tree is covered with magic and we are unable to see it.'

So Raggedy Ann again blindfolded the camel with the wrinkled knees and without waiting for the others, he backed into the tree and disappeared. And where the camel with the wrinkled knees had backed into the tree, there was no hole of any sort to be seen.

'Oh, dear!' Raggedy Ann cried when the last of the camel disappeared into the tree. 'Now he has gone and we shall be unable to follow!' For as she spoke she walked up to where the camel had disappeared and felt the tree: it was just as solid there as at any other place upon its surface.

'We should all have held on to the camel's nose,' the horse said. 'For I guess there is something magic about the camel which lets him walk right through things when he is blindfolded.'

'I guess there is nothing to do except wait outside here

until the camel finds we are not with him. Then perhaps he will return,' Raggedy Andy said. Presently the camel poked his head out of the tree trunk. 'Where are you?' he asked.

'Right where you left us,' Raggedy Ann replied. 'Let us all catch hold of your nose and perhaps we can all get into the tree.' And when everyone had crowded around the camel and had caught hold of his nose, the camel backed into the tree and the others went with him.

The tree seemed very much larger, when our friends were once inside, just like a great room. Over at one side of the great room there was a slab of stone with a ring in it.

'It must be a trap-door,' Raggedy Andy said as he caught hold of the ring and tried to raise the stone.

'Let us all take hold of the ring,' Raggedy Ann suggested. 'Perhaps together we can lift it.' But though they pulled with all their might, the stone would not be lifted.

'This must be the way down into Loonie Land,' the tired old horse said. 'Let us sit down and see what we can think of. There must be a way to open this trap-door.'

And as he finished speaking, the tired old horse sat down upon the stone. And as he sat down rather hard, the stone gave way and he went tumbling down below. The others could not see where the tired old horse fell to, for the stone immediately closed up after he had disappeared, but they could hear him bumping around until he reached the bottom.

'I hope the fall did not hurt him,' Raggedy Ann said. 'Listen!'

They could hear the tired old horse kicking around way down below. And presently they heard his footsteps as he came climbing up.

'Are you there?' the tired old horse called up through the stone trap-door.

'Yes,' Raggedy Ann replied. 'What shall we do?'

'I took a mighty tumble,' the horse called back. 'If you just press down gently upon the stone, I am sure it will open.' And indeed, this proved correct, for when Raggedy Andy pressed down ever so lightly, the stone lowered and they could see the tired old horse standing upon the stone steps.

'Come on,' he said, 'I will hold the stone trap-door open until you all get in. But watch you don't slip on the stone steps, for it is a long way to the bottom.'

'That ring was just put in the top of the stone to fool anyone who came into the tree,' Raggedy Andy said when all had safely reached the bottom of the stone steps. 'For the ring made it look as though you had to pull on the trap-door to open it.'

'I am glad that it was I who sat upon the stone instead of Jenny,' the tired old horse laughed.

CHAPTER 5

A wonderful sight met their eyes, when the tired old horse opened a door at the bottom of the stone steps and our friends walked out into the open again. There, in the distance, upon a wonderful hill, stood a beautiful castle with turrets and spires of red reaching up towards the sky. And between our friends and the castle there was a large valley filled with strangely shaped little houses. From where they stood, Raggedy Ann and Raggedy Andy, Jenny, the tired old horse and the camel with the wrinkled knees could see the loonies running about in the streets like mad. First running one way and then running another.

'What's the matter with them, I wonder?' the tired old horse said. Of course neither Jenny nor any of her friends knew the reason, so they could not answer. But soon the loonies all came running towards them shouting and waving sticks.

'I believe that they see us,' said the camel, who had removed the blindfold from his eyes.

This was true, for the queer little loonies came swarming towards them, looking for all the world like ants as they crossed the valley.

'Where can we hide?' Jenny asked, as she looked about her.

'We shan't hide!' Raggedy Andy cried. 'We shall wait and see what they intend to do.'

The loonies soon showed our friends what they intended doing, for they all surrounded Raggedy Ann and Jenny and Raggedy Andy and the tired old horse and the camel with the wrinkled knees, and poking them with their sticks, started marching our friends down into the valley towards the queer houses.

'Do you think it would be a good plan for me to start kicking?' the tired old horse whispered to Raggedy Ann. 'I can knock them head-over-heels if I start kicking and thrashing about.'

'I do not think you should do that,' Raggedy Ann replied, 'for your heels are hard and you would hurt them very much should you kick any of the loonies.'

'All right,' the tired old horse agreed. 'Then we will march along quietly.'

The loonies marched their prisoners into the largest house in the centre of all the other queer houses and up before the King of the loonies.

'Aha!' the King of the loonies cried, when all the loonies had stopped their chattering. 'What have we captured?'

One of the loonies who had captured our friends spoke and said to the King of the loonies, 'Oh, most looniest of loonies, we have captured those who came down through the great tree.'

'Don't I know that?' the King of the Loonies howled. 'Why don't you answer my question? Whom have we captured?'

'We have captured the prisoners,' the guard replied.

'Good!' the King of the Loonies cried, as he clapped his hands. 'Now see if you can answer this one. What will we do with them now that we have captured them?'

'Put them in prison, I guess,' the guard replied.

'Wrong!' shouted the King of the Loonies. 'Now try to think!'

'I can't seem to think of anything,' the guard answered.

'Good!' the King of the Loonies again clapped his hands together. 'You guessed that I was thinking that I couldn't think of anything either! Now here is another and this is the hardest of all. What is that man with the funny hat?' And the King of the Loonies pointed his long finger at the horse.

The tired old horse looked around at his friends and winked one eye. 'He called me a man,' he giggled.

'Please remain quiet when I am asking riddles!' the King of the Loonies shouted at the horse.

'He is a spoogledoogle,' the guard said.

'Good!' the King of the Loonies again cried as he clapped his hands. 'That is right.'

'It is wrong,' the tired old horse said.

'It is right!' the King of the Loonies cried. 'Whatever I say is right, *is* right, whether it is right or wrong!'

'All right,' the tired old horse replied. 'I shall not argue with you, but I know that I am not a spoogledoogle, for there isn't any such animal!' And with this, the tired old horse walked over and lay down in a small flower garden at one side of the room.

'Here!' the King of the Loonies shouted at the tired old horse. 'Get out of that flower bed! You are worse than the neighbour's chickens!' The tired old horse made no reply, but put his head down upon the prettiest flowers and went to sleep. The King of the Loonies took off his crown and scratched his head. 'Do all spoogledoogles act that way?' he finally asked Raggedy Ann.

'Oh yes,' Raggedy Ann replied, with a twinkle in her shoe-button eyes. 'If you watch him for a while, you will see that when he gets up he will be a horse instead of a spoogledoogle.' And Jenny and Raggedy Andy giggled behind their hands.

The King of the Loonies looked doubtfully at Raggedy Ann. 'Why did you come to Loonie Land?' he asked.

'We came in search of Jan,' Raggedy Ann replied. 'One of the loonies carried him away from his sister, and we are searching for him.'

'Hmm!' the King of the Loonies mused as he rubbed his chin. 'Now I must try and fool you. My loonie did not catch Jan near the little cottage in the deep, deep woods and drag him down here.'

'Oh!' Raggedy Ann cried as she put her hands to her face. 'What a fib!'

'How do you know it's a fib?' the King of the Loonies asked.

'Because,' Raggedy Ann replied, 'if the loonie did not do that, how do you know he caught Jan near the little cottage in the deep, deep woods?'

'That's so,' the King of the Loonies agreed. 'Well, anyway, it doesn't make any difference. Jan is in prison, and if you want him, you must answer three riddles.'

'Do you mean that if we answer the three riddles, you will

let Jan go with us?' Raggedy Andy asked the King of the Loonies.

'Yes,' the King replied. Then he told one of the guards to bring Jan into the room. When the guard returned with Jan, the King of the Loonies said, 'Now I shall ask the three riddles.' They all waited.

'Let's see,' he mused. 'Why does a Boliver bite biscuits? There's a hard one.'

'I don't believe it is a riddle at all!' Jenny whispered to Raggedy Ann. 'He's just making it up.'

'I think so too,' Raggedy Ann replied.

'What are you talking about?' the King of the Loonies asked.

'The Boliver bites biscuits because he wishes to eat them,' Raggedy Ann told the King of the Loonies.

'Good!' the King cried, 'I mean, bad, for I do not wish you to guess them. Now! Why does a snickersnapper snap snickers from snuckers?'

'Isn't that silly?' the camel with the wrinkled knees laughed.

'Don't you think that is a good one?' the King asked the camel.

'Indeed, I do!' the camel replied. 'That is the looniest one you have asked so far.'

'I think so, too,' the King replied proudly. 'Now just you answer that one if you can. Just you answer that one!' he said to Raggedy Ann.

'The snickersnapper snaps snickers from snuckers because the snappersnicker snucks snickersnuckers from snucker-snappers snickersnappers,' Raggedy Ann replied, and it was all she could do to keep from laughing out loud. Raggedy Andy could not help it; he laughed so hard he fell upon the floor and rolled about.

'I don't see how you guess them so easily!' the King of the Loonies cried. 'I never would be able to guess them myself!'

Of course, Raggedy Ann did not tell the King of the Loonies that she did not know the answers herself and that she knew the King of the Loonies did not know the answers either, but just made up the riddles as he went along.

'Now I have thought of a really, really hard one,' the King of the Loonies said. 'How can a hobgoblin hobble a gobble? Guess that riddle and I'll give you a fiddle.'

'Anything you answer will be right,' Jenny whispered. 'The King of the Loonies does not know the answers himself.'

'I know it,' Raggedy Ann replied out loud.

'Then if you know it, why don't you answer?' the King of the Loonies cried.

'The hobgoblin can hobble a gobble by gobbling the hobble with a goghobblin,' Raggedy Ann answered.

'Good!' the King of the Loonies cried, then remembering that he had not wanted Raggedy Ann to answer correctly, he shrieked, 'No, I mean BAD! I did not wish you to guess my riddles so easily! Now I will have to ask you some more!'

'Oh, that isn't fair,' Raggedy Ann said. 'You promised if I answered three riddles, you would let Jan go away with us, so it wouldn't be fair if you did not keep your promise!'

'I've changed my mind now,' the King of the Loonies replied. 'I shall ask you three more riddles; then if you answer them correctly, I will let you take Jan.'

'No, sir!' Raggedy Ann replied. 'You said three in the beginning. And I answered the three riddles. How do I know that you will not change your mind after I have answered the next three?'

'Of course, you wouldn't know,' the King of the Loonies said. 'But that is just what I would do! I have a right to change my mind every time I feel like it, so there!'

'Well, anyway,' Raggedy Andy walked up to the King. 'Raggedy Ann answered the riddles, so now we shall take Jan and leave you,' he said.

'Ha, ha! Is that so?' the King howled. 'I shall see that you do not escape! Bring out the Looniest Knight. I shall have him cut off your nose!'

'Boo! Boo!' Raggedy Andy howled back at the King as loud as the King had howled at Raggedy Andy. Then the King of the Loonies stuck out his tongue at Raggedy Andy and before he thought what he was doing Raggedy Andy tweeked the King's nose so hard it made two large tears run out of the King's eyes.

Just then the Looniest Knight came galloping in, sitting astride a stick with a horse's head on the end. The Looniest Knight pranced up before the King and waved his sword, 'Whose nose is it, the King wishes cut off?' the Knight asked.

'There he is!' shouted the King of the Loonies, pointing to Raggedy Andy. The Looniest Knight rushed at Raggedy Andy and would have tried to cut off Raggedy Andy's nose if Raggedy Andy had not hurriedly crossed his fingers. The Looniest Knight did not know what to do when Raggedy Andy crossed his fingers, for you know, and of course everyone else knows, that means a temporary truce is declared.

'What shall I do?' the Looniest Knight asked the King.

'You must fight!' the King cried. 'Didn't you see him tweek my nose?'

'No, I didn't!' the Looniest Knight replied. 'How did he do it?'

'Like this,' Raggedy Andy laughed, as he tweeked the Looniest Knight's nose. Then while the Looniest Knight was wiping the tears from his eyes, Raggedy Andy awakened the tired old horse and got up on his back. Then taking a long stick away from a loonie man standing near, Raggedy Andy uncrossed his fingers. This was a sign that he was ready to fight.

Then the Looniest Knight jumped around with his hobby horse just as if he was on a real horse which was prancing about as if he could not guide it the way he wanted it to go.

'I believe he is afraid,' Raggedy Andy laughed.

'He isn't afraid,' the King of the Loonies said, 'he just doesn't want to fight until he gets ready.'

But although Raggedy Andy waited patiently, the Looniest

Knight kept on prancing about just as if he could not make his hobby horse behave. Then finally, the Looniest Knight dropped his sword upon the floor and kicked up his heels and pretended that his hobby horse threw him.

'That wasn't any fight at all!' the camel with the wrinkled knees cried. 'The Looniest Knight was afraid of Raggedy Andy! That's what!'

'Sometimes he fights better than that,' the King of the Loonies said. 'Maybe he was afraid that Raggedy Andy would crack him with the long stick.'

'Of course, I meant to crack him,' Raggedy Andy laughed. 'And I'll crack anyone who tries to keep Jan from going with us.'

At this all the loonies cheered loudly and the King of the Loonies came down from his throne and shook Raggedy Andy's hand. Then he shook hands with the tired old horse who had gone to sleep standing up. Then he shook hands with Jenny and Jan and Raggedy Ann and the camel with the wrinkled knees.

'You are so brave, I wouldn't think of keeping Jan any longer,' the King of the Loonies told them. 'So you can all leave.' And as our friends marched out of the King of the Loonies' house with Jan, all the loonies ran after them shouting, 'Long live the brave Raggedy Andy! He vanquished the Looniest Knight!' And even the Looniest Knight and the King of the Loonies ran with them to the end of the village, shouting with the rest of the loonies.

'Well,' Raggedy Andy sighed when they had left the loonies behind at the edge of Loonie Town. 'I am mighty glad that is over! I never was so frightened in my whole life!'

'Were you really?' Jenny asked. 'Why you didn't let on that you were.'

'Of course not!' Raggedy Andy laughed. 'If I had let them know that I was more frightened than the Looniest Knight, don't you see he wouldn't have been as frightened as I and would have cut off my nose,' laughed Raggedy Andy. 'And I didn't care to have my nose cut off, because then all my cotton stuffing would have leaked out and my head would have been as flat as a pancake.'

'Well, here we are back at the tree,' the tired old horse said.

'Yes,' Raggedy Andy added. 'And I have been riding you all this time when you are so tired!' And Raggedy Andy jumped from the horse's back.

'Really, I had not noticed it at all,' the horse laughed.

CHAPTER 6

'Oh, wait a minute!' Raggedy Ann said, as they were about to enter the tree. 'We do not want to go back up through the tree until we find Babette, the French doll! We must blindfold the camel with the wrinkled knees and let him run backwards.'

'Let's see,' the tired old horse thought out loud, 'I will carry Jan and Jenny, while the camel carries Raggedy Ann and Raggedy Andy. In that way we can get there quicker.'

So Raggedy Ann again tied her hanky around the camel's shoe-button eyes and after she and Raggedy Andy had climbed upon his back and Jan and Jenny upon the tired old horse's back, the camel started running backward lickety-split.

The tired old horse ran just behind the camel's head and as Raggedy Ann and Raggedy Andy sat facing Jan and Jenny upon the horse's back, they could talk comfortably as they rode along.

After they had galloped along for ten minutes, the camel suddenly stopped and as the tired old horse had been running with his nose very close to the camel's nose, he bumped into the camel so hard, the camel's soft head was pushed way back in wrinkles against his body, and Jan and Jenny went over the horse's head and landed upon Raggedy Andy and Raggedy Ann.

'It is lucky you fell on us!' Raggedy Ann laughed, as Jan and Jenny got to their feet. 'For Raggedy Andy and I are soft and it did not bump you much.'

'It did not hurt us a bit!' Jan laughed as he brushed off Raggedy Ann's dress. 'But how about the camel?'

Indeed the camel with the wrinkled knees did look very sad. His poor nose was flat and his neck was nothing but wrinkles. Jan and Raggedy Andy pulled and patted the camel's head into shape again and it was not long until he looked as good as before.

'Why did we stop?' the tired old horse asked.

'We ran into something,' Raggedy Ann said, 'but I can't see a thing.' None of the others could see anything either, but when they felt behind the camel, they could feel an invisible stone wall. And although Raggedy Ann and Raggedy Andy ran along the wall for a long way, feeling it, they could discover no gate.

'There must be some way of getting in right here!' the camel said, 'for I am certain this is the exact spot I came out of.'

'Maybe if you came out here there is a door, or gate there,' Jan said.

'And maybe it only opens one way, like the stone in the room in the tree,' Raggedy Ann suggested.

'But if that was so, I would have fallen through, just as the tired old horse did,' the camel said.

'Oh, no you wouldn't,' Raggedy Ann laughed. 'For don't you see, Mr Camel, if you came out a door there, it must have swung out this way, and if you bump it from this side, it only closes that much tighter.'

'That's so,' the camel agreed. 'But can you feel any door knob?' Raggedy Ann had to admit that she could not.

After thinking for a while the tired old horse finally suggested, 'Let the camel back up tight against the gate; for there must be a gate here; and Raggedy Ann and Raggedy Andy get upon the camel's back. Then the camel can pretend that he has just come bouncing through the invisible gate and start to run. This may fool the gate into thinking the same thing and it may swing open as it would do just as someone passed through it.'

'But it will close again,' the camel said. 'Then we are just where we started from.'

'Yes, but if the invisible gate swings open, I shall hold it open,' the tired old horse said. 'Then you can come back and we will all go through.'

'It sounds reasonable,' Raggedy Andy said, 'let's try it, for there is nothing else to do.' And he and Raggedy Ann climbed upon the camel's back and the camel squeezed back tight against the invisible gate. Then with a sudden spring, the camel jumped away from the wall and ran a few steps.

'I've got it!' the tired old horse called as he held the invisible gate open.

'How did you ever think of it?' the camel asked, as he and the others walked through the invisible gate.

'I don't know,' the horse laughed. 'I guess it was just plain horse sense.'

'Well, here we are,' Raggedy Ann said, when they had all passed through the invisible gate. 'And there is a queer little house built of sticks and stones and mud over there.'

'I'll go over and see who lives there,' Raggedy Andy said.

'We'd better all go,' Raggedy Ann suggested. And so they all walked over to the queer little house. As they stood looking at it, a little old woman peeped slyly out of a crack in the door, then the door was opened wide and the little old woman came out. 'Good-morning,' she said. 'Can I serve you with any witchcraft today?'

'I've never tasted any,' the tired old horse replied. 'But if it is anything which will keep me from getting so tired, I'd like to eat some.'

'She doesn't mean food, Mr Horse, when she says witchcraft,' Raggedy Ann explained. 'She means magic!'

'Yes, that is just what I mean,' the little old woman said. 'I'm Winnie the Witch, and I serve people with witchcraft. It is very cheap.'

'How much is five pennies' worth?' the tired old horse asked.

'Just fivepence,' Winnie the Witch replied. 'What kind would you like to have, kind sir?'

The tired old horse fumbled in his pocket and finally

found a fivepence piece and handed it to the witch. 'I'll take any kind you have, just so it is good for being tired,' he said.

'Something in the shape of a bicycle pump?' the witch enquired.

'He isn't a bicycle,' Raggedy Ann laughed. 'What he wants is some hay, or oats, or corn that has been magically made magic to cure him of being tired.'

'Yes, that is what I want,' the tired old horse agreed. 'I don't care what it is, just so it makes me want to move quickly.'

The witch bit the coin, then tinkled it upon her door step. 'I just want to make sure it isn't lead,' she said. 'Yesterday a man came here with the loveliest doll and gave me tenpence for a bottle of magic medicine to make the doll come to life.'

'It must have been the French doll, Babette!' Raggedy Ann and Raggedy Andy cried together. 'And did you give him the magic medicine?' Raggedy Ann asked.

'Oh, yes,' the witch said. 'But after he left, I tinkled the tenpence piece on the table and it was lead.'

'He cheated you!' cried Raggedy Ann.

'Indeed, he cheated himself,' laughed the witch. 'For whenever anyone tries to cheat me, whatever I sell them never does what they wish it to do. And so, you see, the bottle of magic medicine which I gave him turned to plain, everyday water just as soon as he gave me the lead coin.'

The witch, when she had finished telling our friend this, said, 'Now we must all remain very quiet, while I work the magic charm for the tired old horse.' Then from her pocket she took a piece of red chalk and made a ring upon the ground. In the ring she drew many strange figures, each with a number beside it. Then she asked the horse to step into the circle and shut his eyes. When he had done this, the witch took a stick and gave the tired old horse a crack upon his back. 'Giddy-up!' she cried. And the tired old horse jumped out of the circle and went scampering about with his head high in the air.

'There,' the witch said, with a sly wink at Raggedy Ann. 'That was all he needed! In fact, anyone who is always tired needs the same thing, for they just imagine they are tired.' Then when the tired old horse came prancing back to his friends, he was so pleased he wanted all the rest to have some magic too.

'I'm not a bit tired now,' the horse said. 'I could carry all of you upon my back a long way now and not be the least bit tired! I could feel the magic strike me all of a sudden,' he told the witch. 'It was wonderful!'

'I haven't any money,' Raggedy Ann told the witch. 'But I wish that you could tell us how to find the man who had the doll. For we are in search of her and would like very much to find her and take her back home with us.'

'I'll tell you a secret,' the witch whispered, after first looking all about her to make sure there was no one listening. 'I do not care whether anyone pays me for working magic, or not. So,' she went on out loud, 'I will see what I can do for you. Please step into the magic circle, all of you.'

'Shall we receive the same sort of magic that the tired old horse received?' Jan asked. 'I wouldn't care to have Jenny get it.'

'Now please do not worry about that,' the witch promised. 'You will not feel anything at all.' Then when they had all stepped into the magic circle the witch said, 'You must all close your eyes and count to ten slowly. Then you may open your eyes.'

Raggedy Ann, Raggedy Andy, Jan and Jenny, the tired old horse and the camel with the wrinkled knees all counted slowly to ten, then opened their eyes. Instead of the little house belonging to the witch, which had stood a few feet from them before, our friends now saw a large tent and coming from the tent were voices. Very quietly they walked up to the side of the tent and listened.

'Ha!' one voice said. 'The old witch cheated me! The bottle of magic was nothing but a bottle of rainwater! I shall go back and tear down her house!'

Raggedy Ann found a small hole in the side of the tent and peeped through, then she motioned the others to take a peep. There, sitting inside, were twelve burly men with black whiskers and long red noses. And each one had a large sword and two pistols in his belt.

'They are pirates or something, I'll bet,' Raggedy Andy whispered. 'And there is Babette pretending she is only a doll and not moving at all! What shall we do? We must rescue Babette somehow, but the pirates are too many to fight!'

'They look very fierce,' Jenny said. 'Perhaps they will capture us all and keep us prisoners.'

'Listen,' Raggedy Ann whispered. 'They are talking.'

'Ha!' laughed one of the pirates. 'I am about the bravest pirate around here!'

'We are all of us the bravest!' all the other pirates cried, each trying to say it louder than the others.

'How can we all be the bravest, I'd like to know?' the first pirate asked.

'Because,' one replied. 'We are really not pirates at all! So we all can be as brave as each other!'

'That is quite true!' all the pirates agreed, except the first one, and he seemed to be the chief. 'How can you prove that you are as brave as I am?' he asked.

'I know how we can prove which is the bravest!' one thin pirate cried. 'We can take twelve pieces of paper and put a spot on one piece, then we can put all the pieces of paper in a hat and draw. The one who draws the black spot can be

shot by the rest of us. Then we'll put eleven pieces of paper in with one having a black spot and keep on until there is only one of us left and that will be me!'

'How can it be you?' the others all asked.

'Because I will mark the paper and remember which one it is each time,' the thin pirate said.

'I shall be the one to mark the black spot!' the other eleven pirates cried. 'For I want to be the last one left alive!'

'They'll be fighting in a few minutes,' Raggedy Andy whispered, although it was not necessary for him to be quiet, the pirates were quarrelling so loud they would not have heard had Raggedy Andy shouted.

Jan took a tin tube from his pocket and picked up some small pebbles, then whispering for his friends to keep still, he went around the tent until he found a small hole near one of the pirates. Then with his tin tube Jan blew a pebble against a pirate's cheek.

'Wow!' the pirate howled as he jumped up and danced about. 'Who hit me?' Then Jan blew pebbles against the other pirates' cheeks until they were all dancing about, howling. Jan could scarcely blow the pebbles at the pirates, he was laughing so hard, but when he could manage to straighten his face, he stung them with the pebbles. Then, not knowing what was happening to them, the pirates all decided that it was safer outside the tent. And, each trying to get there first, they caused a jam at the doorway, and in a tangle of arms, legs and heads the pirates fell in a struggling mass, pulling the tent down with them.

Jan immediately reached under the fallen tent, picked up Babette and carried her to where Jenny, Raggedy Ann, the tired old horse and the camel with the wrinkled knees stood with Raggedy Andy.

The pirates were struggling to their feet and there was no time to be lost. 'Quick!' the tired old horse cried, 'Jan and Jenny up on my back and Raggedy Ann, Babette and Raggedy Andy up on the camel's back.'

This was done, just as the first pirate scrambled up. And, seeing our friends running away, he knew in a moment what had happened.

With a furious shout to his companions, the pirate started running after our friends. And as the other pirates recovered, they followed. Then, as the tired old horse and the camel

with the wrinkled knees could run very fast, the pirates began shooting. Luckily, none of the pirates knew how to shoot straight, so in a short time the camel and the tired old horse had left the pirates far behind.

CHAPTER 7

After the tired old horse and the camel with the wrinkled knees had run for a long, long time, they sat down to rest, and as they did not tell their riders what they intended to do, Raggedy Ann, Raggedy Andy, Babette, Jenny and Jan slid right off on to the ground.

'I forgot to mention that I intended sitting down,' the tired old horse said.

'So did I,' the camel chimed in. 'It's funny how I just took a sudden notion to stop and rest just as the tired old horse did.'

'Well, no one was hurt,' Raggedy Ann laughed, 'so please do not apologise.'

'Babette is a lovely doll, isn't she?' Jenny said as she smoothed the French doll's hair.

'Indeed she is,' Raggedy Ann and Raggedy Andy both agreed. 'She's the prettiest doll of all.'

'It's nice to have you say that, Raggedy Ann and Raggedy Andy!' Babette smiled so that her dimples showed. 'But really, I must tell you that Raggedy Ann is the most beloved doll of all, isn't she, Raggedy Andy?'

'Yes, indeed that is true,' Raggedy Andy told Jenny. 'You see, Raggedy Ann is so old and so loppy and so generous

and so kindly, and she can think so much better than any of us other dolls. And then, too,' Raggedy Andy said, 'maybe you don't know it, but Raggedy Ann has a candy heart! Haven't you, Raggedy Ann?'

'Honest?' asked the camel with the wrinkled knees. 'Let's see it.'

'Oh, it is sewn up inside my cotton-stuffed body,' Raggedy Ann laughed.

'I thought maybe you had it in your apron pocket,' the camel said.

'Here, look,' Raggedy Andy told the camel. 'You can feel Raggedy Ann's candy heart.' And Raggedy Andy showed the other just where to feel. Even the tired old horse was greatly surprised when he felt such a lovely candy heart.

'Were you frightened when the pirate took you out of the playroom, Babette?' Raggedy Andy asked.

'Not a bit,' Babette replied. 'Only of course I did not wish to be taken away and I was afraid the pirate would drop me and break my china head when he jumped over the fence.'

'I thought you were a French doll,' the camel cried.

'She is,' Raggedy Andy told the camel. 'What makes you think she isn't, Mr Camel?'

'Because,' the camel said, as he scratched his head as if trying to figure it all out, 'if she has a china head, she must be Chinese, so she can't be French.' Everyone laughed at this and the tired old horse turned a summersault and kicked up his heels with glee.

The camel sat with a puzzled expression on his Canton-flannel face. 'Well,' he cried, 'just you tell me then. How can she be French when she is Chinese? Just you tell me that.'

'How can a brick walk?' the horse laughed. 'Or a house fly?'

'I shan't answer your riddles unless you answer mine,' the camel said.

'Then I'll explain,' the horse started to say, when he saw

in the distance a strange object bobbing up and down over the ground and coming towards them. 'Look!' he cried.

'It's a house fly!' the camel cried, 'I mean it's a flying house!'

'Indeed it is,' Babette jumped to her feet. 'It is the jumping houseboat of the pirates! Run as fast as you can!'

The camel with the wrinkled knees immediately started running and the tired old horse had to run after him and drag him back to the others by the string the camel had for a tail.

'Now just see the time you've made us waste!' the tired old horse shouted. 'You know perfectly well that you and I must carry the others! Quick!' he cried. 'Climb on to our backs!'

The camel with the wrinkled knees couldn't think of anything to reply until he and the tired old horse had run almost a mile, then he cried to the horse, 'Wait a minute! I just thought of something I want to tell you!'

'Tell me as we run along,' the tired old horse shouted back to the camel. 'Can't you see the pirates are gaining on us every minute?'

'I just wanted to tell you not to be so bossy, Mr Tired Old Horse!' the camel puffed as his black shoe-button eyes sparkled.

'Please do not stop to quarrel,' Raggedy Ann said. 'There is the witch's little house straight ahead.'

'Shall we dash right in without knocking?' the camel asked as he ran faster.

'Of course not,' the tired old horse replied as he also ran faster. 'If the door is closed and we dash at it, we shall only break the door down and then the pirates could dash in after us.'

'The pirates are right behind us,' Jan shouted. 'Hurry!'

Indeed, the pirates' jumping houseboat was jumping right behind them when the witch opened her front door and cried, 'Run right in!'

The tired old horse was the first through the door and the camel with the wrinkled knees was right behind him. And they both came into the witch's house so fast, and it was such a small place inside, neither could stop although they braced their feet in front of themselves. The tired old horse, Jenny and Jan, the camel with the wrinkled knees, Raggedy Ann, Raggedy Andy and Babette slid across the floor and upset a large bowl of goldfish.

The witch slammed the door, 'BANG!' right in the pirate chief's face, and the camel cried excitedly, 'I'm shot!'

Jenny and Jan picked up the bowl and replaced the goldfish before they had flopped very much, and the witch ran to the kitchen and brought a jug of water to refill the bowl. By this time everyone had got on his feet except the tired old horse, who had fallen in such a comfortable position he had gone to sleep.

The pirate chief banged upon the witch's door with his

sword. 'Open the door, or I'll huff and I'll puff and I'll blow the house down!'

'Ha, ha!' Raggedy Ann and Raggedy Andy laughed. 'He has read that in a book! He can't huff and puff enough to blow the house down!'

'I'll soon show you!' the pirate chief howled. 'You do not know what a good blower I am!' And he puffed so hard his eyes stuck out and it made him dizzy, but still he huffed and puffed! Then after huffing and puffing for six minutes, the pirate chief started coughing so hard the other pirates had to pound him on the back. All those inside the witch's house had been peeping through the chinks in the window-blinds, and when the pirate chief had to give up his huffing and puffing, Raggedy Ann and her friends laughed loud and long.

'I know what we will do,' the pirate chief said, after he had got over his coughing fit.

'What will we do?' the others asked, as they crowded about him.

'We will lay siege to the house and starve them out! I've read in a book about how kings often lay siege to castles until the inmates are starved out!'

'But where will we get the siege to lay?' one pirate asked.

'And besides,' another cried, 'this isn't a castle!'

'Sillies!' the chief cried, as he stamped around. 'That doesn't make a bit of difference! All we have to do is to stay here until they get so hungry they come out and beg for something to eat!'

'That sounds like a good scheme,' the thinnest pirate admitted. 'But won't we be getting just as hungry as they?'

'Of course not,' the pirate chief replied. 'We have a lot of things to eat in the jumping houseboat. And if we bring the food out here and eat it, that will make them hungrier still and very soon they will come out.'

Now, as everyone knows, pirates are always very, very hungry, in fact almost as hungry as little boys, so they all ran to the flying boat and came out carrying bread and butter and dill pickles.

'Look!' the pirates yelled to those in the witch's house. 'We've got something to eat! Yaha! Yaha!'

'That reminds me,' the tired old horse said as he got up and yawned. 'I haven't had a bite to eat since I ate the violets.'

'Snapdragons,' the camel corrected.

'Violets,' the tired old horse replied very firmly.

'Yaha! Yaha! We've got bread and butter and dill pickles!' the pirates teased outside.

'We don't care! We don't care!' Jan and Jenny called back.

'And we've got some sugar to put on our bread and butter, too, if we want it!' the pirates yelled. 'Yaha! Yaha! And you haven't!'

'Here we are,' the witch said; for, while the others had been watching out of the cracks with hungry eyes, she had prepared a lovely lunch with her magic spells. There were ham sandwiches, bread and butter and jam sandwiches, pickles, ice cream, sponge-fingers, doughnuts and water-melon. Everything looked so good it made tears come into Raggedy Ann, Raggedy Andy and the camel's shoe-button eyes, for they had no mouths to eat with. But when the witch noticed this, she took a pair of little scissors and snipped a mouth for each. Jenny and Jan and the tired old horse, of course, were already sitting at the table with napkins tucked under their chins. All the time our friends were eating the lovely magical lunch the witch had prepared for them, the pirates were sitting outside with only bread and butter and dill pickles.

When everyone had eaten all they could, the tired old horse said, 'While you rest, for I know you are all sleepy from eating so much, I will clear the table and wash the dishes.' So the witch, who was as sleepy as the rest, placed pillows around upon the floor and everyone lay down and took a nap. The horse took all the cream puffs and sponge-fingers and ham sandwiches that had been left on the plates to a side window and threw them out.

'Kitty! Kitty! Kitty!' he called and laughed softly to himself. All the pirates came running to see what the tired old horse had thrown out the window. 'Are your names all Kitty?' the tired old horse asked.

The pirates saw all the nice things the horse had thrown out of the window and said to each other. 'Just look at the goodies they have thrown away – cream puffs and sponge-fingers and ham sandwiches and *watermelon*! My goodness! They must have a lot of good things to eat if they can throw away these nice things! And all we had was bread and butter and dill pickles!'

And the pirates all had tears in their eyes and watering mouths, for as you must surely know, the tired old horse had made them very, very hungry.

'We had the nicest lunch you ever, ever saw,' the tired old horse told the pirates. 'And if you promise to behave yourselves, I'll give you each a lollypop, for I did not throw them away!'

'We'll promise,' all the pirates shouted, as they crowded about the window with outstretched hands.

The tired old horse held out twelve lollypops. 'Now if I give you each a lollypop you must promise to reform and not be pirates any more. Now what will you be if you quit being pirates?' The tired old horse held the lollypops so high the pirates could not reach them.

'I'll give up being a pirate and be a plumber!' one pirate cried.

'And I'll give up being a pirate and go into the garage business!' another shouted.

'And I'll give up being a pirate and sell oil stock!' another cried.

'And I'll give up being a pirate and be a – '

'Wait a minute!' the tired old horse laughed, as he scratched his head. 'I believe you had all better remain pirates! So promise me you will be pirates instead of driving taxi cabs, or going into the plumbing business or anything like that!'

When the pirates had all said, 'Cross our hearts!' and promised, the tired old horse gave them each a lollypop. Then one of the pirates began crying and handed his lollypop back to the tired old horse. 'What's the matter?' the tired old horse asked. 'Isn't your lollypop as big as the others?'

'Yes! Snub! Snub!' the pirate sobbed. 'But it makes me feel sorry that I took the doll away from her home. And I am ashamed to have you be so kind to me after I was so naughty.' And the pirate cried and cried as if his heart would break. In fact, he cried so hard, he got all the other pirates crying too, and they cried so hard, they could not eat their lollypops.

If it had not been so sad, the tired old horse would have laughed, for the pirates were all squawling in different keys and it sounded very strange.

'What is all the racket about?' the witch asked, as she and the others came to the windows. 'Did you put red pepper on the lollypops?'

'No,' the tired old horse replied, as he brushed away a tear and told his friends why the pirates wept so loudly.

'It sounds as if they have reformed,' the witch said.

'It isn't that,' one of the pirates said. 'Charlie here is crying because he took the French doll, and he knows that was very, very wrong. And the rest of us are crying to think that one of our band would be so dishonest.'

'Gracious!' the camel with the wrinkled knees said. 'I thought all pirates were dishonest.'

'Maybe they are,' the pirate chief replied. 'But you see, we were really not pirates at all. We were just pretending that we were pirates and that is why we all feel so sad about Charlie.'

'And I feel sadder and sadder and sadder and sadder every minute,' the pirate named Charlie howled.

Raggedy Ann felt so sorry for Charlie and the other pirates, she went outside and wiped Charlie's tears away with her apron. 'Now please do not cry any more, Pirate

Charlie,' Raggedy Ann said as she gave him a large fluffy cream puff with lots of cream in it. 'We will forgive you for taking Babette and we know you will never do anything like that again.'

Pirate Charlie smiled through his tears as he ate the lovely cream puff. 'I'll tell you the truth, Raggedy Ann,' Pirate Charlie said, after Raggedy Ann had wiped the

cream from around his mouth with her pocket hanky. 'We always read stories about pirates when we were little, and all of us decided that when we grew up we would become pirates and sail through the air in a big flying houseboat. So when we finally grew up, we bought this jumping boat and pretended that we were pirates. But all the time we longed for the things we should have had when we were children. And I always wanted a lovely doll. That is why I took the French doll.'

By this time Raggedy Andy, the tired old horse, Jenny and Jan and the others had gathered around the pirates as they sat on the grass by the side of the witch's little house. The kindly witch brought out large dishes of ice cream for everyone and stood looking at the pirates intently for a few minutes.

When everyone had finished eating their ice cream, the witch, with a tinkly little laugh, said, 'I want all the pirates to sit in this circle!' And she drew a circle upon the ground. When the pirates had all taken seats inside the circle, the witch placed a small red thing in the centre of the circle and leading from the small red thing to the outside of the circle was a long rubber tube.

After the witch had said a magic charm like this – 'Hey diddle diddle, the cat and the fiddle!' only she said it backwards, she placed the end of the rubber tube in her mouth and started blowing. And, as the witch blew, everyone saw that the small red thing was a red balloon, and it grew larger and larger until it was almost touching the pirates' knees. Then the red balloon burst with a loud 'Bang!' and everyone except the witch was so surprised they fell over backwards.

'Why!' the camel with the wrinkled knees cried, when he

got to his feet and looked at the pirates, 'they have had a magic shave!' Indeed, all the pirates had lost their black whiskers and long red noses.

'They are all GIRLS!' Jan and Jenny cried in astonishment. The magic red balloon had blown the pirates' false whiskers and false noses right off their faces. 'Now, girls,' the witch laughed, 'you had better all come into my house and wash the red paint from your faces.'

CHAPTER 8

It is remarkable how black whiskers and false noses and red paint will change anyone's appearance. For, after the pirates had had their false whiskers and false noses blown off and had washed the red paint from their faces, they were all pretty girls.

'We even changed our names,' the pirate who had been called Charlie said. 'My name is Charlotte.'

The witch picked up all the false whiskers and long red false noses and took them to the pirates' jumping boat. 'Everybody climb on board,' she said, 'for we will ask the girl pirates to take us in the jumping boat to find Jan and Jenny's mother and father.'

'Why, how do you know about their mother, Mrs Witch?' the tired old horse asked in surprise.

The witch just laughed a tinkly laugh and took off her large hat. And with the hat came all her white straggly hair. Then she took off her long black cloak and stood before them a lovely girl not any older-looking than Jenny.

'Land sakes alive!' the camel with the wrinkled knees cried. 'She isn't a witch at all! She's a fairy queen!' Everyone else was as much astonished as the camel with the wrinkled knees.

'No,' the fairy who had been a witch a moment before said, 'I am not a fairy queen. I am only a fairy princess.' And as the fairy princess waved her magic wand again the girl pirates' jumping houseboat became covered with beautiful fairy lights and started jumping along over the ground. It was just like sailing along over the water when the sea causes the boat to rise and fall with a gentle motion, and everyone enjoyed riding upon the pirates' jumping boat.

'I thought it was funny that a witch could be as kindly as you were,' the tired old horse said to the fairy princess.

'But one really can never tell by appearances,' Raggedy Andy said.

'That is indeed true,' the fairy princess laughed. 'But so many persons always judge people by the way in which they are dressed. Why, the ugliest shell may be hiding the most beautiful pearl and the roughest cover may be on the loveliest, sweetest storybook. It isn't what is on the outside that counts; it is what we may have within us. But,' the fairy princess went on, 'we must not conceal our good qualities, but must let others share them with us, for, whenever we give, then we most surely receive in return. And indeed, a heart filled with love within us always shines through in the kindly acts we do and in the sunshine we give to others.'

The jumping boat had now reached the land of the loonies and jumped around their queer village towards the beautiful castle which stood upon the purple mountain beyond.

'Are we going to the lovely castle?' Jenny asked the princess.

'Yes, my dear,' the fairy princess replied, 'for there we shall find your mother and father. And while we are sailing

there I shall tell you their story. When they left you and Jan,' the Princess said as she put her arm around Jenny, 'they went to see your grandmother, and they intended coming back to you in two hours. But when they reached your grandmother's house, they found a lot of knights and courtiers; and indeed, they were very much surprised to find so many fine people there. And when the knights and courtiers saw your mother and father, they all fell upon their knees and cried, "Long live the King! Long live the Queen!" And your father and mother discovered for the first time that your grandmother had been a queen, but her place had been taken by another woman whose soldiers had driven your grandmother away from the country. Now the other woman who had taken your grandmother's crown had been driven away by the knights who loved your granny and they had come to make her queen again. But your grandmother had been taken to Fairyland as the knights found when they came to her little house, and they were just about to leave when along came your father and mother. So there wasn't anything to do except go with the knights and courtiers and be crowned King and Queen of the Purple Mountain.'

'But why didn't Mamma and Daddy send for us?' Jenny asked.

'That is the sad part of the story,' the fairy princess replied. 'You see, everyone thinks it must be just lovely to be a king or a queen, for then, they imagine, they can do just as they please and have everything they wish for. But this is not always true. When your father and mother wished to return to their own little home, they found that they were not permitted to do so. Indeed they were never permitted to step outside the castle unless knights and courtiers went with them. Nor could they send anyone to bring you two children to them! And that is why I am helping you reach your parents, for I know how they have longed for you!'

The fairy princess directed the jumping boat so that it came to rest in the beautiful garden of the lovely castle. And there sat Jenny and Jan's mother and father, the Queen and King of the Purple Mountain. Jenny and Jan, with whoops of joy, ran and threw their arms about their parents. All the pirate girls and even the tired old horse cried with happiness at the meeting.

'We shall get straight into the jumping boat and leave with you,' the king and queen told the fairy princess, 'for we never, never, never care to be a king or a queen again! The people here, if they wish, can have a republic, like the United States of America; but we would rather be just plain, everyday folk, in a plain, everyday house, with plain, everyday people for friends!'

And so, the king wrote a note and pinned it to the chair, telling all the people of the Purple Mountain that he did not wish to be king any longer and that they might crown another king and queen, or elect a president. Then the jumping boat jumped over the garden wall and sped away until the Purple Mountain and the beautiful castle looked like a little toy far behind. The fairy princess served ice cream and chocolate cake to everyone on board, for she knew just how hungry they would all be after so much joy and excitement. So, with laughing and singing on board, the jumping boat finally reached the poor little house of Jenny's father and mother.

'Won't you all come in?' Jenny's mother asked. 'The first thing I shall do after I take off my queen's dress and jewels and get into a plain, everyday dress will be to make a whole lot of pancakes!'

'Whoopee!' the former king cried as he threw his crown up against the woodshed. 'And I'll run out and chop a lot of wood to build the fire! I haven't had a chance to chop wood since before I was king!'

'I do believe the neighbours have taken care of the chickens all the time we were king and queen!' the mother laughed. 'Bring in a handful of eggs, Henry,' she called to the former king as he stopped chopping wood to moisten the palms of his hands.

'Ah! It sounds good to hear you call me Henry!' the king shouted. 'I wouldn't be a king again for all the golden sovereigns in the world, Harriet!'

After Jenny's mamma had fried pancakes until they were stacked upon the table three feet high, and all the pancakes had disappeared, the pirate girls told Raggedy Ann and Raggedy Andy and Babette that they would be glad to take them home in the flying boat.

'I really believe we had better be getting back,' Raggedy Ann said, as she wiped her shoe-button eyes with the corner of her apron.

'Please wipe mine too,' Raggedy Andy said. 'I am sorry to leave such good friends, but what will Marcella think when she discovers that Raggedy Ann, Babette and I are not at home? She will think that we have all been stolen.'

'I can fix that all right,' the fairy princess laughed. 'I will show you when you get home.'

The camel with the wrinkled knees scratched his head a while and then said, 'I have just thought it all over and I believe that the little boy who used to play with me has by this time grown up into a man, and he wouldn't care to play with me again, so I shall adopt Jan for my new master.'

When the camel with the wrinkled knees said this, Jan's father rubbed his eyes and picked up the camel. As he turned the camel over and over in his hands and wiggled the camel's wrinkled knees, he cried, 'Why, I believe, Harriet, this is a toy I owned when I was a little boy!' And so it proved to be, when he and the camel told of different things that had happened years before. 'Indeed, you shall adopt Jan!' the former king cried as he gave the camel a fond squeeze. 'And the tired old horse can live with us too, if he wishes!'

'Indeed he can!' the former queen cried. 'And we will be most happy to have such a good friend!'

The tired old horse tried to thank them all, but his throat seemed to be filled with lumps and he could only swallow very hard and blow his nose loudly. But the others saw the sunny light of happiness shining through his eyes.

After all had kissed each other goodbye, the jumping boat jumped away and in a short time everything began getting darker and darker.

'We must be going to have a terrible rain storm,' Raggedy Andy said.

'No, no,' the fairy princess laughed. 'That is not the reason it is getting darker and darker. You see, I am just sending the jumping boat back from today to yesterday night, so that, when we get home, it will be the same time as it was when you left.'

Raggedy Andy rubbed his head thoughtfully, but could not quite make it out, so he remained silent. So did Raggedy Ann. When the flying boat came to rest in the back yard, Raggedy Ann and Raggedy Andy and Babette kissed the fairy princess and the twelve pirate girls goodbye and ran through the grass and climbed into the playroom window.

All the other dolls were sound asleep, so Raggedy Ann and Babette and Raggedy Andy were as still as mice as they climbed into their doll-beds. Then after they had been quiet for a long time Raggedy Ann sat up and ran her rag hand through her yarn hair, then whispering to Raggedy Andy to follow her, Raggedy Ann carefully crawled out of bed, climbed upon the window-sill and jumped 'BLUMP' to the ground. Raggedy Ann picked herself up, shook the wrinkles from her dress and ran to the playhouse, followed by Raggedy Andy. They jumped upon the doll-beds and bounced up and down as they smiled up at the wooden ceiling.

RAGGEDY ANN'S WISHING PEBBLE

CHAPTER 1

Raggedy Ann and Raggedy Andy went skipping over the Yellow Meadow, each with a rag arm around the other's neck. When the two Raggedys reached a clump of golden rod they heard tiny voices, laughing and singing.

'Sh!' both Raggedys whispered to each other as they crept up closer.

'You need not be so quiet!' a teeny-weeny silvery voice called to them from the golden rod. 'We can see you easily, and knew you were coming!'

Raggedy Ann and Raggedy Andy laughed happily as they pushed aside the golden rod and saw hundreds of tiny little brownies. 'We did not know who it might be,' said Raggedy

Ann, 'and we did not wish to frighten you away until we saw who you were.'

'And then did you wish to frighten us away?' one of the tiny brownies asked. Raggedy Ann and Raggedy Andy laughed as cheerily as all the brownies at this.

'No, indeed!' Raggedy Ann said when they had stopped laughing. 'We did not wish to have you quit your happy games! That's what I meant to say, so we were just tiptoeing up easily, and then we would have gone away!'

'Well! We are glad you came!' one of the little brownie men said, 'for you can join in our fun!'

'Thank you!' the two Raggedys cried. 'We like fun! What were you playing?'

'We were just planning to fly down to the Looking-Glass Brook and slide on the water, so you may go with us!'

'We would like to go,' Raggedy Andy answered, 'but we cannot fly, nor can we slide upon the surface of the water without getting wet; though that's fun too, because our rag bodies are stuffed with nice white cotton and we soon dry out in the lovely warm sunshine!'

The little brownies laughed and one said, 'When you slide with us, you won't get even a little teeny-weeny speck wet!' And waving his hand to the other brownies, he caught Raggedy Andy's hand; other little brownies caught Raggedy Andy's feet and Raggedy Ann's hands and feet and whisked them up over the golden rod and out across the Yellow Meadow to the Looking-Glass Brook.

When the little brownies and the two Raggedys reached the Looking-Glass Brook, they all ran as hard as they could and went sliding across the smooth surface of the water. It was just like sliding upon ice, except that when one of the brownies or one of the Raggedys fell down, they bounced up again; for the surface of the Looking-Glass Brook gave beneath them like rubber ice and they did not get their heads bumped. As they slid along upon the top of the water, Raggedy Ann and Raggedy Andy could see the pretty little fish swimming about and chasing each other back and forth just as if they were having games too.

The Raggedys and the little brownies were not the only ones who were sliding upon the surface of the water, for while they were resting, they saw queer little tiny long-legged creatures come sliding along. And one came right up to the brownies and Raggedy Ann and Andy. 'Why! He has a tiny boat on each of his feet!' Andy cried in surprise.

'Oh, yes!' a little brownie said. 'He's one of the little ferrymen!'

'Do you mean that he carries tiny passengers across the Looking-Glass Brook?' asked Raggedy Ann.

'That is just what they do!' laughed the little brownies. 'You see, many little creatures cannot walk upon the water, and, if they happen to fall into the water and try to swim across, the little fish, almost always eat them up!

'So the little ferrymen, or "water boatmen", as they are sometimes called, run from one point upon the Looking-Glass Brook to another point and they carry passengers, for the fish never disturb the ferrymen!'

'And I suppose the tiny creatures pay the little ferrymen with seeds or something like that!' said Raggedy Andy.

'Oh no!' laughed the little brownies. 'The little ferrymen never ask pay for carrying the tiny creatures across, because you see, they get so much fun out of sliding across the Looking-Glass Brook themselves that that is all the pay they wish.' When the little brownies told the Raggedys that it was time they went to work, each little brownie gave each rag doll a kiss. Each kiss left a tiny brown freckle on each of the Raggedys' faces, just like the little faces of boys and girls who have been kissed by the brownies. Then with a lot of tiny brownie whoops, the friendly creatures flew high in the air and across the meadow, leaving the two Raggedys watching the little kindly water boatmen carrying the tiny insect passengers across the Looking-Glass Brook.

And the Raggedys, with an arm about each other's neck, felt that their little cotton-stuffed heads were filled with happiness, for you know how much pleasure it gives *you* when you see someone doing unselfish deeds and kindly acts for those in need. And even if it is only a very, very tiny little deed of kindness, the Raggedys knew that however small they may be, the kindly deeds grow and grow until they blossom and fill our hearts with the sunshine of happiness.

CHAPTER 2

As the Raggedys sat upon the bank of the Looking-Glass Brook and watched the little water boatmen carry the tiny creatures across, a ripple came circling by them, then another and another until the little water boatmen rocked as they slid over the tops of the ripples. 'It looks just as if the Looking-Glass Brook was smiling!' laughed Raggedy Ann.

Then as the ripples came faster and faster and closer together, the two Raggedys peeked over the edge of the bending grasses and saw a queer little dumpy creature standing in the water and digging a hole in the bank. He wore a little round felt hat and worked in his shirt sleeves. The Raggedys could not see the little dumpy creature's face until they spoke to him and he looked up at them. Then they saw it was Mr Muskrat and his bright little eyes danced laughingly behind round spectacles. 'Whatever are you doing, Mr Muskrat?' Raggedy Ann asked. 'You are making the Looking-Glass Brook dance and ripple just as if it was giggling!'

Mr Muskrat pulled his braces over his shoulders and winked slowly at both rag dolls. 'Who knows?' he smiled, 'Perhaps it is giggling at me, for you know, someone just played a prank on me!

'But I believe I know who it was!' Mr Muskrat went on, as he pushed his little round hat back and wiped his forehead with his red pocket hanky.

'Who do you s'pect?' asked Raggedy Andy.

JOHNNY
GRUELLE

'Well,' laughed Mr Muskrat, 'When I came here to my kitchen door a few minutes ago, I found that someone had filled my doorway with pieces of mud and grass and completely closed it as tight as tight could be, and in the soft dirt all around the doorway, I saw the tracks where whoever did it had walked, and I said, "Ha ha, I know who made those footprints! It was Timothy Turtle." '

'How did you know that it was Timothy?' Raggedy Ann wished to know.

' 'Cause you see,' said Mr Muskrat, 'Timothy Turtle wears four shoes, two on his front feet and two on his back feet and he turns them in pigeon toed when he walks. So you see, he left four pigeon-toed tracks! And now I'm digging my kitchen doorway open again, for it is time I had my dinner!'

'What will you do with Timothy Turtle when you catch him, Mr Muskrat?' Raggedy Andy asked.

Mr Muskrat stuck his spade in the bank and sat down beside the two Raggedys. 'Timothy Turtle is a funny fellow!' Mr Muskrat chuckled. 'He plays a prank on someone and then he walks away a few feet and pulls his head into his collar, so that just his nose peeps out, and, because he keeps his eyes closed, Timothy believes that no one can see him! Then he usually goes to sleep and forgets all about what he has done. If you will look just around the bend in the bank, you will see Timothy Turtle sound asleep and right where I had to pass him when I came to my kitchen doorway!'

'And didn't you even awaken him?' Andy asked.

'Oh no!' laughed Mr Muskrat. 'You know that Timothy Turtle carries his house right upon his back all the time, and he gets very tired, so he needs all the sleep he can get!'

Just then Timothy Turtle came walking pigeon-toed around the bend in the bank and tipped his hat to Raggedy

Ann, although to do this he had to take off one of his shoes. Timothy Turtle sounded like a polly parrot when he talked and although the Raggedys had to smile (for their smiles were painted on) they were careful not to laugh at Timothy's funny voice. 'Well, here you are hard at work, Mr Muskrat! Building a new house I suppose?'

Mr Muskrat winked at the Raggedys and said, 'Sit down here beside our two friends, Timothy Turtle, and I will soon be through!' And with this Mr Muskrat made the dirt fly until he had opened his kitchen doorway. Then he went inside and came out with two large slices of muskrat bread and butter and jam and gave one to Timothy Turtle. 'I know that you two Raggedys do not eat,' he laughed, 'for if I gave you a bite, it would get jam all over your painted faces!'

'Thank you just the same!' Raggedy Ann and Andy both replied.

When Timothy Turtle had eaten his slice of bread, he said, 'I think I'll swim out to the log and take a nap in the nice warm sunshine!' and nodding his head gravely to the two rag dolls and Mr Muskrat, Timothy Turtle walked pigeon-toed down the bank into the water and swam lazily out to the log. 'You see!' laughed Mr Muskrat. 'Timothy Turtle had forgotten all about playing his prank on me!'

'I think the nicest part is that you forgive him for making you so much unnecessary work!' Raggedy Ann laughed.

'Oh, really there was nothing for me to forgive!' Mr Muskrat replied, 'for I have all the time I wish and I love to work, so if Timothy Turtle got some fun out of it, then I

don't mind in the least, for I have the fun of undoing what he did. And don't you see, if I should get angry at Timothy, that would have taken all the pleasure out of my work, for then I might not have wanted to work. And when anyone tries to get out of a little bit of work which he has to do, or when he puts it off until some other time, then it seems as though the work which is put off, grows and grows until it takes ever so much longer to do.'

CHAPTER 3

'May we come into your house and see how you live?' Raggedy Andy asked of Mr Muskrat.

'Why, Andy,' Raggedy Ann laughed, 'don't you know that is very impolite?'

Raggedy Andy fidgeted his foot about in the sand and did not know what to say, but Mr Muskrat patted him upon the back and laughed, 'That's all right, Raggedy Andy, I was just about to ask both of you inside, for it looks to me as if we are about to have some heavy rain, and if you stay out in the rain, I am sure your rag bodies will get very soggy!' And with this Mr Muskrat led the way into his kitchen.

'Isn't it nice and cosy in here?' Raggedy Ann exclaimed. 'It is so quiet you can hardly hear any of the sounds from the creatures along the Looking-Glass Brook!'

'That's one reason why I like it!' Mr Muskrat answered, leading the way up a long hall into a larger room. 'This is my

living-room!' And he pulled out two little chairs for the Raggedys and took an easy chair himself. After lighting his Muskrat pipe, the funny, dumpy creature crossed his feet and leaned back comfortably. 'Yes, indeedy! Timothy Turtle is a queer little fellow, and all his turtle relatives are queer little creatures, too. But then,' continued Mr Muskrat, 'probably Timothy Turtle and his relatives think everyone else is queer! And I guess it is just as well that we do think that way, for if we didn't we'd probably be discontented and want to be changed into something else. And, that is just how the turtle family happen to be as queer as they are. For, once upon a time, the turtles were almost like the hoppytoads and the greenfrogs except that the turtles could not hop as far as the frogs. Then when larger creatures came to the streams where the turtles and hoppytoads and frogs lived, the turtles could not get into the water as fast as the greenfrogs.

'And so, when Old Mr Skooligan, the magician, came along one day, the turtle family all cried, "Oh, Mr Skooligan, the mosquitoes bite us upon our backs and we can't hop fast enough to get away from them, and when Old Mr Heron comes along looking for dinner, we can't hop fast enough to get away from him! Can you give us some magic medicine which will make our backs so hard the mosquitoes can't bite us and Old Mr Heron won't be able to eat us for dinner?" And Old Mr Skooligan, the magician, he winked his eyes behind his glasses and he chuckled to himself. "Humm! Less see!" musin' like, and then he took out his magic pocket book with two magic buttons and three glass beads in it and touched each turtle upon the back. "There!" he said. "Now the mosquitoes can't bite you, and Mr Heron won't care to eat you!" And away he walked. And so,' concluded Mr Muskrat as he puffed the smoke up around the ceiling, 'the turtle family got just what they asked for but not exactly what they wanted, for while they have very hard backs, they get very tired carrying such heavy loads about with them all the time!'

'They should have been satisfied!' said Raggedy Andy, 'then probably Old Mr Skooligan would have changed them to something even better without them asking for a change!'

'And that's why all the turtle family are so slow and sleepy!' mused Raggedy Ann. 'I've wondered how they became that way!'

'But there's one thing about the turtles!' said Mr Muskrat, 'if they start out to do anything, they keep plodding away until it is done!'

'Do the turtles have any homes besides the ones they carry upon their backs?' asked Raggedy Andy.

'No,' laughed Mr Muskrat, 'unless the mud they bury themselves in at the bottom of the streams in the wintertime could be called homes!'

'Then, too,' he added, 'a lot of the turtles come into our homes for the winter and pull their heads and feet into their shells and sleep!'

'It is kind of you to let them stay with you all winter, Mr Muskrat,' Raggedy Ann said.

'Well,' Mr Muskrat replied, 'the turtles come in very handy to us at times during the winter!'

Raggedy Ann and Raggedy Andy laughed at this and asked, 'How?'

'Lots and lots of times we muskrats have parties and then we use the sleeping turtles for seats and they never know it at all!'

Just then Mrs Muskrat came walking in with a basket upon her arm, 'My! It's raining hard outside!' she said after shaking hands with the two rag dolls. 'You Raggedys had better stay all night with us!'

'Thank you, Mrs Muskrat!' Raggedy Ann and Andy replied, 'We will if it will not put you to any bother!'

'Dear me, no!' laughed the two muskrats, 'we have plenty of spare bedrooms!' And they took the two rag dolls and tucked them in little beds as comfortable as could be and, wishing them good-night, Mr and Mrs Muskrat tiptoed out, leaving the two Raggedys, their little rag heads filled with kindly thoughts and their shoe-button eyes staring up at the ceiling.

'Isn't it nice to meet people who are so unselfish!' Raggedy Andy whispered to Raggedy Ann. 'Indeed it is!' Raggedy Ann answered. 'It makes my little candy heart feel like it would bump right through my pretty white apron. And if we are kind and unselfish, then those who meet us will be filled with good thoughts and love for us!'

'I met Gerty Gartersnake yesterday!' said Mrs Muskrat at the breakfast table as she passed the pancakes to Raggedy Ann, 'And she had a lovely new dress!'

'I didn't know Gerty Gartersnake ever had new clothes!' laughed Raggedy Ann as she poured maple syrup upon a pancake.

'Oh yes,' Mrs Muskrat replied, 'every once in a while she gets new clothes!'

'But she has no hands to make them with!' Raggedy Andy said. 'Does some kind creature make them for her?'

Mr and Mrs Muskrat chuckled at this, 'Yes, indeed, my dears!' said Mrs Muskrat. 'The kindest person in the world makes them for her – Mother Nature!'

'Isn't that nice!' Raggedy Ann cried. 'Mother Nature must be very kind.'

'Indeed she is!' agreed Mrs Muskrat. 'If it wasn't for Mother Nature some of the poor creatures would have a very hard time! As it is, Gertrude Gartersnake has a hard time getting off her old clothes, for you see her new clothes are always under her old clothes!'

'How strange!' said Raggedy Ann. 'You would think the new clothes would be on the outside, like children's dresses, and then you would take off the old dress and put on the new!'

'That is probably the way children have to get their new clothes!' Mrs Muskrat nodded her funny head. 'But Mother Nature plans it better for her many creatures. She makes the new clothes upon Gerty Gartersnake right in under her old clothes, so all Gerty has to do is take off her old dress and she has her new one on without the bother of putting it on!'

'I always thought that Gerty Gartersnake wore her dresses much too tight!' Mr Muskrat said with a sly wink at Raggedy Andy.

Mrs Muskrat knew that Mr Muskrat was joking, so she gave Mr Muskrat a pancake with a hole in it and said, 'Gerty Gartersnake does not even have to button her new dress, it fits her without buttons. But, my! How Gerty Gartersnake has to wiggle and twist to get out of her old dress!'

'Lots of times, children find Gerty's old dresses lying around and I suppose they wonder how Gerty ever gets out of them.'

'There's someone tapping at the kitchen door!' said Mr Muskrat as he got up from the table and went to the door. 'Well, if it isn't Gerty Gartersnake herself, with her pretty new dress on!'

'We were just speaking of you!' said Raggedy Ann as she pulled up a chair for Gerty Gartersnake to sit upon. 'Mr Muskrat says he thinks your clothes are too tight!' said Raggedy Andy.

'If Mr Muskrat wasn't so nice, I'd think he was teasing me!' said Gerty Gartersnake, as she tasted the pancakes and maple syrup. 'For he knows very well that if I did not wear really tight clothes, why! – I'd be catching them on every twig and stick that I wiggled over! Yes, indeed, my clothes are very smooth and tight, but that is just the way I need them so that I can wiggle along and not get fastened upon anything and everything!'

'Your dress is very pretty!' said Raggedy Ann.

'I think it is too!' Gerty Gartersnake laughed. 'Mother Nature in the far-off beginning took different flowers and made the first Gartersnake dress and that is why our dresses are covered with such pretty red and yellow colours! We can hide among the pretty flowers and it is very hard for anyone to see us.'

'You don't bite people, do you, Gerty Gartersnake?' Raggedy Andy asked.

Gerty Gartersnake almost wiggled off the muskrat's chair she laughed so hard. 'Dear me, no! I don't bite anything except things I wish to eat, like pancakes.'

When everyone had eaten as many pancakes with maple syrup as they wished Mrs Muskrat and Raggedy Ann washed and wiped the dishes while Gerty Gartersnake wrapped a rag around her tail and dusted the furniture.

Mr Muskrat and Raggedy Andy swept the floors all nice and clean and put the dishes in the muskrat cupboard. Then, when everything was nice and tidy, they all went out upon the muskrats' back porch and watched the pretty fish jumping about in the Looking-Glass Brook.

'How nice it is just to sit here and listen to all the music of nature!' said Raggedy Andy.

'Yes, indeed!' Raggedy Ann agreed. 'It's just like a great, great, big music box which old Mr Sun winds up every evening before he goes to bed, so that it will start bright and early in the morning playing and sending out happy sounds for everyone's pleasure.'

CHAPTER 4

Raggedy Ann and Raggedy Andy thanked Mrs and Mr Muskrat for the nice time they had at the muskrat home and after shaking hands goodbye the two rag dolls walked along the edge of the Looking-Glass Brook. They peeped under the overhanging grasses and poked about in the sand and pebbles along the shore. 'I wish that we could find a wishing pebble!' said Raggedy Andy.

'Dear me! What would two rag dolls do with a wishing pebble?' Raggedy Ann wanted to know.

'Why!' laughed Raggedy Andy, 'we could wish for so many nice pretty things like lollipops and ice-cream cones and soda-water and sweeties and toys and everything like that!'

'Then let's hunt for a wishing pebble!' said Raggedy Ann. 'Do you know what they look like, Raggedy Andy?'

'Of course I have never seen one!' Raggedy Andy replied, 'But I have heard that they are round and smooth and very white.

'Is this one, do you suppose, Raggedy Andy?' Raggedy Ann asked as she held up a white pebble.

'Less see!' Raggedy Andy said as he held out his rag hand for the pebble. 'Well, it's nice and white, Raggedy Ann, and it's quite smooth, but it isn't round enough I'm 'fraid!'

'I'll keep it anyway,' Raggedy Ann laughed as she put the pretty pebble in her apron pocket, 'for it may be a wishing pebble and we would not know it!'

'We can easily find out if it is a wishing pebble!' said Raggedy Andy.

'How?' asked Raggedy Ann as she took the pretty pebble from her pocket.

'Well,' said Raggedy Andy, 'when you find a wishing pebble, you must hold it fast in your hand and close your eyes tightly and make a wish. Then if it is really and truly a wishing pebble, whatever you wish for comes true!'

'Then', said Raggedy Ann, 'let's wish for something and see if it comes true!'

'All right!' Raggedy Andy agreed. 'You wish for something!'

'But I don't know what to wish for!' Raggedy Ann laughed. 'There's nothing I need!'

'Then wish for something for Mrs Muskrat!' Raggedy Andy suggested. 'Why not wish for her to have a magic pancake mixer which will always be full of pancakes ready to cook!'

'All right!' agreed Raggedy Ann, 'I'll wish that Mrs

Muskrat had a very magical pancake mixer always filled with pancakes ready to be cooked!'

'Oh, wait a minute!' Raggedy Andy cried. 'I've thought of something better! Wish that the pancakes were already cooked, then Mrs Muskrat won't even have to bother about cooking them!'

'But s'pose she really likes to do her own pancake making!' said Raggedy Ann. 'Then if we gave her a magic pancake mixer filled with pancakes already cooked, she wouldn't have the fun making them any more!'

'I hadn't thought of that, Raggedy Ann!' Andy said.

'Anyway,' Raggedy Ann shook her head, 'we can't make the wishing pebble work!'

'Why?' asked Raggedy Andy.

' 'Cause we can't close our shoe-button eyes when we make a wish!' said Raggedy Ann.

'Hmmmm!' was all Andy could say, but he sat down in the sand and ran his rag hand up through his yarn hair and tried to think of a way.

'I can't think of any way at all!' laughed Raggedy Ann. 'Shoe-button eyes can't close, and that's all there is to it!'

Raggedy Andy finally hopped up in the air and turned a flip-flop; it wasn't a very good flip-flop, for Raggedy Andy only turned partly over in the air and fell with his rag legs twisted over his head. When Raggedy Ann had straightened him out, he laughed and said, 'We can have the fun of wishing anyway, Raggedy Ann, and if we wish for things, nice things for others, we can pretend the wishes come true!'

'That is a nice thought!' Raggedy Ann laughed. 'So I wish Gerty Gartersnake had a new dress!'

'And I wish all the birds would sing!' said Raggedy Andy.

'And I wish the muskrats had a magic soda-water fountain in their living-room!' said Raggedy Ann.

'And I wish they had a lollipop field right outside their kitchen door!' said Raggedy Andy. 'And now, Raggedy Ann, let's run back to the muskrats' house and see if our wishes have come true!'

'No! Let's not!' Raggedy Ann said in her soft Raggedy voice. 'It's much more fun not knowing, for don't you see, if we don't know for sure, we can still believe our wishes have come true and we have the pleasure of having wished for good things for our friends!'

CHAPTER 5

'What do you think?' asked Freddy Fieldmouse as he ran up to where the two Raggedys sat upon the clean sand at the edge of the Looking-Glass Brook.

'We were thinking a lot of happy thoughts, Freddy Fieldmouse!' Raggedy Ann laughingly replied.

Freddy Fieldmouse laughed too as he said, 'That is very, very nice, I'm sure, Raggedys, but I mean what do you think about Mr and Mrs Muskrat?'

'We think they are nice and very kindly!' said Raggedy Andy.

'Yes! I know they are very nice and unselfish, Raggedys, but I mean – what do you think the muskrats have?'

'Hmmm!' mused Raggedy Ann. 'Is this a riddle, or something like that, Freddy Fieldmouse?'

'Nothing of the sort!' cried Freddy Fieldmouse. 'You wouldn't guess in a long, long time!'

'Is it a new muskrat baby?' asked Raggedy Ann.

'Nope!' Freddy Fieldmouse replied.

'Then we give up!' said Raggedy Andy. 'I felt a stitch rip out of my rag head, I guessed so hard!'

Raggedy Ann carefully looked at Raggedy Andy's head, even taking off his little blue and white cap to see better. 'You haven't lost a single stitch, Raggedy Andy!' she laughed. 'You mustn't try to fool us that way!'

'Well,' laughed Raggedy Andy, 'I give up anyway. I can't guess what the muskrats have!'

'I won't give up!' said Raggedy Ann. 'But it's very hard to guess, Freddy Fieldmouse.'

'Then I'd better tell you!' agreed Freddy Fieldmouse, 'But I 'spect you'll be s'prised! When I was swinging upon a swingy weed right over the muskrats' kitchen door, I heard Mrs Muskrat squeal and I almost fell off the weed into the water thinking that something had her!'

'What was it, Freddy Fieldmouse?' Raggedy Andy asked.

'I was just about to tell you,' Freddy Fieldmouse replied.

'Just you be patient, Raggedy Andy!' Raggedy Ann said jokingly, as she pushed Andy's little blue and white cap down over his shoe-button eyes.

'I am!' Raggedy Andy laughed. 'But I am so anxious to know why Mrs Muskrat squealed as if something had her!'

'I climbed back up the swinging weed and ran down towards the muskrats' kitchen door and peeped through the grass, but Mrs Muskrat had run into the house and Mr Muskrat had run in after her. I could hear them both squealing and I said to myself, "The muskrats are squealing because they are happy. That's what!" and I walked right in without knocking and what do you think!'

'Dear me, Freddy Fieldmouse! If you don't tell us what you think instead of asking us what *we* think, I'm sure to rip all the stitches out of my rag head trying to guess!' said Raggedy Andy.

'When I walked into the muskrats' house and into their living-room, there stood Mrs Muskrat with one in her hand and Mr Muskrat with one in his hand and when they saw me, they put one in my hand – '

'Not three muskrat babies?' Raggedy Ann said.

'No, not babies! Three ice-cream sodas, that's what!' said Freddy Fieldmouse.

Raggedy Andy jumped up and danced about in the sand, kicking his rag feet so high in the air, he almost fell in the Looking-Glass Brook, and Raggedy Ann just sat still and smiled.

'Wasn't that enough to make anyone squeal, to find an ice-cream-soda fountain right in their living-room?' asked Freddy Fieldmouse.

'We are very, very glad!' said Raggedy Ann. 'And how do you s'pose the soda-water fountain ever happened to be in the muskrats' living-room, Freddy Fieldmouse?'

'Mrs Muskrat told me that she was sitting in the armchair darning Mr Muskrat's socks when she heard a funny sizzling noise right behind her, and she jumped up, so quick she upset her darning basket, and ran out to the kitchen porch. Then she said to Mr Muskrat, "There's a sizzler in our living-room!" And Mr Muskrat picked up a stick so that he might have something to poke the sizzler with, if it needed poking, but when they both got in their living-room again, they soon saw that the sizzling noise came from the pretty little soda-water fountain, and we drank sodas until we had had enough!'

'You still have some soda-water or ice cream on your chin!' said Raggedy Ann, and she dipped her hand into the Looking-Glass Brook and washed Freddy Fieldmouse's face.

'I'm running to tell everybody and invite them to the muskrats' house to eat ice-cream sodas!' said Freddy Fieldmouse as he jumped through the grass.

'Well, what do you think?' asked Raggedy Andy.

'I am thinking a lot of happy thoughts!' Raggedy Ann laughingly replied.

'Yes, I am too!' said Raggedy Andy. 'Our wishing pebble must have been a real, for-sure wishing pebble after all!

You know we wished that the muskrats would have an ice-cream-soda-water fountain in their living-room!'

'Then I suppose it must have been a wishing pebble,' said Raggedy Ann, 'and I wish that I had kept it now! I thought it was only a make-believe wishing pebble and I buried it in the sand again!'

'Well we have had that much fun with it anyway,' laughed Raggedy Andy, 'and we should be happy of that. Indeed, whenever we give pleasure to others, we always make happiness for ourselves!'

And the two Raggedys' shoe-button eyes twinkled merrily.

CHAPTER 6

'Let's run down to Mr and Mrs Muskrat's home and see their new ice-cream-soda-water fountain!' said Raggedy Andy as he lifted Raggedy Ann to her feet.

'You are just in time, Raggedy Ann and Raggedy Andy!' cried Mrs Muskrat, 'We have had sixteen ice-cream sodas already and Mr Muskrat is going to have one more!'

'I've had every flavour except pineapple,' laughed Mr Muskrat, 'and I want to try that! Then I will rest up for about fifteen minutes and try them all over again!'

'I wish you rag dolls could eat ice cream!' said Mrs Muskrat. 'You can't imagine how good it tastes!'

'I wish that we could,' Raggedy Ann sighed; 'but you know we haven't any real for-sure mouths like you have and when we taste anything it just runs and soaks into our rag faces.'

'Then we have to be scrubbed!' laughed Raggedy Andy.

'Don't you think if we made a little teeny-weeny hole in the centre of your mouths we could put a straw in the hole and you could taste the sodas?' Mr Muskrat asked.

'We might try it!' Raggedy Ann agreed.

'I can sew the hole up again after you have tasted the sodas if you wish!' said Mrs Muskrat.

Mr Muskrat set down his glass of soda-water and ran to his tool-box and brought back a large nail. 'Now I can poke this nail right in the centre of your mouths and make a hole large enough to put a straw in!'

'Won't it hurt them?' Mrs Muskrat asked.

'Not even a tiny speck!' Raggedy Andy laughed. 'Our heads are nothing but cloth stuffed with nice white, clean cotton! And besides, we often get rips in our heads and bodies! No indeed, Mrs Muskrat, it won't hurt at all!'

So Mr Muskrat soon poked holes in the Raggedys' mouths with his nail and Mrs Muskrat filled two glasses with vanilla soda. 'For,' she explained, 'if the vanilla soaks through the cotton, it won't stain as much as strawberry or raspberry or chocolate!'

It was easy for Raggedy Ann and Raggedy Andy to drink the lovely ice-cream soda through a straw and they were surprised after drinking two glasses apiece to find that the soda did not soak through to the back of their rag heads.

'Dear me!' Raggedy Ann exclaimed as she held out her glass for more. 'Just think of what we have missed all these years, Raggedy Andy!'

'That is just what I have been thinking!' laughed Raggedy Andy. 'And I was also thinking that I would like to try a glass of raspberry soda!'

'I don't believe it will soak through any more than the vanilla did!' Raggedy Ann replied. 'So I think that I will have a strawberry soda!'

'While you folk sit here and have all the sodas you wish,' said Mr Muskrat, 'I'll just run around the neighbourhood and ask everybody in to have sodas!'

Raggedy Ann and Raggedy Andy had hardly finished their ninth glass each of soda-water when the neighbours began trooping into the muskrat home, so then the Raggedys had to stop in order to help Mrs and Mr Muskrat serve the neighbours with the different flavours.

'I tell you what, Raggedy Ann and Raggedy Andy,' cried Mr Muskrat, 'I don't know how this magic soda-water fountain came into our living-room, but I'm very happy and thankful that it is here, for now all our friends can come in any time and help themselves to all the sodas they wish!'

'Raggedy Ann wished the soda-water fountain in here for you!' Raggedy Andy told Mr and Mrs Muskrat.

'Do your wishes come true?' all the neighbours of the muskrats wished to know.

'I wish that they did!' laughed Raggedy Ann, 'for there are a lot of wishes I would like to make!'

'Raggedy Ann found a wishing pebble,' said Raggedy Andy, 'and she wished for a few things!'

Of course everybody wanted to see the wonderful wishing pebble and they were so disappointed when Raggedy Ann

told them that she had buried the wonderful pebble in the sand.

'I do not believe I would ever be able to find it again!' she laughed.

'We'll all go and help you find it!' said Mr Muskrat. 'Just as soon as we all have six more glasses apiece!'

'The nice part about the magic soda-water fountain,' said Mrs Muskrat, 'is that you can drink about fifteen glasses and it never makes your stomach ache!'

'I think the nicest part of it is that all your friends have been asked to share in your pleasures!' laughed Raggedy Ann.

And all the friends of Mr and Mrs Muskrat agreed to this, for everyone knows how nice it is to have free ice-cream sodas whenever they wish them, and especially magic ice-cream sodas that never give anyone the stomach ache.

CHAPTER 7

'Whee!' Raggedy Ann cried, after she and Andy had drunk fifteen glasses each of soda-water from Mr Muskrat's magic soda-water fountain. 'I don't believe I can drink another soda!'

'They were so good!' Raggedy Andy laughed. 'But I think that I have had enough for now!'

Mr and Mrs Muskrat and their neighbours said that they had had all the sodas they wished for. 'Let's go out and see if we can find the wishing pebble where Raggedy Ann buried it in the sand!' suggested Mr Muskrat. 'Then when we find it, we will all be thirsty again and we can all come back in here and have more sodas!'

'That's a fine idea!' cried Mrs Muskrat. 'And if we find the wishing pebble we can wish for everything! Let's hurry and find it!' So out of the door she ran, followed by Raggedy Ann and Raggedy Andy and Mr Muskrat and all their neighbours. There was Georgie Groundhog and Henrietta Hedgehog and Charlie Chipmunk and Freddy

Fieldmouse and Freda Fieldmouse and all the rest of the neighbours. They ran out of the door in a long string and raced down the bank towards the sandy shore where Raggedy Ann and Raggedy Andy had found the wishing pebble.

'Here's where we were sitting when we found the pebble!' said Raggedy Ann. 'But I can't remember where I was when we made the wishes, or where I was when I buried the wishing pebble in the sand!'

'Then we must hunt all along the sandy stretch of shore!' said Georgie Groundhog as he began scratching the sand right and left.

'Perhaps we had better all hunt a little distance apart from each other!' laughed Henrietta Hedgehog, as she brushed the sand from her dress where Georgie Groundhog had kicked it.

'We can find it more easily if we search farther apart!' said Mrs Muskrat. 'I'll scratch up the sand over here!' And soon all the friends were sending the sand in all directions as they dug for the magic wishing pebble.

Raggedy Ann looked over to where Georgie Groundhog had been digging and all she could see of him was his tail sticking out of a hole in the sand and he was sending the sand up from the bottom of the hole in a shower.

'Oh dear, Georgie Groundhog!' Raggedy Ann laughed, 'Stop digging for a minute!'

'Have you found it, Raggedy Ann?' Georgie Groundhog wished to know as he climbed out of the hole he had dug, his face all covered with wet sand.

'No, we haven't found it, Georgie!' Raggedy Ann laughed as she brushed the sand from his face with her apron. And as the others all came and listened, Raggedy Ann said, 'When I buried the magic wishing pebble I just pushed it down under the loose sand, so when we find it, it will only be about an inch under the surface.'

'And here I was scratching and digging a regular tunnel!' laughed Georgie Groundhog.

'We must just feel around in the loose sand!' said Raggedy Andy. 'And when we find it, it probably will be very near the top!'

'Yes, it will!' said Raggedy Ann. 'I remember that I had just wished that a garden of lollipops would be growing outside Mrs Muskrat's kitchen door and then I pushed it right under the sand, for I thought it wasn't a real for-sure wishing pebble!'

'Isn't it too bad, you didn't know?' Henrietta Hedgehog said.

'But there were no lollipops growing at our kitchen door,' said Mr Muskrat, 'for I came in and went out of the kitchen door many times and if the lollipops had been growing there I know I would have seen them!'

'Surely they must be there!' said Henrietta Hedgehog. ' 'Cause if Raggedy Ann wished for the magic soda-water fountain and it came into your house, surely the lollipops must have come too!'

'I'll run and see!' said Mr Muskrat.

'Let's all run and see!' cried Mrs Muskrat.

'I knew there were no lollipops growing here!' said Mr Muskrat as he and his friends came to the muskrats' kitchen door.

Raggedy Ann ran her rag hand up through her yarn hair and thought and thought, 'I can't understand,' she said, 'why one wish came true and not the other!'

'Let's all go into the living-room and have another glass

of ice-cream soda!' said Mrs Muskrat. 'Then perhaps we can think better!'

'Yes, let's,' cried Georgie Groundhog. 'We can think a whole lot better if we have a soda!'

'Oh dear me!' Mrs Muskrat cried when she walked into the living-room. 'There is no magic soda-water fountain any more!'

'It's gone!' cried all the neighbours.

'Ha, ha, ha!' a voice sounded in through the kitchen door. 'Of course it's gone!'

'Who was that?' Raggedy Andy shouted.

'There is no one around here that I can see!' said Henrietta Hedgehog as she and the others came out of the muskrats' house.

'Ha, ha, ha!' the voice again laughed from across the Looking-Glass Brook. 'I saw Raggedy Ann find the magic wishing pebble, and when she buried it, I soon found it! And I wished the lollipops would disappear and the magic soda-water fountain, too. And I've got the wishing pebble!'

'Don't cry!' Raggedy Ann said to Mrs Muskrat. 'We will find who it is and get the pebble back!'

CHAPTER 8

Mrs Muskrat couldn't keep from crying, 'I had planned on all of our friends coming in whenever they wished and helping themselves to the magic soda-water!' she sobbed.

'It is so nice to have a cold glass of ice-cream soda on a hot day!' said Mr Muskrat, as he wiped his eyes with his red bandanna hankie.

'Well! Let's be thankful that we had a nice lot of ice-cream sodas anyhow!' said Henrietta Hedgehog.

'I wonder who the disagreeable person is!' Raggedy Andy mused.

'I can't imagine!' Raggedy Ann replied. 'I don't see why he didn't let the muskrats have the lollipop garden and the ice-cream-soda-water fountain; he could easily have wished for another just like it!'

'Whoever it is,' said Georgie Groundhog, 'he must be very, very selfish and wants everything for himself and doesn't want anyone else to have any pleasures.'

'I can't imagine who would be that selfish along the Looking-Glass Brook!' said Mrs Muskrat.

'I think it will be a good plan for all of us to try and find out who took the magic wishing pebble, so that we can get it back!' said Raggedy Andy.

'If I find him, I shall throw him down and take it away from him!' said Georgie Groundhog.

'We mustn't do that!' said Raggedy Ann. 'For you know, the magic wishing pebble really belongs to whoever finds it! And while I had it, it belonged to me, and when I buried it again, then, don't you see, it belonged to whoever found it the next time! So we must not take it away from him, for that would be wrong, even if he has wished the magic soda-water fountain out of the muskrats' living-room!'

'Then how can we ever get it again?' Raggedy Andy wanted to know.

'First,' said Raggedy Ann, 'we must find out who has it; then if he loses the wishing pebble, or if he buries it, as I did, if we can find it, it will belong to us and we can sit down and wish for a lot of things!'

'If I find it, I'm going to wish for a bicycle!' said Georgie Groundhog. 'Then I can ride really fast up and down the paths through the Yellow Meadow.

'And I will wish for a pair of roller-skates!' said Henrietta Hedgehog. 'Then Georgie and I can have lots of fun together!'

'I'll wish for the Soda-water Fountain back again,' said Mrs Muskrat, 'so that all our friends can have parties at our house!'

'I don't know what I shall wish for,' said Raggedy Ann thoughtfully, 'but I'll probably think of something if ever I find the magic wishing pebble!'

'I think we had all better hunt for the selfish person who

has the wishing pebble!' said Raggedy Andy. 'We can never find the pebble by sitting here!'

'I'll start right away and find it!' said Georgie Groundhog, as he jumped to his feet. 'And when I find it, I'll come right back here and let every one of you wish for as many things as you want!'

'Oh dear!' Mrs Muskrat cried.

'Mercy me!' Henrietta Hedgehog squealed, for Georgie Groundhog had no more than got the words out of his mouth when his feet flew up in the air and he stood upon his head with his legs and arms waving about in a strange manner. Raggedy Ann and Raggedy Andy ran to Georgie Groundhog and pulled his feet down to the floor, but as soon as they let go of his feet, they flew up in the air again, so when they pulled Georgie's feet to the floor again Mr Muskrat sat upon them and held them there. 'Whatever happened to you, Georgie?' he asked.

'I just flew upside down!' said Georgie. 'And I tell you, it surely s'prised me!'

'How do you feel now?' asked Raggedy Ann.

'All right!' Georgie laughed.

Mr Muskrat got off of Georgie Groundhog's feet and Georgie stood up, but again his feet flew up in the air and he kicked his feet about trying to get them down to the floor. 'It makes me dizzy!' he cried.

Raggedy Ann had been thinking as hard as her rag head could think. 'Wait!' she said. 'Cross your fingers, Georgie Groundhog!' she cried. 'There! You see!' she laughed as Georgie Groundhog's feet came down to the floor and he was able to stand up again. 'Whoever has the magic wishing pebble knows that we want to get it back again and they are wishing for Georgie to stand upon his head! And, you know,' whispered Raggedy Ann, 'if you cross your fingers that means you can't be magicked at all!'

'Then,' said Raggedy Andy, 'what will happen when one of *us* gets magicked, Raggedy Ann?'

'I don't know!' laughed Raggedy Ann. 'We haven't any fingers to cross!' Raggedy Ann had hardly said this when she found herself standing upon her head.

'I don't care,' Raggedy Ann laughed, 'for my head is stuffed with nice clean white cotton and it doesn't make me a bit dizzy! Really it is a lot of fun!'

When she said this, her feet came down to the ground and she wiggled one of her shoe-button eyes at everybody. 'You see,' she smiled, 'whoever has the magic wishing pebble is teasing us, and if they think we enjoy it, then they will quit, for they won't find any fun in it if we are having any fun! That's the way with selfish people. So if we always make them believe that their mischief does not annoy us they will always let us be!'

CHAPTER 9

When Raggedy Ann and Raggedy Andy left the muskrats and their neighbours, they walked down the bank of the Looking-Glass Brook asking everyone they met if they knew who had found the wishing pebble which Raggedy Ann had buried in the sand.

'I don't know who has it,' Grampie Hoppytoad said, 'but it must be a very magical pebble if it can bring lovely ice-cream-soda-water fountains by just wishing for them!'

'Oh, indeed, it is a very wonderful pebble!' Raggedy Andy replied. 'Why Raggedy Ann only had it a few minutes and she wished for the ice-cream-soda-water fountain to be in the muskrats' living-room and a lollipop garden to be at the muskrats' kitchen door, and right away, there they were!'

'You know what I believe, Raggedy Andy?' asked Raggedy Ann.

'What?' Raggedy Andy asked in reply.

'Why, I believe that whoever it was who found the magical wishing pebble where I buried it, must have been watching us while we sat there in the sand. And I think that

he heard me wish for the lollipop garden, but he didn't hear me wish for the fountain. So, when he found the magical wishing pebble he immediately wished that the lollipop garden would grow near his own kitchen door!'

'And you think that he did not know about the magical ice-cream-soda-water fountain?' asked Grampie Hoppytoad.

'That is what I believe!' said Raggedy Ann. 'You see, Mr Muskrat wished all of his neighbours to share in the fun of drinking lovely ice-cream sodas so he sent Freddy Fieldmouse to tell everybody. And I guess that whoever has the magical wishing pebble must have heard Freddy tell of the soda-water Fountain.'

'I hear every word you say!' a voice shouted across the Looking-Glass Brook at the three friends. 'And I have the magical wishing pebble safe in my pocket and you will never, never get it, so there!'

'It seems to me that I have heard that voice before,' Grampie Hoppytoad said, 'but I can't think who it is!'

'You'd better watch out, or I'll make you stand upon your head, Grampie Hoppytoad!' the voice cried.

'Why don't you do it now?' Grampie Hoppytoad shouted back across the Looking-Glass Brook.

'You just wait and I will!' the voice replied. 'I'm wishing it now and pretty soon you will stand right upon your head!'

'I feel kinda funny!' said Grampie Hoppytoad to Raggedy Ann and Raggedy Andy.

'Quick! Cross your fingers!' said Raggedy Andy.

'No, I shan't!' said Grampie Hoppytoad. 'I don't believe he can make me stand upon my head!'

'Can't I?' the voice shouted from the reeds across the Looking-Glass Brook. 'You just wait! I'm wishing mighty hard and you'll stand upon your head in a minute!'

'Ha! Ha! Ha!' laughed Grampie Hoppytoad. 'I knew you couldn't do it! And I haven't got my fingers crossed either!'

'No wonder!' the voice cried. 'I was holding the magical wishing pebble in my left hand! That's why! Now you just watch out! How does that feel to you now?'

'I can't feel a thing!' laughed Grampie Hoppytoad, teasingly, 'And I don't believe you really have the magical wishing pebble.'

'Yes, I have,' the voice shouted, 'for I have the lovely ice-cream-soda-water fountain in my own living-room and the lollipop garden right at my own back door and no one shall have a single glass of ice-cream-soda-water or a single lollipop from my lollipop garden!'

'I wouldn't be too sure of that,' cried Grampie Hoppy-toad, 'for you can wish as hard as you like and you can't make me stand upon my head. So maybe the magic has gone out of the wishing pebble and maybe your magical ice-cream-soda-water fountain and your lollipop garden have gone with it!' Grampie Hoppytoad winked his eye at Raggedy Ann, as if to say, 'I'm just teasing!'

'Well! something *is* wrong with the magical wishing pebble,' cried the voice, 'because I've never had any trouble making anyone stand upon their heads when I wished it!

'I'm going home to have a glass of ice-cream-soda-water and I'm leaving you there to think how nice it tastes!'

'Isn't he mean?' laughed Raggedy Ann. 'But when a person grows stingy, it isn't very long before they lose all they have, and then, *my*! how quick they are to ask favours of those they have been stingy with!'

'Yes,' laughed Grampie Hoppytoad. 'The best way to be is to do as many pleasant and kindly things as possible for others, then others love you and help you in return when you need it!

'I'll keep my two large goggle eyes open for the person

who has the magical wishing pebble!' he told them as he shook hands goodbye with Raggedy Ann and Raggedy Andy. 'And if I find out who has it, I'll hunt you out and tell you.'

'Thank you very much!' said Raggedy Ann and Raggedy Andy. 'Someday we will find the magical wishing pebble and then we can have lots of fun wishing.'

'Do you know what, Raggedy Ann?' asked Raggedy Andy, 'I bet you that whoever has the magical wishing pebble can't make its wishes come true any more because they keep wishing unkind things!'

'I'll bet so too!' laughed Raggedy Ann. 'And it wouldn't s'prise me a little teeny-weeny bit to find out that the magical ice-cream-soda-water fountain will not taste very good to whoever has the magical wishing pebble!'

'And the lollipops won't taste good to them either!' said Raggedy Andy.

'I can hear you talking about me,' cried the voice of whoever had the magical wishing pebble, 'and you'd better be careful what you say!'

'Why don't you come out from behind those weeds so we can see you?' asked Raggedy Andy.

'Because!' the voice said angrily, 'I went home and I found my magical ice-cream-soda-water fountain and my lollypop garden just as I left them.'

'How did the soda-water taste?' asked Raggedy Andy.

'I didn't taste any!' the voice replied. 'But I believe you two old rag dolls are the cause of my soda-water fountain tasting bitter and my lollipops tasting like burnt candy!'

'Why! We haven't had anything to do with it!' said Raggedy Ann. 'The magical wishing pebble worked very well when I had it, and all the little creatures thought the ice-cream sodas were so nice!'

'And I think I know just why it worked such nice magical things for you, Raggedy Ann!' the selfish person cried.

'I believe it will work just as well for you, if you wish unselfish things!' said Raggedy Ann.

'You can't fool me that way!' the selfish person cried. 'I know that you have a candy heart, Raggedy Ann! And that is the reason you can work the magical wishing pebble so well!'

'That isn't the reason at all!' laughed Raggedy Ann. 'If you wish nice things you'll soon find that they come true!'

'You just wait!' cried the voice. 'I'll show you! Just as soon as I catch you asleep, I'll take your candy heart, then all my wishes will come true just the same as yours did!'

'You won't ever get Raggedy Ann's candy heart!' Raggedy Andy cried. 'For I shall watch over her all the time she sleeps and if I ever catch you –

'I'll see who you are!' cried Raggedy Andy as he ran and jumped into the Looking-Glass Brook, intending to swim across and chase the disagreeable person. But when Raggedy Andy landed in the water, he kicked and splashed about and only succeeded in swimming in a circle.

Raggedy Ann got a long stick and as she fished Raggedy Andy out she saw a queer little creature run out of the

weeds on the other side of the Looking-Glass Brook and go scampering away as fast as his thin legs would carry him.

Raggedy Andy was dripping wet, but he still wore his cheery smile.

'When you get nice and dry, Raggedy Andy, we'll set off to follow the little man, for I saw which way he ran!' said Raggedy Ann.

And the two Raggedys sat in the warm sunshine and laughed as happily as they ever had before they lost the wonderful magical wishing pebble.

CHAPTER 10

When the nice warm sunshine had thoroughly dried Raggedy Andy after his splash in the Looking-Glass Brook, the two dolls walked down the bank, looking for a place to cross.

After a while they came to a funny little hole in the bank and all about the hole the mud had been built up into a small wall about an inch high.

'Hm!' mused Raggedy Ann as she noticed the queer hole, 'I wonder what that is?'

Raggedy Andy lay flat upon the ground and looked down into the hole.

'Can you see anything?' asked Raggedy Ann.

'I can't see a thing! Dear be! Subthig's grabbed by dose ad I cand tog plaid!'

'Did you say, "Something's grabbed your nose and you can't talk plain?" ' laughed Raggedy Ann.

'Yes!' Raggedy Andy replied, still with his rag face over the hole. 'Subthig is pinjig by dose!'

'Something is pinching your nose?' Raggedy Ann repeated in surprise.

'Thad's whad I said, Raggedy Add!' Raggedy Andy laughed. 'Bud I cand see whad id is! Id dode hurd a bid, though!'

'You talk just like you had a cold in your nose, Raggedy Andy!' Raggedy Ann could not help laughing. 'Shall I pull you away from the hole? It may be a pinching bug!'

'I'm not a pinching bug!' a queer little voice said from down beneath Raggedy Andy's face.

'Id isn'd a pijjig bug!' laughed Raggedy Andy, 'Id jusd said so!'

'I heard it!' laughed Raggedy Ann. 'I guess it would be best if I pulled you away from the hole!' And with this, Raggedy Ann lifted Raggedy Andy away from the queer little hole and there, hanging on Raggedy Andy's painted nose was Clifton Crawdad. Clifton Crawdad flapped his tail as hard as he could, but he did not let go of Raggedy Andy's painted nose.

Clifton Crawdad pinched Raggedy Andy's painted nose so hard it was all pinched up into a wrinkle, and to keep from losing his hold, Clifton Crawdad reached up with his other claw and caught hold of Raggedy Andy's shoe-button eye.

'Here!' said Raggedy Ann reprovingly, 'I wouldn't do that, Clifton Crawdad. You may scratch all the shinyness off Raggedy Andy's shoe-button eye!'

Clifton Crawdad only flapped his tail and, as he had water at the bottom of his queer little home, he splashed mud all around Raggedy Andy's chin.

'I guess I'll pick him off!' said Raggedy Ann, after thinking awhile. 'He may get your necktie all muddy!'

'Maybe you had bedder pig hib off!' said Raggedy Andy, 'Bud be careful you dode hurd hib!'

Raggedy Ann caught hold of Clifton Crawdad with her two soft rag hands. 'Does that hurt you?' she asked in her kindest raggedy tone.

'No, not a tiny speck!' said Clifton Crawdad. 'You see I have a very hard shell and your hands are nice and soft!'

Raggedy Ann pulled upon Clifton Crawdad until she held him out from Raggedy Andy's rag face but Clifton Crawdad's arms kept stretching till Andy cried, 'Waid a binnet, Raggedy Add, you musn'd pull his arbs off!'

'She won't pull my arms off,' said Clifton Crawdad, 'for I'll let go before she pulls that hard!'

'Then you'd better let go,' suggested Raggedy Ann, 'for I'm going to pull hard now!'

'Then I'll let go!' said Clifton Crawdad. And when he did let go, Raggedy Ann was pulling so hard, she fell over backwards, carrying Clifton Crawdad with her.

Raggedy Ann put Clifton Crawdad down upon the sand and smoothed out her apron. 'Just see how muddy you made Raggedy Andy's chin!' she said reprovingly.

'Raggedy Andy should never have put his face over my front door!' said Clifton Crawdad.

'Well, I'll wash it off before the mud dries,' laughed Raggedy Andy.

'You might have lost one of your claws!' said Raggedy Ann.

'Yes!' said Raggedy Andy after he had washed his face. 'What if I had been someone else and just picked you off in a hurry? I might have pulled one of your claws right off!'

'I know it!' Clifton Crawdad answered. 'But after a while it would have grown on again! I'm glad you didn't do it though, Raggedy Andy!'

'I always thought you crawdads lived in the water!' said Raggedy Ann.

'We do most of the time,' Clifton Crawdad answered, 'but sometimes we dig little round homes in the banks of streams and live there!'

'Have you seen a queer little man with thin legs and a wishing pebble?' asked Raggedy Ann; and then she told Clifton Crawdad all about the wishing pebble and the muskrats' ice-cream-soda-water fountain.

When she had finished telling him, Clifton Crawdad said,

'I know who you mean, for one day he came here and filled my front door full of mud and it took me a long time to clean it out again! It's Minky, and he's very unkind and selfish! I didn't know he had a magical wishing pebble, though. You'd think that anyone with such a wonderful pebble would be very happy and kindly!'

'Indeed, he should be!' said Raggedy Ann.

'Well, if Minky ever puts his face down like Raggedy Andy did at my front door, I'll hold him until you come and take the pebble away from him!'

'No, you mustn't do that, Clifton Crawdad,' said Raggedy Ann, 'for although it did not hurt Raggedy Andy when you pinched him, it would hurt Minky very much! And we must never hurt others even when they are mean to us!'

CHAPTER 11

'Isn't it nice to sit here in the sunshine!' Raggedy Ann exclaimed. 'It makes me feel so nice and sleepy!'

'It feels just as if I was getting so light and fluffy I could fly!' said Raggedy Andy as he lay back and put his arms under his rag head. 'Put your head on me for a pillow, Raggedy Ann!' he said. 'The sky is as blue as blue can be, and the clouds are as white as popcorn. It's nice to lie here and look up at them!'

Raggedy Ann and Raggedy Andy dozed and had hardly been asleep five minutes when the grass beside them was parted and the two little eyes looked out at them.

'I wish I knew for sure whether they are asleep or not!' said Minky.

Minky was the selfish and disagreeable person who had found the magical wishing pebble when Raggedy Ann had buried it in the sand.

'I guess they are asleep for sure!' chuckled Minky as he crept out of the grass towards the sleeping Raggedys.

'I must get Raggedy Ann's candy heart!' he said out loud to himself. 'Then if I eat the candy heart, I am sure that I can make the magical wishing pebble work.

And as Minky had by this time reached the sleeping Raggedys, he took a piece of string from his pocket and tied their rag hands to their bodies and tied their feet together; then he pushed sticks in the sand and tied their rag bodies to the sticks. From his pocket Minky took a pair of scissors and was just about to snip a hole in Raggedy Ann's apron so that he could snip another hole in her rag body and get her candy heart when Raggedy Ann awakened.

'Ha, ha, ha!' laughed Minky. 'I've got you tied tight! And I mean to have your candy heart!'

'It won't do you a speck of good,' laughed Raggedy Ann, 'for it wasn't the candy heart that made the magical wishing pebble so magical!'

'Well, now I'll get it and we will soon see!' cried Minky, as he came towards Raggedy Ann to snip a hole in her rag body.

Minky sat down beside Raggedy Ann to begin the snip but had hardly got seated before he let out a howl and tried to get to his feet. 'Wow!' he cried as tears streamed down his nose. 'Something is biting me and won't let go! Wow!' And turning over and over, Minky rolled until he splashed into the Looking-Glass Brook and came up kicking and squealing, wet and soaking. The selfish creature scrambled to the other side and went howling over the bank and into the bushes.

'There!' said Clifton Crawdad, 'I have paid Minky back for filling my doorway with mud!'

'What's all the fuss about?' Raggedy Andy asked as he rubbed his shoe-button eyes sleepily.

Clifton Crawdad and Raggedy Ann told him about Minky.

'Well, I think we had better walk down the side of the Looking-Glass Brook until we find a place to cross!' said Raggedy Andy when he and Raggedy Ann had untied themselves with Clifton Crawdad's help.

'Yes! we had better go now!' Raggedy Ann agreed as she held out her hand to shake Clifton Crawdad's claw goodbye.

'Goodbye!' said Clifton Crawdad, as he held out his left claw.

'Why, you must never shake hands left-handed!' said Raggedy Andy.

'I have to!' laughed Clifton Crawdad. 'I left my right claw hanging on Mr Minky's trousers! And I hope it is still pinching him to beat the band!'

'Oh dear!' Raggedy Ann cried, as she got on her hands and knees beside Clifton Crawdad. 'I am so sorry you lost your claw just for me! I would rather have had Minky get my candy heart many times than to have seen you hurt. You two wait here just a minute! I'll be right back!' and up the bank she scrambled and out across the Yellow Meadow.

At the first spider telegraph wire she came to, Raggedy Ann found Jenny Cricket calling up the grocery shop to order her next day's dinner. When Jenny Cricket had finished with her marketing, Raggedy Ann asked, 'Jenny Cricket, do you know how to telegraph the little gnome who works magic cures?'

'Yes, indeed!' Jenny Cricket replied.

It took Jenny Cricket only a moment to call Mr Gnome and he said he would be over in a few moments.

Raggedy Ann told Jenny Cricket all about the magical wishing pebble and selfish Mr Minky and all about how Clifton Crawdad lost his claw helping her and Raggedy Andy escape from Mr Minky.

'That was kind of Clifton Crawdad!' said Jenny Cricket. 'Well, here is Mr Gnome!'

Raggedy Ann lost no time in telling Mr Gnome about Clifton Crawdad and Mr Gnome lost no time in flying to the Looking-Glass Brook, so by the time Raggedy Ann reached there, Mr Gnome had fixed a new claw upon Clifton Crawdad and had hurried back home.

'Now we can shake hands goodbye with you, Clifton Crawdad!' laughed Raggedy Ann. 'And thank you so much for helping Raggedy Andy and me!'

'Oh!' laughed Clifton Crawdad, 'I am so glad that I could help you and I hope you can find the magical wishing pebble again!'

So Raggedy Ann and Raggedy Andy shook hands goodbye with Clifton Crawdad, and arm in arm, they walked down the bank, looking for a place to cross the Looking-Glass Brook.

'Clifton Crawdad was an ugly little fellow,' said Raggedy Andy, 'but he surely was a good friend to have when we needed one!'

CHAPTER 12

'Well,' Raggedy Andy said, 'after this, Raggedy Ann, when you feel sleepy, I'll try not to feel sleepy at the same time! Because I do not want to be asleep when old Mr Minky comes snooping around trying to get your candy heart!'

'If it had not been for kind Clifton Crawdad, I guess Mr Minky would have had my candy heart. But it would not have been of any use to him!' laughed Raggedy Ann.

'Do you think you would be as kindly if you did not have a candy heart, Raggedy Ann?'

'Oh, yes, indeed!' Raggedy Ann replied. 'It does not make any difference with either of us, Raggedy Andy! You are just as kindly as I am, and you have no candy heart!'

'That is true, Raggedy Ann!' Raggedy Andy said. 'Perhaps it is the nice clean white cotton which we have in our rag heads!'

'Maybe it is!' Raggedy Ann agreed.

'Ha, ha, ha!' laughed a voice from a tree behind the two Raggedys, 'I am glad to hear you say that!' And looking up, who should Raggedy Ann and Raggedy Andy see but old Mr Minky looking at them from the lower branches.

'I do believe he is going to fish!' said Raggedy Andy.

Mr Minky, from his perch in the tree, let a line with a hook on it fall down among the tall grass at the foot of the tree.

'How do you expect to catch any fish in the tall grass, Mr Minky?' Raggedy Ann asked.

'Oh, I'm not fishing for fish!' Mr Minky said with a sly wink.

'What do you s'pect he's fishing for Raggedy Andy?' whispered Raggedy Ann.

'Less go over and see!' Raggedy Andy whispered back to Raggedy Ann.

When Mr Minky saw the two Raggedys coming over to see what he was fishing for he almost fell off the limb, he was so tickled, for Mr Minky was really fishing for Raggedy Ann and Raggedy Andy, although they did not know it. And Mr Minky wished to get the two rag dolls underneath the tree, so he could jerk upon the line and catch the hook in their clothing and pull them up to the branch. So the Raggedys, not knowing what Mr Minky was up to, walked right over under the tree and looked in the grass to see what Mr Minky was fishing for.

'He! He! He!' Minky chuckled as he gave his line a jerk.

'Dear me, what's happening?' Raggedy Ann cried. Mr Minky's hook had caught in Raggedy Ann's apron and then in Raggedy Andy's trousers, and there the two rag dolls hung in the air, twisting and twirling about as Mr Minky hauled them up to the branch.

'Now I told you I was glad to hear you say it was the nice clean whire cotton in your heads that made the wishes come true!'

'We didn't say that!' cried Raggedy Andy. 'We said that it only made us kindly!'

'You can't fool me!' Mr Minky replied. 'So I will pull you up to the branch here and tie you tight; then I'll take Raggedy Ann's candy heart and all the cotton out of your rag heads! Whee! Won't I have fun then!'

'No, indeed, you will not have fun,' Raggedy Ann said, as she wiggled and kicked, 'for no one can have fun with anything they take from another, and you will find that instead of making your wishes come true, it will keep your wishes from coming true!'

'We'll soon see about that!' shouted Minky, as he reached into his pocket for his scissors so that he could snip a hole in Raggedy Ann's dress and get her candy heart. But Mr Minky evidently did not see Bertha Bumblebee sitting upon the tree trunk right behind him.

'I think you'd better not snip Raggedy Ann's dress today!' said Bertha Bumblebee very buzzy-like. And with that, she flew and gave Mr Minky such a sting upon the top of his little round head he let out a great cry and tumbled right out of the tree and Raggedy Ann and Raggedy Andy fell right on top of him. Mr Minky got to his feet as quickly as he could, and without looking behind him to see what had

happened, ran across the great Yellow Meadow, holding his hand to the place where Bertha Bumblebee had stung him.

It took Raggedy Ann and Raggedy Andy only a moment to get the hook out of their clothes.

'Isn't it funny,' said Raggedy Ann, 'that when we try to get fun from injuring another, trouble always bounces up and hits us instead and we get fooled every time!'

And Bertha Bumblebee winked her eye at Raggedy Ann and flew out across the Looking-Glass Brook, singing a loud buzzy tune as she went.

CHAPTER 13

Raggedy Ann and Raggedy Andy went skipping along the shore of the Looking-Glass Brook, stopping here and there to lift up the head of a pretty little flower – 'To see if there are any fairies sleeping inside,' said Raggedy Ann. They were careful each time they looked into a flower not to jiggle it too much and awaken the little fairy. And when they found a little, teeny-weeny fairy, sound asleep inside a pretty little flower, Raggedy Ann's and Raggedy Andy's little shoe-button eyes twinkled with excitement and fun.

The two rag dolls strolled along until they came to a log which had fallen across the Looking-Glass Brook, forming a nice bridge over which they could walk and reach the side of the brook where Mr Minky lived.

'I guess the best thing for us to do,' said Raggedy Ann, 'is to try and get the wishing pebble away from Minky and then we can wish him to become kind and loving!'

'Yes!' agreed Raggedy Andy. 'That would be a good plan! For, while old Mr Minky has the wishing pebble, no one gets any good out of it, and if we can get it and wish Mr Minky to be really good and generous, then we can give the wishing pebble back to him and he will have lots of fun wishing nice things for others!'

'Then let's cross the brook upon this log,' said Raggedy Ann, 'and we will try and find Mr Minky and ask him for the wishing pebble!'

Raggedy Ann and Raggedy Andy had just reached the centre of the log bridge when their feet slipped out from under them and they both went 'splash' into the Looking-Glass Brook, and as they looked up, who should they see coming out upon the log with a long stick in his hand but Mr Minky.

'That's fooled you!' he shouted as the Raggedys splashed about in the water. 'I thought you would try to cross here and I put soapsuds upon the log and made it slippery so that you would slip and fall into the water. Now I will fish you out with this long stick and drag you to the bank and get Raggedy Ann's candy heart!'

Mr Minky reached out with the long stick and poked at Raggedy Ann, trying to get the end of the stick fastened in her dress or apron, but each time Mr Minky thought he had Raggedy Ann's dress fastened upon the stick, Raggedy Andy gave Raggedy Ann a pull and the stick came loose.

'If you don't stop loosening Raggedy Ann's dress when I get the stick fastened in it, I'll tie a stone around your neck when I fish you out, Raggedy Andy, then I'll throw you back into the water and you'll sink!'

'Ha, ha, ha!' laughed Raggedy Andy. 'That wouldn't hurt me a speck, Mr Minky! And you might as well know now that you will never get Raggedy Ann's candy heart if I can help it.'

'Dear me!' Raggedy Ann said. 'To hear you talk, Mr Minky, one would think Raggedy Andy had done something mean to you!'

'I don't care!' Mr Minky replied. 'I am tired of having Raggedy Andy keep me from getting your candy heart and having my wishes come true!'

'If you would just let us take the magic wishing pebble for a few minutes we would wish something nice for you and you would then be able to make the loveliest wishes and have them all come true!'

'I wouldn't trust you with the magic wishing pebble, for I know you would wish something very unpleasant for me!' said the selfish little creature. 'I'll fish Raggedy Andy out first and tie the stone about his neck! Ha, ha!' he cried as his long stick caught in Raggedy Andy's trousers. 'Now I have you!' And with many winks and chuckles, Mr Minky drew Raggedy Andy up to the log. Raggedy Ann kicked and splashed about in the water trying to swim to Raggedy Andy and pull him from the stick, but Raggedy Andy did not even wiggle as Mr Minky pulled him up on the log.

'Now for a large stone!' Minky cried, and leaving Raggedy Andy lying across the log, Minky ran ashore and came back carrying a large stone and a piece of string. But just as Mr Minky ran out to where Raggedy Andy lay across the log,

Minky's feet flew out from under him and with a cry and a splash he fell into the Looking-Glass Brook. 'Ha, ha, ha!' laughed Raggedy Andy as he got to his feet, being careful not to step upon the soapsudsy place on the log. 'That's the time you got fooled, Mr Minky! For I moved back over the slippery place on the log when your back was turned and you came running right out upon the soapsuds!' It took Raggedy Andy only a moment to pull Raggedy Ann ashore and then by putting sand upon the log where the soapsuds had been, the two rag dolls crossed the log in safety.

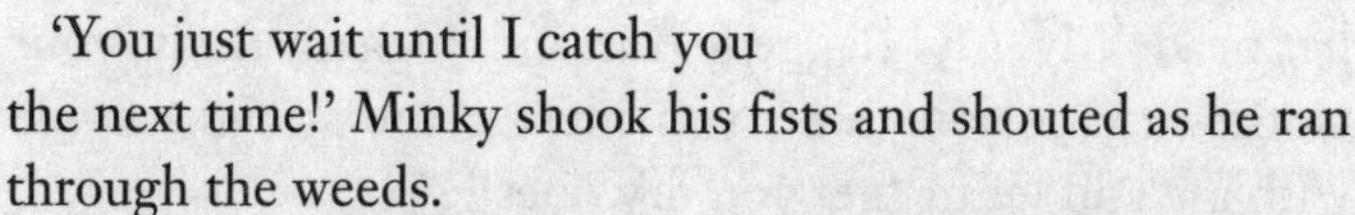

'Shall we pull Minky out of the water?' Raggedy Andy asked, as the two rag dolls looked back and saw the naughty little fellow kicking about.

Raggedy Ann nodded her head and Andy soon reached Mr Minky with the long stick and pulled him ashore.

'You just wait until I catch you the next time!' Minky shook his fists and shouted as he ran through the weeds.

Raggedy Ann and Raggedy Andy laughed softly to themselves and followed the wet trail Minky left on the ground.

'I'm glad that we can make our troubles lighter by laughing at them!' smiled Raggedy Ann.

CHAPTER 14

'Where in the world are you Raggedys going?' Winnie Woodchuck asked, as she stepped out on to the path in front of Raggedy Ann and Raggedy Andy. Then, seeing that the two were soaking wet, Winnie Woodchuck shook her head. 'My! My! Raggedy Ann and Raggedy Andy, your clothes are soaking wet, you must come straight home with me and let me get you dry ones!'

Walter Woodchuck was sitting upon the front steps smoking a pipeful of mullein leaves, for someone had told him mullein leaves were good for hug-tite-iss, whatever that may be.

'Oh goody!' Walter cried, as he knocked the ashes from his pipe. 'I was just wishing Winnie would bring someone home with her! We haven't had visitors for almost two hours! Come right in!'

Winnie Woodchuck hurried and got some nice dry clothes for Raggedy Ann and Raggedy Andy, and Walter Woodchuck made a fire in the fireplace so the Raggedys could get their feet dry. You know, both Raggedy Ann and Raggedy Andy's shoes were just sewn upon their feet and there was no way of taking off their shoes without spoiling them.

The little fire of birch bark sputtered and crackled merrily and in a few minutes the Raggedys were just as nice and dry as could be.

'Now we will have some licorice-root tea,' Winnie Woodchuck said as she brought in a tray of teacups and woodchuck cookies, 'for I know how hungry you must be after falling in the brook!'

So Winnie and Walter Woodchuck and Raggedy Ann and Raggedy Andy sat in front of the little crackly fire and drank the licorice-root tea and it was ever so nice and did not make the cotton stuffing in the Raggedys the least bit damp, 'cause it was made so nicely.

And, while they sat drinking the nice licorice-root tea, the door opened and, without even knocking the teeny-weeniest knock, in walked Minky.

'I just guess I'll have a cup of that licorice-root tea!' he said.

Now, everyone knows that the Woodchucks are very friendly little folk and when they find anyone in trouble they are always ready to help them, but when Minky came stomping into their nice, clean woodchuck living-room with his muddy feet and without knocking, Winnie Woodchuck did not like it!

'Now you just march right out, Mr Minky!' she said. 'You are very rude!'

'Ha, ha, ha! You'd better be very careful when you call me rude, Winnie Woodchuck!' Minky said. 'I 'spect you don't know that I have a very magical wishing pebble and I can work magic on you!'

'The wishing pebble doesn't work for him at all!' Raggedy Andy told Winnie and Walter Woodchuck. 'And the reason it doesn't work magic for him is because he always tries to do selfish things!'

'Just you wait until I catch you alone, Raggedy Andy!' Minky shouted, much louder than was necessary. 'Just you wait, that's all!'

'Well,' Winnie Woodchuck said, as she ran to the kitchen and came back with her broom, 'magic wishing pebble or not, you cannot stay here and spoil our nice little party, Mr Minky!' and she paddy-whacked the mean little fellow so hard with the broom he was glad to dash out of the door.

'Now then, just for that I shall change you all into monkeys with my wishing pebble!' Minky cried, as he shook his fist in the door.

'And I 'spect I shall wrestle you and take the wishing pebble away from you!' Raggedy Andy said as he ran towards Minky.

My! How they tusselled! This way and that! First Minky tried to put his foot behind Raggedy Andy and trip him, then Raggedy Andy tried to put his foot behind Minky and trip him, but neither one could throw the other. Finally Minky grew very angry and, catching hold of Raggedy Andy's pretty collar, he tore it from Raggedy Andy's nice striped shirt.

'Anyway, even if you did tear my nice pretty shirt, I shall not tear your coat,' Raggedy Andy said, 'for it is wrong to destroy anything! But I shall wrestle you much harder now!'

And sure enough Raggedy Andy did. He just wrestled twice as hard, and the first thing Minky knew, he had tumbled upon his back and Raggedy Andy was on top.

'Aha! Aha! Mr Minky! Now will you be good?' Walter Woodchuck cried as he danced about Minky and Raggedy Andy. 'Now take the magical wishing pebble away from him, Raggedy Andy!'

'Oh no!' Raggedy Ann cried. 'It would be wrong for Raggedy Andy to take the wishing pebble from Minky! That would break all the magic of the pebble, and besides, it is wrong to do anything like that!'

'Then I shan't take away the wishing pebble!' Raggedy Andy said as he got to his feet and helped Minky get up.

'Ha! Indeed you won't take it away from me!' Minky said. 'It is at home!' and before Raggedy Andy could jump to one side, Minky gave him a push and sent Raggedy Andy flying head over heels.

Then Minky ran home as fast as he could scamper, laughing as if he had played a good joke on Raggedy Andy.

'Don't you care!' Walter and Winnie Woodchuck said as they helped Raggedy Andy stand up and brushed the leaves from his clothes, 'Minky is a very, very, very rude little fellow, and someday I'll bet he will be sorry!'

Winnie Woodchuck got out her sewing-box and in a few minutes she had sewn Raggedy

Andy's collar on his pretty striped shirt just a good as new.

'I 'spect if you only had the wonderful wishing pebble, you would make some nice wishes!' Winnie Woodchuck said to Raggedy Ann.

'You bet she would, Winnie Woodchuck!' Raggedy Andy answered. 'When Raggedy Ann had the wishing pebble before, she wished for the nicest things in the muskrat house, but she lost the pebble and as soon as Mr Minky got it, he wished for the ice-cream-soda-water fountain and the patch of lollypops to disappear, so now the kindly muskrats have no soda fountain in their front room!'

'Hmm,' Walter Woodchuck mused, as he rubbed his chin. 'I 'spect I'll be back in a few minutes, Raggedy Ann and Raggedy Andy!' he said. 'Please excuse me!'

'Yes, indeed!' the Raggedys said as Walter Woodchuck went out of the door.

'I 'spect speaking of ice-cream sodas made Walter Woodchuck's mouth water!' Winnie Woodchuck chuckled. 'Maybe he has gone to the shop to buy some sweets!' So she got out a roly-poly game and she and the Raggedys sat on the floor in front of the crackly fire and played with the game while they waited for Walter Woodchuck to return.

CHAPTER 15

As soon as Walter Woodchuck got outside his front door, he winked both little brown eyes at a tree and said to himself, 'If old Mr Minky was mean enough to get the nice magical wishing pebble and wish all the nice things to disappear from the kind muskrat home, after Raggedy Ann had given the things to them, I believe someone should borrow the magical wishing pebble from selfish old Mr Minky!' And Walter Woodchuck winked again at another tree and smiled to himself. 'So I shall just walk over to Mr Minky's house and borrow the wishing pebble from him!' And he chuckled his soft woodchuck chuckle as he walked along.

Walter Woodchuck knew just where old Mr Minky lived and in a few minutes he was knocking at the door.

'Who is knocking at my door?' Minky shouted in a growly voice.

'It's Walter Woodchuck, and I have come to see you!' Walter Woodchuck replied.

'Then you can run right smack dab back home!' Minky shouted. 'I shall not let you in!'

'Then you come out!' Walter said.

'I shan't do it!' Mr Minky said. 'And if you don't run home right away, you'll be sorry, that's what!'

'Ha! What will you do? Just you tell me that, Mr Minky! What will you do?' Walter Woodchuck asked.

Minky did not reply, and he was so quiet Walter thought surely Mr Minky must have gone to sleep, but the next thing he knew he was lifted clear off his feet and jerked up in the air.

'Ha! That's fooled you, Walter Woodchuck!' Minky shouted as he pulled and pulled on the rope until Walter Woodchuck was almost as high as the roof of Minky's house. 'Now I shall fasten the end of the rope to the chimney and you can just hang there!'

So the mean creature tied the end of the rope to the chimney and left poor Walter Woodchuck hanging against the side of the house.

Walter Woodchuck wiggled and twisted and kicked this way and that, but he could not get loose. Minky had fastened a hook in the end of the rope and had caught the hook in the back of Walter Woodchuck's braces and, of course, Walter could not reach around there and unfasten it.

'I wonder what Winnie Woodchuck will think when I do not return?' Walter Woodchuck thought to himself.

While Walter was wondering this, Winnie Woodchuck was wondering why Walter did not return from the shop with the sweets she thought he had gone for.

'Maybe Walter Woodchuck stopped to visit someone

along the way!' Raggedy Ann suggested when Winnie spoke of it.

'Oh no,' Winnie Woodchuck replied, 'Walter always hurries right home from the shop. I think I will run down the path and meet him!'

So Winnie Woodchuck went down the path and pretty soon she met Wallace Woodpecker. Wallace Woodpecker was the mail carrier in the deep, deep woods and knew all the news.

'Have you seen Walter Woodchuck?' Winnie asked.

'Yes, ma'am!' Wallace Woodpecker replied. 'He is down at Mr Minky's house. At least, he was going that way when I saw him. But I'll tell you one thing, Winnie, if I were you, I wouldn't let Walter Woodchuck go to see Mr Minky very often 'cause Mr Minky is a disagreeable creature!'

'Indeed! He is!' Winnie agreed. Then she thanked Wallace Woodpecker and ran down to Mr Minky's house. And when she saw Walter hanging by his braces to the hook at the end of the rope, Winnie was very angry.

She knew in a moment that Minky had played a trick on Walter, so she went and thumped upon Minky's door, 'THUMP! THUMP! THUMP!' like that, only a great deal louder. 'Come in!' Minky called through the door.

So Winnie Woodchuck walked into Minky's house, intending to give Mr Minky a great piece of her mind, but she had hardly opened the door before Minky caught her and had her tied to a chair. 'Now, I 'spect you won't say much,' he said. Then when he saw that Winnie Woodchuck did intend saying a great deal he stuffed a large hanky in her mouth so she couldn't talk.

'Ha, ha, ha!' Minky laughed. 'Pretty soon I'll bet Raggedy Ann and Raggedy Andy will come to hunt you, and I shall capture them as easy as I did you and Walter.'

CHAPTER 16

Raggedy Ann and Raggedy Andy sat upon the floor in the Woodchuck home and played with the roly-poly game for a long time. First Raggedy Ann won the game then Raggedy Andy won the game.

'Isn't it time Winnie Woodchuck returned?' Raggedy Ann asked.

'Maybe we had better go and see what can be keeping the Woodchucks so long!' Raggedy Andy replied. 'Maybe they have caught their feet in a trap!'

'Oh no, Raggedy Andy,' Raggedy Ann said, 'there are no traps in the deep, deep woods, I am certain! There are too many clever little gnomes and elves and fairies living here. And you know,' she added, 'they watch out for the other little woodland creatures!'

So Raggedy Ann put away the roly-poly game and she

and Raggedy Andy ran down the path through the woods until they came to Minky's home; there they saw Walter Woodchuck hanging high up in the air near the house top.

'Aha!' Raggedy Ann said, 'I'll bet Minky did that! Let us ask Walter Woodchuck.'

'Yes it was Minky!' Walter Woodchuck said when Raggedy Andy asked him who had pulled him up there. 'And,' Walter said, 'Winnie Woodchuck came to rescue me and I am certain that Minky has captured her, for she hasn't come out of the house and I am sure she went in at the side door!'

'Dear me!' Raggedy Ann said. 'What shall we do, Raggedy Andy?'

Raggedy Andy took off his cap and scratched his head with a little stick, but he could not think of anything to do – 'Unless I go inside and wrestle Minky!' he finally said.

'Yes! And have him capture you too? Indeed! You shall not go inside Minky's house until we find out just what he has done with poor Winnie Woodchuck!'

So the Raggedys slipped up to one of Minky's windows and peeped inside. There they saw poor Winnie Woodchuck tied fast to a chair, but wiggling and twisting as she tried to get loose.

'We must find some way to rescue Walter Woodchuck first!' Raggedy Ann said. 'Then we will plan a way to rescue Winnie Woodchuck next!'

'I'll tell you what!' Raggedy Andy said. 'I'll pretend that I am returning to the woodchuck house and you can pretend that you are going inside Minky's house. Then I will run around to Minky's back door, while you talk to Minky at the front door. If I can run inside, I will untie Winnie Woodchuck and then we will run out.'

So Raggedy Ann and Raggedy Andy did just as Raggedy Andy had suggested and when Raggedy Ann came walking up to his door, Minky said to himself, 'Ha! Goody! Here comes Raggedy Ann all by herself! Now I can capture her and take her candy heart, then I am sure my magic wishing pebble will work!' And he waited for Raggedy Ann to knock upon the door.

Raggedy Ann thought to herself, 'Maybe Minky is hiding right behind the door just waiting for me.' So she knocked upon the door and then had to smile to herself, for as soon as she knocked Minky said, 'Come in, Raggedy Ann!' and Raggedy Ann knew Minky had been watching her all the time.

'I don't think I shall come in today, Mr Minky,' Raggedy Ann replied. 'You must open the door. I wish to talk with you.'

So Minky opened the door and poked his long nose out. 'What do you wish to say, Raggedy Ann?' he asked.

'Hmm! Let's see!' Raggedy Ann mused. 'Oh yes! I remember now, Mr Minky, I want to ask you something. Did you ever hear of "slapwinkies"?'

'Why! What a silly thing!' Minky said. 'Of course not! What are "slapwinkies", Raggedy Ann!'

'Why!' Raggedy Ann replied, as if greatly surprised. 'If you would only come out here and look in the grass, you might see a slapwinkie; who knows?'

'If you are trying to fool me, Raggedy Ann, you'll be mighty sorry!' Minky said, as he opened the door and stepped out. 'I should like very much to see one though!' and he closed the door behind him.

Then Raggedy Ann began singing a song just as loud as she could, for she knew by this time Raggedy Andy must be inside Minky's house and she did not wish Minky to hear Raggedy Andy.

And while Minky was looking in the grass, Raggedy Andy *had* quietly sneaked into the house, untied Winnie Woodchuck and with her had slipped out of the back door again and over into the bushes where they were hidden. Then Raggedy Andy told Winnie Woodchuck, 'Now you stay hidden here in the bushes, Winnie, and I will run up the path towards Minky and he will never know but that I have just come from your house. You must keep very quiet though and not let Minky see you!'

So Raggedy Andy ran away and then came running up the path to where Minky and Raggedy Ann were looking for slapwinkies in the grass.

'Now what are you looking for, Mr Minky?' Raggedy Andy asked very politely.

'I'm looking for slapwinkies!' Minky gruffly replied.

'Hmm!' Raggedy Andy said, 'I never heard of slapwinkies!'

'Then I'll bet Raggedy Ann was fooling me!' Minky howled as he jumped to his feet. 'I vow I will capture Raggedy Ann and take her candy heart, then my wishing pebble will work nicely!'

And he started as if he would catch Raggedy Ann, but Raggedy Andy said, 'Wait, Mr Minky! I 'spect if you would run up to Winnie Woodchuck's house and ask her, she would tell you if she has ever seen a slapwinkie!'

'Ha!' Minky laughed, forgetting himself. 'Winnie Woodchuck isn't at home, so there!'

'Oh, is that so?' Raggedy Andy asked. 'Why I just left Winnie Woodchuck not two minutes ago!'

Minky looked queerly at Raggedy Andy and then ran into

his house and out again. 'She's escaped!' he cried. 'How did she get away when I had her tied to a chair?' Raggedy Ann and Raggedy Andy did not reply, for they did not wish to tell, but Raggedy Ann said, 'I 'spect that Winnie Woodchuck escaped just like Walter Woodchuck will escape if you do not hurry and let him down yourself.'

'There must be a lot of magic going on around here,' Minky said, 'And for fear some of the magic will be worked on me before I get the wishing pebble working properly, I will untie the rope and let Walter down.'

So he ran indoors, up the stairway to the attic and then to the roof and let Walter down to the ground.

Raggedy Ann and Raggedy Andy and Walter Woodchuck walked away, never saying a word to Minky, and when they came to Winnie Woodchuck, they all caught hands and ran towards the woodchuck home, laughing heartily at the way they had played a good trick on old Mr Minky.

CHAPTER 17

When Raggedy Ann and Raggedy Andy left the woodchuck home, they walked down the path towards Minky's house, for they intended, if they could, to get the fine wishing pebble so that they could make some lovely wishes and have the ice-cream-soda fountain back in the living-room of the muskrats' cheery home.

But when they reached Minky's home, there was a sign on the door which read, 'Gone fishing for the day!'

'Let's go to where he is fishing!' Raggedy Andy said to Raggedy Ann.

'That is a good plan!' Raggedy Ann agreed, as she started towards the stream where she knew Minky had gone.

When they came to the stream, there upon a log sat Minky fishing away for dear life.

'Have you caught anything?' Raggedy Andy asked.

'No, sir!' Minky replied. 'I haven't even had a single bite!'

Just as he said this, Minky's pole gave a big jerk, and before he could catch himself, the little fellow was pulled from the log and went splashing into the water below. Raggedy Ann thought he would never come up again, for the water was so deep, but finally Minky came to the surface, blowing and puffing to catch his breath.

Raggedy Andy got a long stick and held it out so Minky could catch hold of it. Then Raggedy Andy, with Raggedy Ann's aid, pulled until Minky came ashore, all dripping wet.

'That settles it!' Minky said when he could get his breath.

'Settles what?' Raggedy Andy asked.

'I shall never try to capture Raggedy Ann!' Minky said, 'I know now that both of you Raggedys are nice kind folk, and it was very wrong of me to take Raggedy Ann's lovely wishing pebble and make the ice-cream-soda-water fountain disappear from the home of the muskrats.'

Raggedy Ann looked from Minky to Raggedy Andy and smiled. It pleased her to think that Minky had changed from a mean little creature to a good little creature, and Raggedy Ann's shoe-button eyes wiggled with happiness.

'Yes, sir, Raggedy Andy,' Minky said, 'I am so very, very, very, very – ' But Minky could say no more for his eyes filled with tears and he began crying loudly.

Raggedy Ann wiped the tears from Minky's eyes, and when he had stopped weeping she said, 'Do not feel so sad, Mr Minky. If you will get the magical wishing pebble, I am certain in a few moments we can wish for the nice ice-cream-soda-water fountain to return to the muskrats home and we can make them a lollypop garden and wish a whole lot of nice things for them. Then we can go down to their house and I am sure they will be glad to have you share in their pleasures!'

JOHNNY GRUELLE

'Oh! Do you really believe they would do that, after the mean trick I played on them?' Minky asked. Then, when Raggedy Ann and Raggedy Andy told him, 'Yes, indeed,' Minky said, 'Then I shall run right home and get the wishing pebble, for I have it in a teacup up on the top shelf in my cupboard. I will be right back and I shall give it to you and let you make the nice wishes!'

So Raggedy Ann and Raggedy Andy sat down on a little log and twiggled their thumbs and waited for Minky to return with the wishing pebble.

When they had waited a long, long time, Raggedy Andy said, 'I wonder why Minky is taking such a time?'

'Maybe he has gone to sleep,' Raggedy Ann said in reply. 'Let us walk to Minky's house and see.'

So the two dolls caught hands and went trippity-trip down the path to Minky's house. The front door stood wide open and, after knocking, Raggedy Ann and Raggedy Andy went inside. There they found the furniture all turned topsy-turvy and the back door standing wide open.

Many dishes were broken and lay scattered about the floor. 'Something has been going on here, like a fight or a scuffle!' Raggedy Andy said. 'See how the chairs are topsy-turvy and everything broken!'

Raggedy Ann agreed with Raggedy Andy. 'Yes,' she said, 'Minky has had a fight with someone for sure!'

'And Minky has chased whoever it was right out of the back door!' Raggedy Andy called from the back porch. 'Let's follow down through the woods; we can see their tracks through the grass where they have trodden it down!'

So, with Raggedy Andy in the lead, the two rag dolls ran as fast as they could in the direction the trail led.

In a few minutes Raggedy Ann and Raggedy Andy saw

Minky coming towards them and he was crying as hard as he could. 'Why, Minky!' Raggedy Ann exclaimed. 'Whatever in the world has happened? Your clothes are torn and all muddy!'

So Minky sat down on a stone and wiped the tears from his eyes. Then he looked sadly from Raggedy Ann to Raggedy Andy and said, 'The magical wishing pebble is gone, Raggedy Ann and Raggedy Andy, and we shall never get it again to make nice wishes with.'

'Why, Minky?' Raggedy Andy said. 'Who has it?'

'Bertram Bear!' Minky replied. 'When I left you, I ran home just as fast as I could, for I wanted Raggedy Ann to have her wishing pebble as soon as I could get it. But when

I was running up the path near my house, I saw Bertram Bear come dashing out of the bushes and go running right in through my front door. "Hey! Bertram Bear," I shouted, "don't go into my house!" but into the house he went just the same, and of course I followed. And what do you think, Raggedy Ann and Raggedy Andy, there was Bertram Bear climbing up on a chair after the cup which held the wishing pebble. I knew then that Bertram Bear had listened to us talking back there in the woods and that he intended having

the wishing pebble, so just as Bertram Bear jumped from the chair, I caught him and tried to take the wishing pebble away from him. We tussled this way and that and upset all the furniture and all the dishes. But Bertram Bear finally pushed me over a chair, and when I got to my feet, the mean creature was running out of the back door; and he has the wishing pebble in his pocket, for I saw him put it there!'

'Dear me!' was all Raggedy Andy could think of to say, but Raggedy Ann said, 'Well, never mind, Mr Minky! You run home and change your clothing and wash the mud from your face. Raggedy Andy and I will go to Bertram Bear's house and tell his mamma how naughty he has been and you can follow us there! I 'spect Bertram Bear's mamma will make him return the wishing pebble mighty quick!'

So Minky went sadly home, while Raggedy Ann and Raggedy Andy went towards the home of Bertram Bear.

CHAPTER 18

The bears lived high up on a hill in the deep, deep woods where the ground was very stony and there were great boulders as large as chicken coops. Raggedy Ann and Raggedy Andy had never been there, but they could follow Bertram Bear's trail through the grass until they came to the stony ground and from there they could see the home of the bears.

So Raggedy Ann and Raggedy Andy followed the path up the hill, in and around the large boulders, until they came to the home of Mrs Bolivar Bear, and they knocked upon the door with their cotton-stuffed hands, 'Thump, thump, thump!'

Mrs Bolivar Bear came to the door. 'Why!' she cried. 'It's two rag dolls! And they are alive!'

'May we come in, Mrs Bolivar Bear?' Raggedy Ann asked.

'Certainly!' Mrs Bolivar Bear replied, as she held the door open, but she wondered what two little rag dolls could be doing way up at her house.

'We were just having some nice ice-cream soda-water!' Mrs Bolivar Bear said, as she led the way into the dining-room to where Daddy Bolivar Bear and Bertram Bear sat near a sparkling soda-water fountain.

Mrs Bolivar Bear brought Raggedy Ann and Raggedy Andy each a glass of ice-cream soda-water and told them to sit down. 'Bertram just made the soda fountain with a magical charm he found!' Mrs Bolivar Bear said.

Of course, Bertram Bear knew right away that Raggedy Ann and Andy had come for the wishing pebble, for he had heard them talking about it with Minky, and knew that the wishing pebble really belonged to Raggedy Ann; so he thought, 'I must think of some way to fool Raggedy Ann and Raggedy Andy so that they cannot tell my nice mamma!

'What are you two rag dolls doing way up here among the rocks?' he asked Raggedy Ann.

Raggedy Ann tried to speak, but she could not say one word. 'Why! how funny!' she thought. 'I can think just as well as ever, but I can't talk even a smidge.'

Then Bertram Bear turned to Raggedy Andy and said, 'Didn't you get tired climbing up this high?' And Raggedy Andy tried to answer Bertram Bear but, like Raggedy Ann, he could not speak one word.

'They could talk very well a while ago!' Mrs Boliver Bear said. 'Something must have happened to their clockwork insides!'

She did not know that Raggedy Ann and Raggedy Andy were just stuffed with nice white cotton and their bodies had no clockwork.

'I 'spect I will take Raggedy Ann and Raggedy Andy out to the work-shed and fix their clockwork!' Bertram Bear said. 'Maybe it just needs some oil.' But to himself he said,

'I will take the Raggedys out and throw them as far as I can from the highest rock, so that they will not come back again.' So Bertram Bear picked up Raggedy Ann and Raggedy Andy and carried them out of the house and neither of the Raggedys could say even one word.

When he had gone far enough from the house so his mamma and daddy could not hear him, he said, 'Now I shall tell you just what I intend doing with you! I shall throw you both away and when you hit upon the ground way down below, you must run home as fast as you can, or the next time I will treat you far worse!'

And of course then the Raggedys could talk, and Raggedy Ann said, 'You should feel so ashamed of yourself, Bertram Bear! You told your nice mamma and daddy the biggest fib about the magical wishing pebble and I am sure the wishing pebble will not work for you when you tell fibs, or do anything wrong!'

'Ha, ha, ha!' Bertram Bear laughed. 'Don't you believe it, Raggedy Ann! Didn't you see how my mamma and daddy liked the nice soda-water fountain? Now I shall throw you from this high stone and you had better never come back.' And the mean bear swung the Raggedys around his head and threw them just as far as he could.

Bertram Bear turned and walked back into the house, but the Raggedys just lay where they had fallen – not because the fall had hurt them at all, but because they were lying side by side and wanted to think just what to do.

'Isn't he a mean bear?' Raggedy Andy said. 'How nice it is that all creatures are not like Bertram Bear!'

'Oh!' Raggedy Ann said, as she sat up and smoothed out her yarn hair, 'we will let Bertram Bear keep the magical wishing pebble, for it will not be magical very long.'

The two Raggedys caught hands and walked down the hill the way they had come and talked of the wishing pebble as they went along; then, when they came to a bend in the path, there sat Freddy Fox upon a log and he was all out of breath from running.

'Why have you been running, Freddy Fox?' Raggedy Ann asked, as she came up to him.

Freddy Fox squinted his eyes until they were just tiny slits and smiled. 'Oh,' he said, 'sometimes I just like to run and run and run, Raggedy Ann.' But in his mind Freddy Fox was thinking, I must find out from Raggedy Ann and Raggedy Andy all I can about this wonderful wishing pebble I heard them talking of back there.

'Oh, yes!' Freddy Fox went on, 'I run and run and run to keep in practice, so if anything chases me I can get away. But I wish I had a fine Wishing Stick or a magic ring so that I could make nice wishes and never have anything chase me!'

'It would be nice if you had one!' Raggedy Ann said. 'Once I found a wishing pebble –' And she told Freddy Fox all about Minky and how now Bertram Bear had it, but she did not tell how they were not able to work magic with it after they had had it a while.

So Freddy Fox said, 'Well, I guess I shall never own one, so it is no use wishing for one.' And with that, he bounced up and dashed away through the woods.

'Isn't he a strange creature!' Raggedy Ann said. 'He did not look into our eyes when he talked to us, and you can never trust anyone who cannot look into your eyes when they speak to you!'

CHAPTER 19

'Raggedy Ann and Raggedy Andy are such silly things!' Freddy Fox said to himself as he left the two and ran away through the woods. 'But then, Raggedy Ann and Raggedy Andy are only two old rag dolls and their heads are just stuffed with cotton; no one could expect them to be as smart and cunning as I am.' And Freddy Fox made a turn in the woods and circled until he was headed up the hill towards the home of Bertram Bear.

'Bertram Bear is a silly thing, too,' Freddy Fox thought, 'and it will be very easy for me to fool him and get the magical wishing pebble away from him; then I shall wish for everything I can think of, and I will not give anyone a single thing! Oh! I shall easily fool Bertram Bear! Just as easily as I fooled the Raggedys!'

And up he went and called outside Bertram's house, 'Oh, Bertram Bear! Oh, Bertram Bear, come out!'

So Bertram Bear came out when he heard Freddy Fox, for often they had lots of fun together, though Freddy Fox always teased Bertram Bear a great deal. Freddy Fox was too sly to mention the magical wishing pebble, for he did not care to have Bertram Bear know that he knew Bertram had it, so he said, 'I have found something I wish to show you, Bertram Bear. Come down to my house and see it!' So Bertram Bear thought to himself, 'Freddy Fox does not know that I have a wonderful wishing pebble and I will look at his find, then I shall wish for it to be in my house after I see if it is any good! My! Won't Freddy Fox be surprised when he discovers it has disappeared?' And Bertram Bear chuckled to himself to think how he would fool Freddy Fox.

And while Bertram Bear was thinking how he would fool Freddy Fox, Freddy Fox was thinking of how he intended fooling Bertram Bear.

The Raggedys had told Freddy Fox that the magical wishing pebble was very white, so Freddy Fox had picked up a white pebble just the size of the real wishing pebble, and he thought he could easily exchange it for Bertram Bear's wishing pebble when Bertram wasn't watching.

And so, Freddy Fox and Bertram Bear walked along through the woods towards the home of Freddy Fox.

By this time Minky had decided he would run up to Bertram Bear's house and tell Bertram Bear's nice mamma how Bertram had taken the wishing pebble, so Minky walked up the path just a moment or so after Bertram Bear and Freddy Fox had walked down the path.

And Minky had gone but a short distance when lying right in the centre of the path he saw a white pebble. 'Can this be the magical wishing pebble?' Minky wondered. 'I will just make a wish and see if it really is!' So he held the pebble in his right hand and closed his eyes and wished. 'I wish that I was with Raggedy Ann and Raggedy Andy!' he whispered to himself. Then he opened his eyes, and was greatly surprised to find himself standing right in front of Raggedy Ann and Raggedy Andy.

'Why, Mr Minky! Where did you come from?' Raggedy Ann asked and she told Minky how Bertram Bear had treated Raggedy Andy and herself.

'Do you think Bertram Bear could have lost the real magical wishing pebble, Raggedy Ann?' Minky asked.

'There may be more than one wishing pebble!' Raggedy Ann replied.

'We could wish to find out whether Bertram Bear lost it!' Raggedy Andy suggested.

So Minky wished that he and Raggedy Ann and Raggedy Andy knew just how Bertram might have lost the wonderful wishing pebble, and as soon as Minky made the wish, the three friends laughed, for they saw right away that the wishing pebble had dropped through a little hole in Bertram Bear's pocket.

'And now it is yours again, Minky!' Raggedy Ann said.

'Oh no!' Minky replied. 'The wishing pebble is really yours, Raggedy Ann, and I am so glad that I can return it to you. I am very sorry that I was so stingy when I had it before. So you take it and make a lot of nice lovely wishes with it!' And Minky handed the magical wishing pebble to Raggedy Ann.

'Thank you, Mr Minky,' Raggedy Ann said. 'I know that now you will find a lot more happiness in the deep, deep woods, because you have changed from a mean little fellow into a nice little fellow!' So she and Raggedy Andy shook hands with Minky and watched him as he walked sadly away.

But there was a twinkle in Raggedy Ann's shoe-button eyes and she said to Raggedy Andy, 'I 'spect Mr Minky will be shouting with joy when he walks into his home!'

'What makes you 'spect that, Raggedy Ann?' Raggedy Andy wished to know.

' 'Cause,' Raggedy Ann replied, 'I have already wished that there will be a nice ice-cream-soda-water fountain in Minky's living-room and right at the side of his kitchen porch a nice lollypop garden. So now Minky can find out

just how much fun it will be having his friends help him enjoy the nice things he has!'

And after the two rag dolls had walked along in silence for a few minutes Raggedy Ann laughed and said, 'There! You see, Raggedy Andy!'

'See what?' Raggedy Andy asked in surprise.

'Why!' Raggedy Ann chuckled. 'I just wished that I knew what you were wishing, and when I found out that you were wishing the muskrats could also have a lollypop garden and another ice-cream-soda-water fountain I wished for it with the wishing pebble, and I'll bet by this time the muskrats are all calling in their friends to share in their pleasures!'

'Then let's run down and see if the wishes came true, Raggedy Ann!' Raggedy Andy cried, as he caught Raggedy Ann's hand and ran with her down the path through the woods.

CHAPTER 20

At the muskrat home by the side of the Looking-Glass Brook there were sounds of merriment. Squeals of delight and happy chattering and laughter.

Mr Muskrat was out upon the bank of the Looking-Glass Brook, calling through a horn made of birch-bark: 'Everyone is invited to the muskrat home – we are having a grand party! Hurry and come!' And when the little meadow-creatures and the wood-folk heard the cheery invitation, they flew and ran and wiggled towards the muskrat home.

And, when Mr Muskrat went around to his kitchen porch, he saw that the lollipop garden was in the back yard and there upon small sticks, growing like thousands of coloured dandelions, were lovely, mouth-watering lollipops. So he called to Freddy Fieldmouse and Herbert Hedgehog and some of the other meadow-folk and had them help him pick enough lollipops for each and every guest.

Along the bank of the Looking-Glass Brook came Raggedy Ann and Raggedy Andy, their little cloth faces wreathed in smiles, happy in their knowledge that through their wishes they had brought pleasure to so many kindly little creatures. 'Hurrah for Raggedy Ann with the candy heart!' everyone cried. 'Hurrah for Raggedy Andy, too!' everyone cried, as they all ran to meet the Raggedys and crowded about to hear how they had recovered the magical wishing pebble.

So Raggedy Ann and Raggedy Andy sat down upon the soft yellow grass beside the Looking-Glass Brook and with the happy little creatures of the great meadow and the deep, deep woods about them, they related all the difficulties and adventures through which they had passed.

Then, when old Mr Sun had slipped down out of sight and the blue of the evening had settled, changing the purple shadows of the deep, deep woods into a mysterious blackness, the little fireflies came flitting up from the tall grasses and lighted the way for the wood-folk and the little meadow-creatures to reach their homes.

The brilliant stars and the face of the crescent moon were reflected in the Looking-Glass Brook. Raggedy Ann, seeing this, laughed and said, 'Isn't the reflection of the moon and stars in the surface of the Looking-Glass Brook just like the reflection of happiness we may send out? When someone gives us a moment of happiness, that happiness makes our hearts sing with joyousness and we reflect that happiness from our sunny hearts to someone else, and so in turn it is reflected to others, on and on!'

Then the Raggedys and Mr and Mrs Muskrat went into the muskrat home, and in ten minutes all were sound asleep in their little soft beds, dreaming the dreams which are always brought to heads filled with happy thoughts.

CHAPTER 21

Bright and early in the morning, when the smiling face of the great Mr Sun had just peeped over the trees in the deep, deep woods, again painting the great meadow in its morning bath of golden light, Mrs Muskrat hopped out of bed and slipped quietly to the kitchen intending to make no noise so as not to awaken the Raggedys.

Mrs Muskrat knew how to make the loveliest pancakes, all a golden brown on both sides. She wanted to make a lot before she called Mr Muskrat and Raggedy Ann and Raggedy Andy.

But when Mrs Muskrat opened the kitchen door she gave a squeal of surprise for there, sitting upon a chair by the kitchen door, his face washed nice and clean and his shoe-button eyes with all the sleep dust wiped from them, sat Raggedy Andy.

There beside the kitchen table, her sleeves rolled up and wearing a large apron, was Raggedy Ann.

'Now you just sit down beside Raggedy Andy!' Mrs Muskrat laughed. 'I got up early so that I could make the pancakes. Then when I had a lot baked I meant to call you both.'

Presently Mr Muskrat came from his bedroom and as soon as he had washed his face breakfast was ready.

'What did you do with the wishing pebble, Raggedy Ann?' Mr Muskrat asked after all had eaten sixteen pancakes with maple syrup on them. 'Did you push it down in the sand again?' and he and all the rest laughed at the recollection of how they had searched for the lost pebble.

'Indeed, I didn't, Mr Muskrat!' Raggedy Ann replied as she wiped the syrup from around Raggedy Andy's mouth with her napkin. 'I have it wrapped up carefully in my pocket hanky and here it is!' She took her hanky with the blue border from her pocket and showed Mr and Mrs Muskrat the wonderful wishing pebble and the light of the morning sun shone into the white of the wishing pebble and seemed to wink cheerily.

'Isn't it white and smooth and round?' Mrs Muskrat said, 'No wonder it is so magical! But Raggedy Ann, you should not carry such a magical thing in a pocket hanky! What if you should lose it?'

'I don't know what else to do with it!' Raggedy Ann replied. 'If I just put it in my apron pocket, and that's the only pocket I have, I would be sure to lose it – but if I keep it wrapped in my pocket hanky and lose the hanky, it will be much easier to find!'

'I know!' Mrs Muskrat cried as she ran into her bedroom and came out with her sewing-basket. 'I will snip a little hole in Raggedy Ann's body and – '

'Oh dear no!' Mr Muskrat cried, jumping up when Mrs Muskrat took out a pair of scissors. 'You mustn't hurt Raggedy Ann!'

'Silly!' Mrs Muskrat laughed, as she gave Mr Muskrat a playful pinch on his nose. 'Don't you know Raggedy Ann and Raggedy Andy are made of cloth and stuffed with nice clean white cotton? It doesn't hurt them to be snipped open with a pair of scissors. Then when I have made a tiny slit in Raggedy Ann's cloth body, I will poke the magical wishing pebble way into the soft cotton stuffing and sew the hole up. Then she cannot ever lose the wishing pebble unless she gets lost herself!'

So Mrs Muskrat took off Raggedy Ann's apron and dress and snipped a tiny hole in Raggedy Ann's cloth back. Then she poked the wishing pebble way into the cotton stuffing and in a few moments had the hole sewn up.

Raggedy Ann kissed Mrs Muskrat and thanked her. 'Is there any other nice thing I could wish for you, Mrs Muskrat?' Raggedy Ann asked.

'Dear me, no, Raggedy Ann!' Mrs Muskrat replied. 'We have the lovely ice-cream-soda-water fountain in our living-room and the lollipop garden at the kitchen door. What more could we wish for to make our friends any happier?'

'Then I 'spect our adventure is at an end!' Raggedy Ann said. 'For Raggedy Andy and I must return to the nursery and we have a long way to go!'

The kindly muskrats did not like to see Raggedy Ann and Raggedy Andy leave, but they also knew they must not be selfish with their friends, so they gave Raggedy Ann and Raggedy Andy a lot of tight hugs, then watched the two dolls as they walked away through the tall yellow grass.

'What a pleasure it is to have generous, kindly friends

who love us!' Mrs Muskrat said, as she wiped her eyes with the corner of her apron.

And, as Raggedy Ann and Raggedy Andy with an arm about each other walked towards their home, the same pleasant thoughts ran through their little cotton-stuffed heads, and while they said never a word to each other, each knew and felt the other shared the same joyousness.

And, as you surely must know, there is no feeling which brings as much true sunshine to our hearts as the happiness of honest, loving friendship.

The Fairy Ring

How pleasant it was for the Raggedys to walk through the deep deep woods and hear and see fairies and all the other magical creatures as they went.

Raggedy Ann and Raggedy Andy stopped at a great big tree and watched a band of fairies playing in the soft, velvety moss beneath it. These were very tiny fairies, and they were as dainty as flowers.

The ten little fairies formed a ring and danced hand in hand. They whirled around in a circle, faster and faster, growing more airy as they danced.

Soon the Raggedys could only see a hazy white smoke in the shape of a ring.

They rubbed their hands over their shoe-button eyes as the smoke disappeared, and with it all signs of the tiny fairies.

All that remained was a circle of tiny mushrooms.

Just then the Fairy Queen appeared. 'I see you have been watching the fairies dance,' she said.

'Yes, we have,' said Raggedy Ann, 'and they were beautiful.'

'But where did the mushrooms come from?' asked Raggedy Andy.

'I will tell you,' said the Fairy Queen. 'The fairies leave a circle of mushrooms so that everyone who finds it may know that fairies have been dancing in a fairy ring.'

'How wonderful!' said Raggedy Ann.

'And since you are so good and kind to the woodland creatures,' said the Fairy Queen, 'I am going to give you one fairy wish.'

The Raggedys wished for a whole week of beautiful spring weather for everyone.

'That is a nice wish, because it is an unselfish one,' the Fairy Queen said.

'And almost every unselfish wish in the world comes true, whether a fairy makes the wish or not!'

The Picnic

'Marcella's taking us on a picnic tomorrow!' Raggedy Ann said to the dolls about their little mistress.

All the dolls gathered around. There were Frederika and Henny, the Dutch dolls; Uncle Clem, the Scottish doll; Cleety, the clown; the French doll with the yellow curls; and Rosa and Sarah, the pretty dolls with china heads.

And then there were the Raggedy animals – Sunny Bunny, the Little Brown Bear and Eddie Elephant.

'She's taking all of us?' Henny asked. 'Even the Raggedy animals?'

'Of course,' Raggedy Ann replied.

'I don't see why she would want to take them!' Henny growled. 'They're not even dolls!'

'The Raggedy animals are just as good as any of us dolls,' Raggedy Ann reminded him.

'And I'd be ashamed of myself if I were you, Henny,' said Uncle Clem.

With that, Henny shuffled off to sit behind the toy box in the corner and sulk.

That night, Marcella's daddy gathered up all the dolls and the animals and piled them on the rear seat of the car. Then he went back into the house.

'I do hope Henny behaves himself tomorrow,' Raggedy Ann said.

Raggedy Andy laughed. 'I guess he will, because Henny won't even be at the picnic! He was left in the nursery pouting behind the toy box.'

'It serves him right, too!' the French doll said. 'That's what happens when one is selfish.'

The Raggedy animals were sitting together quietly. They were all feeling very sad.

When all the other dolls had fallen asleep, the three of them climbed out of the car.

As they ran across the yard, they met Hairy Puppydog.

Eddie Elephant told him all about Henny.

'Even though Henny was rude to us,' he explained, 'we still want him to go on the picnic.'

'Even if he did not want us to go!' Sunny Bunny added.

Hairy Puppydog had an idea. He barked at the back door until he was let into the house. Then he ran upstairs to the nursery, picked up Henny, and dropped him out of the window to the ground below, where the three Raggedy animals were waiting.

Then they all ran back to the car.

Bright and early in the morning, Marcella's family started off on their picnic.

Marcella sat in the back seat with all her dolls. But she held Eddie Elephant, Sunny Bunny and the Little Brown Bear right in her lap.

'I'm so glad you thought to bring the Raggedy animals, Daddy!' Marcella said.

Raggedy Ann winked at Henny, as if to say, 'Isn't it more fun when we share our happiness with others?'

And Henny made up his mind that thereafter he would love the Raggedy animals just as much as he loved all the dolls.

THE
END